"I'd like to go to bed right now."

The expression in Saul's eyes was unmistakable. "And take you with me, dear Miss March...."

"It might be best to pretend you never said that." Claudia picked her words with care. "I should have made it clear from the outset that I could never play a dual role. Becky's governess by day and your... companion by night is out of the question for me."

The silence in the room was ominous. She couldn't look at him.

"I'm sorry..." she began.

"That's enough," he said savagely. "I'm not one of your pupils, Miss Schoolteacher. I caught your drift the first time around. Have no fear—in the future you can lead your life of blameless instruction totally unsullied by me!"

Books by Catherine George

These books may be available at your local bookseller.

For a list of all titles currently available,
send your name and address to:

Harlequin Reader Service
P.O. Box 52040, Phoenix, AZ 85072-2040
Canadian address: P.O. Box 2800, Postal Station A,
5170 Yonge St., Willowdale, Ont. M2N 5T5

CATHERINE GEORGE

devil within

Harlequin Books

TORONTO • NEW YORK • LONDON
AMSTERDAM • PARIS • SYDNEY • HAMBURG
STOCKHOLM • ATHENS • TOKYO • MILAN

Harlequin Presents first edition September 1984
ISBN 0-373-10722-6

Original hardcover edition published in 1984
by Mills & Boon Limited

CHAPTER ONE

It was a toss-up as to which one was in the worse condition, her car or her passenger. Claudia drove on doggedly through the rain, giving an occasional anxious glance at her friend Liz from time to time as the other girl shivered uncontrollably, her coat collar tightly clutched against her flushed face. Claudia was relieved when they finally left the crowded outskirts of rush-hour Coventry behind and were on the way to the quieter town of Kenilworth. While the little sports car was in fourth gear all was reasonably well, but Claudia had grave misgivings as she changed down at the approach to traffic lights outside the town. Grinding and shuddering, the car lurched to a halt, but at least consented to go on idling.

'It sounds worse than I feel,' said Liz hoarsely. She coughed dryly. 'I'm truly sorry about this, Claudia. This 'flu bug must have been a present from one of our dear little pupils.'

'Don't worry, it can't be helped.' Claudia smiled comfortingly, her eyes on the lights as they turned green. 'Say a prayer, Liz, this clutch needs all the encouragement it can get!'

There was a snort from Liz as Claudia eventually managed to get the car into gear with much jerking and bouncing and they were on their way again, though at hardly more than a crawl.

'I feel so rotten, spoiling our trip to the Lakes like this,' said Liz miserably. 'I suppose you won't go on your own?'

Claudia hooted.

'How? Even if you were fit we'd have no transport, love. It'll be a miracle if I get this car home, let alone up to Kendal!'

'You'd better take it to a garage in Kenilworth,' advised Liz. 'No point in chancing the extra few miles.'

Claudia shook her head.

'I'd rather my own little man had a look at it. He knows the car.' She peered through the steamed-up windscreen. 'I think the rain's eased a little. I hate to suggest it, Liz, but could you manage if I dropped you at the bottom of your road? If I try anything ambitious like a three-point turn I fancy the car might die.'

'Yes, of course. Give me a ring when you get home—*if* you get home!'

'Thanks for the vote of confidence!' Claudia brought the car carefully to a halt and said goodbye to Liz with strict instructions on aspirin, hot drinks and immediate bed as she eased the car on its way again.

From then on the journey was nerve-racking. The car shuddered and ground its way along until five miles and almost an hour later Claudia finally reached the garage where she normally took the car for servicing, lucky to find her usual mechanic before he left. Obligingly he pushed the car into the workshop and gave it a cursory examination, then shook his head apologetically as he wiped his hands on an oily rag.

'Sorry, Miss March. I'll need to strip it down, of course, but it looks to me like a clutch job, and late on a Friday like this—well, it's just not on.'

Claudia shrugged philosophically.

'When could you have it ready?'

'Not before Tuesday evening, I'm afraid.'

She nodded, and stooped to remove her umbrella and bulging briefcase from the car.

'Can't be helped. I'll give you a ring on Tuesday afternoon to make sure. Goodnight.'

The man watched with pleasure as the tall, slim figure in the belted trenchcoat weaved its way through the echoing cavern of the garage workshop, her tawny hair streaming in a sudden gust of wind as she paused in the doorway to put up the umbrella before plunging out into the miserable evening.

The chill, driving rain of late October met Claudia in full force, and she hunched her shoulders against it as she walked quickly across the Market Square past the small museum, the ground treacherous with the slick wet pulp of fallen leaves. The clock in the square tower of St. Margaret's Church struck the half hour as Claudia hurried through the small town, battling her way down the narrow street of small shops, all closed now except for the pizza parlour and the King's Head at the bottom as she turned the corner to reach the relative shelter of the neatly-tended gardens of the block of flats where she lived. It fronted on to the busy main road, but Claudia had been lucky enough to get one of the smaller apartments on the top floor at the back, its view of the town's rambling green park amply compensating for a decided lack of space. Keeping to her habit of ignoring the lift, she mounted the four flights of stairs quickly with the ease of long practice, letting herself into her small domain with a sigh of relief.

While the kettle boiled Claudia rang Liz as instructed, then hung her raincoat on a hanger in the claustrophobic little bathroom, towelling her hair while she looked at her post, the expected electricity bill accompanied by a thick white envelope addressed to her in a familiar hand. Claudia tore it open to find a wedding invitation from Richard Freer. She sat down, staring at it. She and Richard had met when she was a freshman at Cambridge, and from the very first all their free time had been spent together, the bond between them strong and unshakeable, more like a friendship between two members of the same sex than an affair of the heart. After graduation their jobs had taken them to different parts of the country, and gradually the ties between them had loosened over the years, nevertheless it gave Claudia a sharp pang to read the copperplate evidence of Richard's marriage to someone else. Scrawled across the back was a message. 'Thought you'd like to be the first to know'. Did he indeed!

Claudia tossed the card on her battered second-hand desk and made her coffee, flopping in front of the television news to drink it, the usual dose of depression hard to take after a day designed to test anyone's strength of character. On the last day before half term her lively Upper Fourths had been more concerned with a week's freedom than any nuances in the boring old relationship between Antonio and Bassanio in *The Merchant of Venice*. More like hooligans than the privileged young ladies who attended Highdean School for Girls, they had been exuberantly impossible, and only rigid self-control had kept Claudia from screaming at them like a fishwife. After a trying day it had been a blow to find that Liz Arnold, who taught Latin at the same establishment, was obviously feeling rotten with the first stages of 'flu, which meant goodbye to their planned half-term holiday touring the Lake District together.

Dispiritedly Claudia went into the cupboard-like kitchen and began to cook bacon and egg, her culinary enthusiasm at low ebb. The car had been the final straw. Crawling back from Coventry in the rush hour with a rapidly expiring clutch had been no joke, and the garage mechanic had only confirmed her own diagnosis. Liz had an irritating tendency to preach about the little car, which was admittedly elderly, but Claudia's priorities had been firmly apportioned when she was first appointed as Junior English Mistress at Highdean after graduating. She wanted her own home. Any economies would have to be made in other directions, mainly transport. For years she had travelled by bus, but a short time ago had bought her dashing little green car, which had proved only as unreliable as its age would lead one to expect. Without it the week of the half-term holiday yawned in front of her as arid and empty as the Sahara—but a lot colder and a lot wetter by the sound of the rain beating against the window.

After her meal Claudia felt better, and settled down to read the daily paper while she drank more coffee. As she turned the pages idly a small boxed advertisement in the Situations Vacant section took her eye.

GOVERNESS REQUIRED for girl of five in British family home, Minas Gerais, Brazil. Mature, highly qualified applicants only. Athletic accomplishments an advantage.

Claudia's interest was caught, her imagination instantly fired by thoughts of hot yellow sunshine pouring down on a lush, verdant landscape from a burning blue sky, in vivid contrast with the wet greyness outside. She searched her memory for facts from schooldays' geography, dredging up something to the effect that Minas Gerais was a Brazilian state where gold, iron ore, precious and semi-precious stones were found in abundance. It had a wild and romantic sound. She bit the tip of one finger, gazing absently at the quiz game on the television screen, wondering just how mature was mature in this particular instance. She was twenty-seven, hardly young and foolish, her qualifications were impeccable, slightly overpowering for teaching five-year-olds perhaps, but for the rest she played tennis, squash, swam and did twenty minutes' exercise every day.

Impulses were a luxury Claudia never normally allowed herself, but suddenly she felt reckless and sprang to her feet, dialling the London telephone number given in the advertisement. She found it belonged to the Park Lane Hotel in Piccadilly, and after referring to the advertisement she was put through to a pleasant, feminine voice which said 'Good evening' briefly.

'I saw your advertisement for a governess,' began Claudia.

'I'm sorry, but I already have a full quota of applicants. The advertisement has been in for several days.'

'Oh, I see. I've only just seen it.' Claudia's disappointment was keen, to her surprise.

'However, since you've troubled to ring,' went on the voice, 'you may as well give me a brief outline of your qualifications.'

'Nine A-grade O-levels, three A-grade A-levels, and a first from Trinity, Cambridge. I teach English.'

There was a distinct pause.

'With those credentials you certainly merit an interview, but the only time I have free is at two tomorrow afternoon. Could you come here to the hotel to see me at that time?'

Claudia's long grey eyes widened.

'Why, yes. Yes, I can.'

'May I have your name?'

'Claudia March.'

'Let them know at reception when you arrive, Miss March. My name is Treharne—Miss Beatrice Treharne. Goodbye.'

Claudia sat down on the corner of her desk, staring at the telephone in surprise. She had never really believed for a moment that her phone call would result in anything as concrete as an interview, and her spirits rose considerably as she thought of the next day. Miss Treharne had sounded pleasant, and if nothing else, the trip to London would at least enliven the weekend a little.

Claudia was up early next morning, giving herself plenty of time to achieve an efficient, well-groomed appearance. She decided on a plain white shirt to go with the grey flannel suit kept for parent's evenings and speech days, and coiled her waving, shoulder-length hair firmly on top of her head. Make-up was left to a minimum. She never used much on her clear pale skin, but liked a touch of charcoal shadow to emphasise the pure, clear grey of her heavily-lashed eyes, added a hint of colour to her high cheekbones and her full, generous mouth and felt ready to face Miss Treharne with confidence.

The weather was worse, if anything, than the day before, and Claudia put on her trenchcoat over the suit and added the checked wool scarf that matched her umbrella. In the cold, clear light of day she felt almost embarrassed at doing something so uncharacteristic as chasing off to an impulsive interview for a post she had no intention of taking even if it were offered to her. Liz would have a fit at the mere thought of Claudia taking off for some isolated mountain fastness in a country she knew little about except its coffee, carnival and fantastic football. The train journey to Paddington went by at unusual speed as she stared unseeingly at the sodden passing landscape, slightly aghast at her own temerity in even contemplating giving up a steady, remunerative job for such a pie-in-the-sky alternative. She knew very

well that if she and Liz had been off to the Lakes as
planned, or if the car had behaved itself and there had
been no unsettling invitation from Richard—or even if
the weather had been less atrocious, she might never
have noticed the advertisement. Nevertheless she had,
so she might as well enjoy her trip to London and treat
the interview as just an item on a programme of things
to do on her day out.

Once in London Claudia made her way to Bond
Street by tube, emerging to indulge in an orgy of
window-gazing for an hour, then eating a quick snack
at a sandwich bar before wending her way through the
crowds to Piccadilly and her appointment. Icy rain was
sheeting down once more, in gusting showers that
spattered like hail on her umbrella before she reached
the warm haven of the hotel lobby.

Claudia gave her name at reception and was given
the number of Miss Treharne's room. She took off her
raincoat in the lift and had a quick look in the small
mirror in her handbag, combing back a few errant
strands of hair smoothly. Outside the appropriate door
she took a deep breath and knocked, opening it as she
heard a voice ask her to go in.

She found herself in a small sitting room. A slim,
erect woman with elegantly dressed grey hair rose from
a brocade sofa at her approach, her dark eyes
examining Claudia with frank interest. The woman
smiled warmly, the eyes kind above the frankly Roman
nose, and immediately Claudia felt at ease.

'Miss March? How do you do. I'm Beatrice
Treharne.'

'How do you do, Miss Treharne.' Claudia's eyes lit
with an answering smile as she sat in the easy chair the
other woman indicated, settling herself comfortably
while Miss Treharne resumed her place on the sofa,
notebook in hand.

'I'll just get the necessary details down, full name,
age, address, etc.,' said Miss Treharne briskly. 'Then
we'll have a little talk.'

Claudia duly supplied the information, covertly
studying the other woman while she made notes. Her

age was difficult to guess, late fifties possibly, her figure trim in the expensively simple cashmere suit in mist-blue, real pearls in her ears and at her throat. She removed a pair of gold-framed spectacles and smiled at Claudia, her manner casual and friendly.

'Now, Miss March, have you any experience in this type of work?'

'Not with this age-group. I teach English to the junior and middle-school girls at Highdean, an independent girls' school near Coventry. But I do have some experience in dealing with five-year-olds, even though I've never actually taught children of that age.'

'I see.' Miss Treharne was thoughtful. 'Your qualifications are impressive, even top-heavy for the task, though, of course, there is the possibility that you could be required to prepare my great-niece right up to Common Entrance, should you stay the course—and should her father's work keep him abroad that length of time.'

'I understand.' Eight years, thought Claudia. A long, long time.

'Where did you come by your experience of small children?'

'I was brought up almost from birth in a children's home. As I grew older I lent a hand with the younger ones.'

Miss Treharne frowned slightly and consulted her notes.

'Where did you go to school, Miss March?'

'From five to eighteen I went to one of the Girls' Public Day School Trust, from which I won an Exhibition to Trinity Cambridge. My present post has been my only job since then.'

Miss Treharne hesitated delicately.

'You had an expensive education, Miss March, for a child from an orphanage.'

Claudia looked at the other woman candidly.

'I was lucky, Miss Treharne. One of the governors of the orphanage was a very rich old gentleman willing to pay the necessary fees for a student likely to prove worthy of his support.'

'And you won his sponsorship.' Miss Treharne smiled, a twinkle in her dark eyes.

'By means of slogging,' said Claudia ruefully. 'I rarely had time for anything else—I worked myself into the ground all the way through school, then even harder at Cambridge, where I survived with the aid of a very sparing diet, Oxfam as my couturier and working as a waitress through the holidays.'

'Why a waitress?'

'Free food!' Claudia's eyes danced involuntarily.

Miss Treharne chuckled.

'Of course. Slow of me. Now, Miss March, tell me something of your interests and spare-time activities.'

Miss Treharne was obviously genuinely interested, and Claudia found it easy to talk about the rather quiet life she had led, and her enjoyment of tennis, squash, swimming, walking, reading, the cinema and, very occasionally, the rare treat of a visit to the theatre or dining out.

After scribbling a few more notes Beatrice Treharne settled herself more comfortably against the soft cushions.

'You've told me about yourself, my dear, so I'm sure you'd like to have some idea of the kind of post offered. My nephew, Saul Treharne, is employed as Engineering Superintendent of a privately-owned goldmine in a town by the name of Campo d'Ouro in the state of Minas Gerais, Brazil. His little daughter, Rebecca, has only lived there with him for the past few months. Since her mother was killed, in fact.' She paused, as if choosing her words with care. 'I feel bound to furnish some information that may strike you as personal, but is nevertheless necessary to illustrate some of the problems involved.'

Claudia's interest quickened, and she inclined her head in polite agreement.

'Saul and Elaine—Rebecca's mother—were divorced when the child was very small and Elaine proved very awkward about 'reasonable access' to the child by her father. Consequently Saul is virtually a stranger to his daughter, which has not made Becky's adaptation to her new way of life very easy.' Miss Treharne's aquiline features wore a troubled expression. 'There are excellent schools in Brazil, of course, but as Becky flatly refuses to admit any knowledge of Portuguese, or to try to learn, Saul has no alternative but to employ a British governess. I myself had no hesitation in making my home in Campo d'Ouro with Saul when Elaine died, as I'd spent many holidays there and always loved the place. Not only that, I knew the child would need some feminine influence in her life, though unfortunately I'm not qualified to teach her.'

'I see.' Claudia was intrigued, and listened intently as the other woman went on.

'I must stress that whoever is selected for the post must be very sure of what the life entails. Campo d'Ouro is sixty miles from Boa Vista, the nearest town, and often in the wet season the only road becomes impassable. There is no cinema or theatre, and little in the way of entertainment, few young people with whom to associate. There's a club where you could play your tennis and squash, and if you play bridge you will be welcomed with open arms, but beyond that very little in the way of diversion.' With a sudden change of subject she asked, 'Are you fond of children, Miss March?'

Claudia was on firm ground here.

'Yes,' she said with conviction. 'Otherwise I would never have chosen to teach. I feel strongly that teaching should be a vocation fully as much as a job, after all I spend far more time in the company of the young than with adults.'

Miss Treharne nodded in approval, then looked at Claudia in speculation.

'At the risk of being personal, my dear, may I ask if you have any ties in this country?'

'If you mean emotional ones, no,' said Claudia serenely. 'I have women friends, of course.'

'Surely an attractive young woman like you must have some interest in the opposite sex!'

Claudia smiled, shrugging.

'Well, yes, naturally. I knew a lot of men in college, and had a fairly close relationship with one of them. At the moment my acquaintance is restricted to two schoolmasters, both of them from Coventry. I go out to a meal or to the theatre with one or the other of them occasionally, but the conversation inevitably turns to education rather than anything more romantic.'

'Extraordinary!' Miss Treharne shook her head, then sat just looking at Claudia for a minute or two, studying the overtly intelligent attraction of the girl's clear-cut face as though memorising it, before nodding with a smile, as if satisfied with her conclusions.

'Thank you, my dear. Should you be offered the post would your headmistress accept a half-term's notice?'

Claudia's eyes narrowed.

'I couldn't say,' she said guardedly. 'A full term is the usual period.'

'I would need the lady's name and telephone number for reference purposes, of course,' went on Miss Treharne. Claudia supplied them, her mind working overtime as the other woman continued. 'I will be open with you, Miss March. You are a great deal younger than the age my nephew had in mind, not perhaps as—well, motherly as he would have wished. However, I shall now ring him in Campo d'Ouro and give him an account of all the candidates I've interviewed and leave the choice to him. I shall let you know whether or not you were successful as soon as I can. My time is very limited as I leave for Brazil in two days and must utilise Monday for Christmas shopping—an exhausting prospect!' She rose to her feet, holding out her hand, a pleasant smile on her handsome face. 'Goodbye, my dear, it's been a pleasure to meet you. Thank you for coming at such short notice.'

Claudia went down in the lift with her mind buzzing. It was too early to think of catching the train home, so she decided to treat herself to a cream tea in the Art-Deco opulence of the hotel's Palm Court Lounge. After her brief, but highly interesting time with Miss Treharne she needed breathing space to think before the return journey home. Home. That was the real key-word, of course. Her mind not really on her elegant surroundings, Claudia enjoyed a cream-laden mille-feuille pastry and drank three cups of Earl Grey, her mind very much preoccupied with the interview. It had been the word 'home' in the advertisement that acted like a spur to her impulse in answering it. There had also been the romantic, Jane Eyre connotations of the term 'governess', of course. But, discounting the glamorous temptation of Brazil, or possibly the idea of it given by all those old Hollywood musicals, what really drew Claudia like a magnet was the thought of being part of a family, actually living in a private home.

To date all Claudia's life had been spent in institutions or lodgings, and apart from odd nights spent at Liz's house she had never actually lived as part of a household. Her own small flat was a home of sorts, of course, but a quiet, solitary place—a retreat. A contrast from the orphanage, to be sure, but a bit lonely at times.

Once on the train Claudia sat in a window seat, oblivious to her surroundings as the train rattled on through the darkness, wondering how she would respond if, by some quirk of fate, the unknown Mr Treharne should pick her name from the hat. The salary offered was adequate, particularly as no living expenses would come out of it, and Claudia did endless sums in her head, weighing the pros and cons of taking on the job. Her answer to the advertisement had been almost a joke, a reaction to an unpleasant day, but somehow at this stage the whole idea had begun to assume very real possibilities. No reference had been made to any social standing, but surely the days were gone when a governess occupied a nebulous position in a household, neither family nor servant, but relegated to some indeterminate niche somewhere between the two. Claudia smiled at a sudden vision of lonely meals on trays in some large foreign house where she was neither fish, flesh, fowl, nor good herring. Miss Treharne had seemed much too warm and kind a person to condemn anyone to that type of existence.

But what of Mr Rochester himself—Saul Treharne, the unknown quantity? At least it had been made clear from the outset that there was no prospect of a mad wife in the attic, but Claudia was frankly curious as to what kind of man he was—the kind of man his wife felt necessary to leave, presumably, which weighed rather heavily against him. On the other hand, the fact that he was prepared to go to the expense of a governess for his child awarded him high marks in Claudia's book. She speculated idly on whether he was young, middle-aged, tall, short, charming, brusque, the list of possibilities grew so absorbing Claudia almost missed getting off the train at Leamington Spa.

Once back in her warm little flat, however, some of the appeal of the job began to fade as she cooked herself a simple meal and ate it in comfort in front of a film on television. Afterwards she curled up with a new paperback novel bought at the station bookstall earlier, pleasantly tired after her hectic day, her mind wandering from the book, more inclined to linger on the events of the afternoon.

Gradually it was borne in on her that, adventurous and tempting though the job sounded, if she *were* offered it she would have to refuse. Sighing regretfully, Claudia faced facts. As things were at the moment she had a good job, security, a pleasant little retreat she could call her own—well, almost—friends of both sexes, a secure life many women, and perhaps even a few men, might envy. There was very little chance she'd get the job anyway, but if she did it could result in disaster. She might not fit into the Treharne household, Mr Treharne might take an instant dislike to her, and vice versa, and the child might prove utterly impossible to teach. And then Claudia March might find herself back in the U.K. post-haste without a job or a home, and with no relatives to turn to.

Claudia roused herself eventually and jumped up to wash her dinner things. No point in counting chickens before they were hatched. It was hardly likely that Miss Treharne had recommended her, for a start; after all, she *had* made rather a point of saying Claudia's age was against her. And there was no guarantee that Mr Treharne would have agreed even if she had. Sensible Claudia put the matter out of her mind and went to bed early with her book, falling asleep before getting past the first chapter.

Sunday was the one morning of the week when Claudia allowed herself a lie in, and it was almost ten next day when the telephone woke her. She stumbled out of bed yawning, wrapped her dressing gown round her and went into the other room to pick up the receiver.

'Hello,' she said sleepily, then came to life as she recognised her caller.

'Miss March? Good morning, Beatrice Treharne here. I hope I didn't wake you.'

'No, of course not,' said Claudia, fingers crossed. 'Good morning.'

'Forgive my early call, but I felt I should contact you as soon as possible.'

With a sinking feeling in her stomach Claudia kept silent, knowing in her bones what Miss Treharne was about to say.

'I spoke with Saul, my nephew, last night and discussed the applicants in general, and although I must be honest and admit he had reservations about your youth, he has agreed to offer you the post on my recommendation.'

Claudia perched on the edge of the desk, feeling wretched.

'Why, that's—that's very kind of you,' she said slowly at last. 'I never thought for a moment I'd be suitable, Miss Treharne. I thought it over very carefully last night on the offchance, but came to the conclusion that I don't feel it's possible for me to accept your offer.'

There was a pause.

'I see,' said Miss Treharne thoughtfully. Claudia could have sworn she sounded disappointed. 'Do I gather you don't care for the idea of the job itself, or is there some other reason?'

'It's not the job,' said Claudia quickly. 'The idea of teaching one child from scratch is attractive, a challenge, and the opportunity to visit Brazil a great temptation.'

'Then what is the stumbling block, my dear?'

'To reduce it to the basic—security, Miss Treharne.'

Claudia rubbed her eyes wearily. 'I own a flat on which I pay a mortgage so that I have a home to call my own. It cuts mercilessly into my salary, but I have a secure job, and my life-style, if not exactly exhilarating, is pleasant, and the money I earn is sufficient to save a little for my future—or to put it another way, my old age.'

'Miss March, that's a very staid outlook for a girl like you!' Miss Treharne sounded shocked.

'I don't have much alternative—I have only myself to depend on. If I come out to you in Brazil things might not work out well, and after a year, or even less, I might find myself back in this country out of a job, and with nowhere to live.'

'I appreciate your point of view, my dear, but there must be some way of getting round this particular obstacle.' There was a pause, then Miss Treharne went on matter-of-factly, 'Don't dismiss the whole idea out of hand, Miss March. Give me a little time to ponder, then I'll ring you back, so keep an open mind in the meantime. Is that convenient?'

'Yes, of course. Goodbye.' Claudia put the phone down, sighing, and went off to have a bath, wondering what Miss Treharne would come up with when she rang back. Perhaps she intended to consult her nephew again in the meantime to ask for advice. Claudia remained convinced that her only course of action was to opt for the status quo, with its assurance of safety and security.

The telephone rang an hour later and Miss Treharne got down to business straight away.

'I wish you were nearer, Miss March, then we could discuss this in a civilised way over a meal, but as my time is so short we shall have to make do with this disembodied form of exchange.'

Claudia sat down at her desk, listening with attention as the other woman went on.

'I've given the matter careful thought over the past hour or so, Miss March, and I shall lay my cards on the table. Being single myself I'm in a better position to appreciate your views on security than a man could, especially a man like my nephew, who is singularly self-sufficient in all ways; too much so.'

Claudia was interested.

'Please go on, Miss Treharne.'

'Unlike you I do possess relations, some of whom in fact are the Fonsecas, the owners of the goldmine in Campo d'Ouro, but above all I have Saul, who is more a son to me than a nephew since his parents died. Nevertheless I can readily appreciate how very different life would be if I were alone in the world. In short, Miss March, if you will take the job I am prepared to pay you a lump sum out of my own pocket, over and above the salary Saul is offering.'

Claudia's eyes opened as Miss Treharne named the sum.

'Oh, but I couldn't. . . .' she began.

'I haven't finished yet. You would have to undertake to stay with Becky for a minimum of two years. You could sublet your flat, then you could return when the time was up if you wished, and your home would be still there. In addition you would have the security of a nest egg to live on while job-hunting.'

Claudia was glad she was sitting down. She tried wildly to think of something to say.

'I'm at a loss, Miss Treharne,' she said eventually. 'Your offer is very generous. But why are you making it? There must have been several other candidates equally suitable for the job.'

'There were indeed. Highly eligible, sensible, middle-aged ladies all of them. I'll be honest and admit that I just liked you more than any of the others. Remember, this isn't just a job. You would be living in our house as part of the family, and I, in particular, would be in your company more than anyone else. I feel you and I would get on well together, despite the age difference, and even on such short acquaintance. Do you agree?'

'On that count I do, sincerely, but——'

'Don't say any more, my dear. Turn it over in your mind and let me know some time later today. Before seven if you can.'

Promising to be in touch as soon as possible, Claudia put the phone down and decided some food would help her brain to function clearly. She grilled a steak for her Sunday lunch, then afterwards she pulled on her old sheepskin jacket and went out to do her thinking in the park. The rain held off, but there were few people about as Claudia walked at a brisk rate through green parkland and clusters of trees, leafless already after the hail and strong winds of the previous week. The wind was still high, and Claudia turned up her fur-lined collar against its cold attack, thrusting her hands deep in her pockets as she moved swiftly with her usual long-striding pace, her mind occupied with how she should answer Miss Treharne.

There was no point in consulting Liz, even if her friend was well enough, as Claudia knew in advance how she would react. Liz would make no bones about thinking the whole idea idiotic and out of the question, so there would be no help from that quarter. Claudia looked up sharply as the first heavy drops began to fall from the leaden clouds now darkening the sky, annoyed to find herself at the farthest point possible from home. She broke into a run as the drops merged in a driving, drenching downpour, and arrived back sodden and shivering as she let herself into the little flat, gasping and depressed suddenly by its solitude. Dozens of other people lived in the building, yet Claudia felt at that moment she was the only person in the world as she stood at the window, her dripping hair forgotten as she stared down a long, mental vista of speech days and sports days, parents' evenings and school bazaars. Was the life of Miss Jean Brodie really the life Claudia March wanted for herself?

Her mind made up, she switched on all the lights and picked up the phone, dialling the number of the Park Lane Hotel.

'Miss Treharne?' she said, after she was put through. 'Claudia March here. I've come to my decision.'

CHAPTER TWO

LESS than two months later Claudia was finally airborne in a Varig jet bound for Rio de Janeiro. 'Flying down to Rio', she thought with a little smile as the plane soared above the lights of London. She was glad it was dark. This way it was impossible to see England's green and pleasant land recede from view to reinforce any last-minute pangs of uncertainty. Not that she had many. Her bridges had been left intact, not burned, behind her. One of Liz's many cousins had taken over Claudia's flat for the time being while he did a post-graduate course at Warwick University, so if life in Campo d'Ouro proved too hard to take after two years, all she need do would be to cut her losses and retreat in good order. She relaxed as the plane reached its cruising speed and the seatbelt warning light flashed off. Soon she was able to enjoy the meal served en route to the refuelling stop at Lisbon, the elderly lady in the next seat being more inclined to sleep than talk afterwards, to Claudia's relief.

The past few weeks had flown by at unbelievable speed. Miss Todhunter, the Principal of Highdean, had been very kind and understanding about accepting a mere half-term's notice, and otherwise the only problem had been the fairly frivolous one of finding warm-weather clothes in mid-winter Britain. The search for these had been in the company of Liz, who was openly upset at Claudia's departure, and full of gloomy prognostications on the madness of accepting the new job. Even so she had been an enormous help, and it was sad and difficult to leave everything loved and familiar just before Christmas, though Claudia consoled herself with the thought that it would probably be easier to make friends with her new charge over the festive season than during a less exciting time of the year. Mr Treharne had given her carte blanche with regard to

Rebecca's education, and anything she needed in the way of books and educational aids, all of which had already been shipped to Campo d'Ouro. Any time left over Claudia had occupied with a crash course in Portuguese, which she hoped would help start her off on the right foot.

She slept fitfully during the flight, and was awake well before the plane was due to land in Rio. She ate a little of the continental-style breakfast served to her, the butterflies in her stomach preventing any real enjoyment of the meal, then freshened herself up, ready to greet the day. The Rio agent of the Fonseca goldmine would be meeting her at the airport, according to the terse, formal missive most recently received from her new employer, and in reply Claudia had given a brief description of the almond green dress and jacket she intended to wear for travelling so that Senhor Helio Braga would be able to identify her without trouble. As the plane began to lose height Claudia gazed from the window in tense fascination as the beautiful, island-studded Bay of Guanabara came into view in the first gilding rays of the rising sun. As they flew lower the glittering light illumined the summit of Corcovado, the mountain peak where the great white statue of Christ the Redemptor stood, its great arms outstretched in eternal blessing over the city of Rio de Janeiro.

When she was finally in possession of her luggage and had emerged unscathed from her encounter with Customs, she was approached by a portly, middle-aged gentleman with olive skin and greying dark hair, his white suit and shining black shoes immaculate. He bowed and introduced himself as Helio Braga, his English strongly accented and formal. Claudia was deeply thankful to see him, glad to dispense with her jacket now that Senhor Braga had identified her, and within minutes the polite, efficient Brazilian took charge of Claudia's cases and carried them to his waiting car while she brought up the rear with her hand-luggage. He explained regretfully that his instructions were to escort the Senhora to Santos Dumont, the internal airport, where almost immediately she would

board another plane for the hour-long flight to Boa
Vista in Minas Gerais.

They reached Santos Dumont with only minutes to
spare, and before Claudia had time to do more than
express hurried, sincere thanks to him, Senhor Braga
had bidden her farewell, and she was airborne once
again, this time in a much smaller plane which took off
above the same beautiful bay but headed inland above
the mountains behind the city. The flight, over endless
vistas of mountain peaks, was brief, but bumpy, and
Claudia began to regret the sketchiness of her breakfast,
her stomach distinctly queasy long before the plane
landed in Boa Vista. The airport was picturesque, small
compared with those in Rio, the small terminal building
reminiscent of a conservatory, with its expanse of glass
and banks of potted plants and greenery everywhere, all
of them exotic and unfamiliar. By this time Claudia had
begun to feel that travelling was a way of life, and
wondered wearily how long it would take to reach
Campo d'Ouro. As she followed the test of the voluble
passengers into the airport terminal she felt an odd
tightening of her stomach muscles, an abrupt realisation
that she was on alien soil, among strangers in a foreign
land. The feeling intensified as no one appeared to take
charge of her. Wondering whether to go off in search of
her luggage, or to stay put for the time being in the
hope that someone would turn up to collect her,
Claudia opted for the latter and chose a central
arrangement of flowering plants where she had a fairly
good view of the small terminal in general. She stood,
outwardly composed, watching the passing crowd, her
interest genuine enough, but scarcely strong enough to
dispel the curl of disquiet deep inside her. If I knew the
Portuguese for 'lost property', she thought dryly, I
could deposit myself there until someone remembers
I'm supposed to arrive today!

Claudia's composure was beginning to wear thin.
Inwardly she battled with a feeling of misgiving, not
daring to admit to herself for an instant how lost and
alone she was beginning to feel, concentrating instead

on making bets with herself as to which of the men within sight was Saul Treharne. Her concentration was so effective she almost jumped out of her skin when a voice, male and British, spoke almost in her ear. She turned sharply, her eyes, accustomed to meeting most people at their own level, obliged to travel upwards, a considerable way upwards, to meet expressionless dark blue eyes in an even darker face that might have been described as handsome, but was marred by a broken nose and the rigid compression of the mouth above a cleft chin, too masculine to merit the word dimple. Devil within, no doubt, thought Claudia, her spirits sinking a little as she ventured a polite smile in response to the man's query of 'Miss March?'

'I'm Claudia March,' she said, dampened a little as she received no smile in response to her own.

'Treharne,' said the man, and stooped to pick up her grip. 'Saul Treharne.'

Mr Rochester in person. Claudia held out her hand, inclining her head.

'How do you do, Mr Treharne.'

Saul Treharne touched her outstretched hand with the hard, calloused palm of his own for the briefest of contacts, then gestured to the far side of the terminal.

'I'm pressed for time, Miss March,' he said shortly, 'so let's collect your luggage and get back to the jeep—unless you feel like a very swift cup of coffee before we start?'

Claudia was well aware he expected her to refuse, but some wayward urge of defiance prompted the saccharine-sweet smile she turned on him.

'How thoughtful! Thank you, that would be lovely. I drank only tea and fruit juice on the flight, so this will be my very first experience of Brazilian coffee.'

Without a word he turned and headed for the snack-bar, leaving her to hurry in his wake, the two tiny cups of coffee already steaming on the bar by the time she caught up. The *cafezinho* he pushed towards her was a demitasse of liquid intended to be drunk in true Brazilian style, very hot, very strong and, in Claudia's case, very sweet, though she noted that her taciturn companion took his undoctored. It took less than a minute to dispose of the drinks before Saul Treharne hustled her on her way again to collect the three large suitcases brought with her. Despite Claudia's protests he took charge of all four pieces of luggage as he ushered her from the air-conditioned terminal into the heat outside, his long strides testing even her unusually long legs as he forced her to hurry to keep up as they approached the vehicle Saul had referred to as 'the jeep'. To Claudia's relief it was far removed from her idea of an army jeep, more like a British Range Rover, standing high up off the ground and necessitating a greater show of leg than she would have preferred as Saul heaved her up into the passenger seat with scant ceremony.

While he was stowing her luggage in the back Claudia took firm control of the hot resentment that was threatening to gain the upper hand, compressing her own lips together every bit as tightly as those of this oversized, bad-tempered man who was making no effort to conceal his disapproval of his aunt's choice of governess. He could at least have expressed some sort of welcome, however lukewarm, asked her about the flight, or even her opinion of her first taste of Brazilian coffee. She kept her eyes straight ahead as Saul Treharne leapt up into the driving seat and started the jeep, reversing in a wide sweep before driving out on to a highway that, to her disappointment, led away from the town of Boa Vista that was just discernible in the heat-hazed distance as a frieze of tall buildings, chalk-white against the cobalt blue of the sky.

'We don't pass through the town?' she asked, disappointed.

'No. This road is called the BR3, which would eventually take you back to Rio, but don't be misled. We branch off it a few kilometres away.' Something in his tone made her glance at him sharply, but his face was blank, concentrated on the road ahead.

Claudia sat in rapt silence as the road wound smoothly between undulating hills, pierced at intervals by sharper, more jagged mountain peaks. The vegetation was green but sparse, broken sporadically by clusters of palms and shrubs, the earth a rich rust red with a scent entirely its own, nutty and distinctive as it pervaded the jeep's interior. To her surprise Saul told her to wind up her window, doing the same with his own.

'Is it really necessary?' she asked. 'I enjoy driving with an open window.'

'You won't in a minute.' He gave her a brief, sidelong look. 'Just along here we turn off the BR3 and take the road to Campo d'Ouro.'

Claudia soon realised the difference, obliged to hang on to the door handle as the jeep swerved off on a road very different from the highway. The metalling was non-existent in places, the road deteriorating at times to little more than a track, winding through mountainous terrain which abruptly became wilder, harsher, the road swooping in serpentine curves, occasionally doubling back on itself, at other times running straight along a mountain ridge, with vertiginous views on either side into rock-filled ravines far below. Fine red dust seeped into the jeep, infiltrating the finely-knitted fabric of Claudia's dress and coating her face with a fine red film. Her stomach heaved as Saul drove at what seemed like manic pace along the tortuous road, but she ignored it, breathing deeply, determined to hide any physical weakness from this cold, indifferent man.

The lack of cordiality in the atmosphere began to play on Claudia's nerves at last, and she decided it was time to put things on a slightly more normal footing, at least make some reference to the main reason for her very presence in Brazil.

'How does Rebecca feel about my advent, Mr Treharne?' As she looked up at his irregular profile he frowned, taking out a cheroot and lighting it with one hand dexterously.

'I don't think she quite understands why you're coming,' he said distantly. 'I've tried to explain the function of a governess, but either she refuses to understand, or she genuinely has no idea about lessons.'

Claudia bit her lip, the scent of the cheroot escalating her feeling of nausea alarmingly.

'In fact, she loathes the whole idea,' she said wryly. 'I hope I can alter her outlook.'

'My aunt obviously has great faith in your ability to do so.' Again the assessing sidelong look. 'Otherwise, Miss March, we would never have invested so heavily in engaging you.' He turned away to negotiate a particularly blind bend and set the jeep at a sharply rising incline on the other side.

There was an odd edge to his words that intensified another lurch of her stomach as it protested against the last manoeuvre. Claudia could feel sweat breaking out in the palms of her hands and dampening the line of her hair where it was brushed back from her face. To her relief Saul wound down a window and threw out the offending cheroot, closing the window again quickly against the insidious dust as they hurtled down a steep, rutted incline, only to climb up immediately to one of those straight sections of road that seemed to stretch between the peaks like a tightrope. Claudia closed her eyes tightly against the dizzying drop to the ravine-bed far below, wondering how much longer this interminable journey was likely to go on, unaware that Saul was frowning at her pale face.

'Would it, in your opinion, impair your authority if we were all to be on first-name terms?' he said surprisingly. 'Rebecca included, I mean. It might be better if she never thought of you as "Miss March", but someone who's more a friend than a teacher.'

'I have no objection, of course.' Claudia looked at him speculatively. 'I think I'd like to get things clear. Does that mean that you will use *my* first name, and vice versa?'

'When necessary. You can call Aunt Bea "Miss Treharne" if you prefer.'

Saul lost interest in the subject as he glanced at his watch and cursed under his breath, accelerating until Claudia felt as though every bone in her body was grinding against its neighbour. After a few minutes of this treatment her ill-used stomach finally rose up in revolt.

'Mr Treharne,' she gasped, forgetting any instruction about first names. 'Please stop. Now!'

A sharp glance at her greenish-white face obviously convinced Saul it was necessary, and with a squeal of brakes the jeep came to a halt and Claudia was out of the vehicle before it stopped, parting violently with the contents of her stomach in a convenient ditch at the roadside. When she finally considered it safe to stand straight a clean khaki handkerchief was thrust into her hand and, still gasping and sniffing, she mopped her face, unaware that her ministrations were adding rusty streaks to her appearance. Her temper was scarcely improved when she looked up to find Saul doing his obvious best to hide the first sign of a smile she'd been privileged to witness on his face, the corners of his mouth definitely twitching instead of shut like a steel trap.

'Are you better?' he enquired gravely.

'Only relatively,' she said ungraciously. 'Is it much farther?'

'About ten kilometres.'

'Then would it be possible to proceed at a slightly less bruising pace? My stomach is more accustomed to gentler roads—not to mention slightly more sedate driving!' Claudia was unable to resist the last bit, but a shrug was her only answer as Saul hoisted her back into the jeep and got in to resume the journey at about half the previous speed, which made the silent journey interminable, but at least physically viable as far as Claudia was concerned.

A final bend brought them into sight of Campo d'Ouro, which was built mainly on two hills, the red-roofed white houses clinging to steeply sloping streets among patches of verdant plant life, interspersed here and there with tall palm trees. A twin-towered church stood at the crown of each hill looking down on the town, themselves dominated by the great cross at the summit of Morro d'Ouro. Claudia looked in silence, her discomfort forgotten as she stared in fascination at the scene, unreal as a picture postcard, very different from her preconceived idea. Saul steered the jeep sharply to the right and began to climb a steep road which curved well away from the town, past large houses screened from view by shaded gardens, finally driving in through open green-painted gates to come to rest in the drive of the house at the highest point of the hill.

He helped Claudia down to the flagged patio running around the base of the house, and while he unloaded her luggage she stood still, just looking at the house that was to be her home for the next two years. At first glance it appeared to consist of two floors, but as Claudia looked more closely she could see that the ground floor was merely a basement, with green-painted trellis softening its walls and continuing upwards to shade a portion of the verandah of the house from the sun. Her eyes were dazzled by light and colour as yellow-gold sunlight poured down from a brilliant blue sky on the blindingly white walls and red roof, even the dull green of the trellis embellished by a profusion of crimson and purple blossoms where bougainvillaea entwined lovingly with its lattice.

Saul motioned her to precede him up the flight of stone steps leading to the verandah, which proved to be virtually an extra room of generous proportions, enclosed on three sides by the house, only its fourth side open to the sun, and even this was partially screened by the flower-laden trellis. As Claudia reached the verandah the blessedly familiar figure of Beatrice Treharne was waiting to greet her, erect and immaculate as remembered, a smile on the features Claudia now realised bore a strong resemblance to those of her less friendly nephew.

'Welcome to Campo d'Ouro, my dear,' she said with warmth, taking Claudia's hand. 'You must be exhausted after that mammoth journey. How was your flight?'

Claudia returned the smile with infinite gratitude, a slight lump in her throat at the kindness of Miss Treharne's greeting, so markedly different from the reception accorded her by Saul Treharne.

'The flights were just fine,' said Claudia cheerfully, 'though the last one from Rio was a trifle bumpy. It was the journey by road that proved the true endurance test.'

Miss Treharne cast a look of reproach at her nephew

who had just mounted the steps with the last of Claudia's luggage.

'I really don't quite see why you felt it necessary to fetch Claudia in the jeep, Saul,' she said severely. 'After all, Luc had put the Mercedes at your disposal.'

'I'm happier in the jeep,' he said impenitently. 'Unfortunately Miss March is a poor traveller—the road proved to be her undoing.' He stood looking at Claudia with a trace of amusement on his dark features, an improvement admittedly on the almost hostile indifference of earlier on, but it nevertheless acted on her bruised spirit like salt rubbed into a wound.

'I wouldn't say the road was entirely to blame,' she said evenly, but her comment fell on stony ground as Saul ignored it, obviously impatient to be away.

'I must be off—I've been too long away from the job as it is. No lunch for me, Aunt Bea, I'll be home in time for dinner.' He ran down the steps with a tread surprisingly light for so tall a man, and seconds later the revving of the jeep's engine disturbed the still morning air as he reversed it out of the drive into the red, dusty road.

Saul's departure left Claudia feeling limp and suddenly very conscious of her dishevelled appearance, though better able to appreciate her surroundings. The verandah was a welcoming place, with comfortable wicker furniture cushioned in cream and russet and a large glass-topped table holding a work-basket and a writing-case. Beatrice Treharne smiled.

'This is where we eat most of our meals and where I spend most of my time; a combination of living, dining and playroom.' Her eyes twinkled. 'But I'm sure that a bath is of much more interest than décor at the moment, isn't that right? Come with me, and I'll show you your room.'

Claudia followed the trim figure in the crisp blue cotton dress through glass doors into a square, cool hall, its floor polished to a diamond brightness. A number of doors led off it, one of them giving on to a dim corridor where Miss Treharne threw open three doors in quick succession.

'Becky's room, the bathroom you share, then your room, my dear. I hope you find it comfortable.'

After the microscopic dimensions of her strictly functional little flat in the Midlands the rooms looked large and spacious to Claudia, with their high ceilings and gleaming floors, bare except for a rug or two. The two bedrooms were very similar, though Becky's furniture was of light wood and there were teddies and a rag doll on a large chest, while Claudia's room had furniture in what she later learned was Portuguese Colonial style; dark wood intricately carved, with wrought-iron hinges and handles. Flower-printed curtains and bedcovers added to the impression of freshness in both rooms, the finishing touch in Claudia's a white pottery bowl containing pink roses on the dressing table.

'It's charming,' she said with sincerity, touched by the thoughtful flowers, then yawned, suddenly and violently. 'Oh dear, do forgive me! The aftermath of my journey, I'm afraid.'

'Have a nice leisurely soak in the bath,' advised the other woman kindly. 'Join me on the verandah when you're ready. Lunch is cold today, you won't be holding anything up.'

One thing was puzzling Claudia.

'I've seen no sign of Rebecca, Miss Treharne.'

'I sent her to play with the Fonseca children earlier on. She's having her lunch with them and you can make her acquaintance later when you feel better equipped to face the world.' An understanding smile lit Miss Treharne's eyes. 'I felt you might prefer to meet us in instalments, so to speak.'

Grateful for Miss Treharne's forethought, Claudia lay in the big white tub in the bathroom, admiring the austerity of the marble-floored room as she lay supine in the warm water, her body utterly relaxed. Her thoughts, however, were busy, a mélange of new impressions dominated by the brooding figure of Saul Treharne. She had previously visualised him as older; kind and ineffectual, a man incapable of holding his wife. Claudia breathed in deeply, a frown drawing her slanting brows together. Ineffectual was the last word applicable to Mr Treharne! Forceful, irritating, over-powering even, ineffectual never. She roused herself and washed her hair vigorously, conditioning it for dear life, wondering whether it would ever be rid of all the dust gathered on the journey. When it was dry and shining again the effect on her spirits of merely feeling clean was immediate, and dressed in sleeveless yellow cotton, her bare feet in mules of plaited white kid, Claudia left her room and retraced her way back to the verandah, pausing in the square hall to speculate where the other doors led. She found Beatrice Treharne sitting at the verandah table, which was now set for lunch. She looked up from the letter she was writing, an approving smile on her handsome face.

'A veritable transformation, Claudia—you look a different person. Come and sit down.' She rang a little pottery bell. 'Would you care for a drink before we eat?'

'No, thank you.' Claudia sat gazing past the blossom-laden trellis at the view beyond. 'How wonderful to have a verandah like this!'

'We tend to live on it in hot weather, but at night we eat in the dining-room.' Miss Treharne indicated another pair of glass doors. 'The insects are a bit annoying in the dark if one has much of a light. Ah, here comes Maria.'

A tall, strapping black girl, a wide smile on her genial face, brought in a tray and set down an avacado half stuffed with prawns at each place. Miss Treharne waved a hand towards Claudia and said something in Portuguese to the girl, presumably telling her that Claudia was Becky's new governess. The girl nodded her head and beamed.

'Muito prazer,' ventured Claudia, and was rewarded with an even wider smile from the girl.

'Igualmente, senhora, muito prazer.' She bustled out, her spotless blue print dress and white apron fairly crackling with starch.

'What a very pleasant-looking girl,' commented Claudia, then turned to her plate with anticipation.

'Vinaigrette sauce or garlic mayonnaise?' offered her hostess.

Claudia hesitated, eyes narrowed, then shook her head regretfully.

'I adore both, but until my stomach forgives me for my journey I'll use discretion and leave my prawns au naturel.'

'It's that road. It's a killer, and I've no doubt Saul drove like a charioteer, as usual.' Miss Treharne shook her head and began to eat, pausing a little with a glance at Claudia before going on. 'I trust you won't find my remarks unduly personal, my dear, but I think it's necessary to say that although my nephew may appear—well, somewhat dour on times, his bark is generally worse than his bite. I mention this because you will find that Rebecca is still somewhat in awe of him, and I devoutly hope you may be able to change her attitude.'

Claudia smiled in agreement, and forbore to mention that in her opinion Saul's attitude had room for improvement too, though it was possible he was more human where his small daughter was concerned.

'That reminds me,' went on Miss Treharne. 'Has Saul mentioned what Becky is to call you? I don't want to start her off on the wrong foot.'

'Mr Treharne suggested we all use first names.' Claudia avoided the other woman's eye. 'I find it rather—well, difficult to regard him as Saul, but as far as Becky is concerned I think it's a good idea. Perhaps she might accept me more easily that way. Naturally I wouldn't presume as far as you're concerned, Miss Treharne.'

'Then it rather cancels out the whole thing, doesn't it? You could call me "Aunt Bea" like the other two; pretend I'm another of your aunts.'

Claudia kept her eyes on her plate as she occupied herself with the last of her prawns.

'What have I said?' asked Bea gently. 'Have I touched on a sore spot?'

'Not really.' Claudia gave an odd little smile. 'It's just that I'm totally lacking in the relative department—absolutely no aunts at all.'

'How tactless of me,' said Bea, vexed. 'I'd forgotten.'

'Normally it's a case of not missing something I've never had. But just occasionally I feel I'd like to have known my mother.'

'You should have a fellow feeling for Becky, then,' said Bea, sighing. 'She still cries for her mother now and then, even after several months. Though why I'll never know. Elaine was more concerned with having a gay time with that new husband of hers . . .' She stopped, looking annoyed with herself. 'Do forgive me, I tend to get carried away on the subject of Becky's mother.'

'Did—did Mrs Treharne not care for it here?' Claudia felt a pang of shame at being so curious.

'She never lived here. Do have some cold chicken and potato salad, my dear, by the way. Saul is related to Luc Fonseca, who owns the mine, and when the previous Engineering Superintendent retired Luc asked Saul if he cared to take on the job. Saul jumped at the chance, but in the meantime Elaine had become pregnant and he had to leave her behind. The idea was for her to join him as soon as the baby was born. But she never would. A man she'd known before re-entered her life and, to cut a long story short, eventually Saul agreed to a divorce, only to find Elaine very awkward about letting him see Becky.' Bea frowned, sighing. 'This is why Saul was virtually a stranger to Becky when Elaine was killed, and to the child he's someone who took her away from everything familiar and brought her to live among more strangers. She's improving, but now and then we get scenes.'

'Scenes?'

'When she can't get her own way. Elaine's method of upbringing seems to have been to ignore the child half the time and to spoil her unmercifully at others, which sometimes results in demands for attention, naturally.'

'Poor child!' Claudia touched her napkin thoughtfully to her lips, beginning to wonder just what she'd let herself in for.

'Now,' said Bea briskly, 'have you finished? Would you care for trifle, or cheese and biscuits?' She rang her little bell.

'I think it might be wisest to rest on my laurels,' said Claudia regretfully. 'Would it be possible to have some tea?'

'Of course. I generally have tea out here after Saul returns to the mine. Time hangs heavy sometimes.'

Maria appeared with a daintily set tea-tray and removed the used plates and serving dishes with swift, quiet efficiency.

'Does Mr Treharne normally come home to lunch?' asked Claudia, wondering if her arrival was the reason for his absence today.

'Sometimes. But he's out all day quite a lot, too. That's part of the problem with Becky. She just doesn't see enough of Saul to get accustomed to him.' Bea shook her head, sighing. 'Perhaps you will be able to improve things, Claudia.'

'I shall certainly try—what's that?' Claudia looked up sharply at the commotion outside, a tearful voice raised in voluble protest as its owner was shepherded up the side of the house to the kitchen entrance.

'Becky.' Bea sounded resigned.

'Not over-enthusiastic about meeting me,' suggested Claudia with a smile.

Bea rose to her feet in determination. 'I'll just go and sort her out.'

'Oh no—please!' Claudia looked at her in appeal. 'Could we let her come in her own time? If she's hauled in front of me like a criminal she's bound to resent me from the start.'

Bea subsided reluctantly, and began to pour out tea.

'Have you discussed your timetable with Saul, my dear? When and where as regards the lessons?'

Claudia shook her head. 'Mr Treharne was not over-talkative, I'm afraid.'

Bea looked apologetic.

'I must explain that the very fact he came to meet you at all was unfortunate. I was coming to Boa Vista in the Fonsecas' car with a chauffeur. Becky, however, took it into her head to hide this morning and in minutes the whole household was in uproar, the maids thinking she was lost, or worse, judging from their hysterics. My command of Portuguese doesn't cover disasters yet, so I was forced to ask Saul to come home to deal with things, and needless to say he was in the middle of some knotty problem down at the Reduction plant, and one way and another the entire situation became too fraught for words.'

'What had happened to Becky?'

'She was crouched down behind a whole stalk of ripening bananas in one of the empty outhouses, where Saul eventually located her. When she realised her father had been fetched home to look for her she became hysterical and clung to me like a limpet, so I had to stay.' Bea sighed, shaking her head. 'Saul was deeply upset by her fear, beneath that wooden mask of his, and then, of course, he had to come and fetch you from Boa Vista when he was needed back here, so you can see why——'

'He wasn't exactly at his best when he finally arrived at the airport,' Claudia finished for her.

'Precisely. The disturbing fact about the whole incident is that Saul wasn't in the least stern with Becky, yet when she saw him she screamed as though he was likely to beat the living daylights out of her.'

'Why is she afraid of him?'

Bea shrugged, her face troubled.

'He tries very hard to be gentle and friendly with her, but she sees comparatively little of him except at weekends, and then of course he's so big and—well, forbidding-looking most of the time. I'm sure it's not anything more deep-rooted than that.'

Privately Claudia felt a great deal of sympathy with the child. She found Saul Treharne more than a little daunting herself, and she was a big grown-up girl, not given much to trepidation about people at all, at least not until now. The fictional Mr Rochester in *Jane Eyre* was a pussycat compared with the dour, unfriendly man who had met her today without a word of welcome. Not that she was any Jane Eyre, either, decided Claudia—it would take more than a bit of boorish behaviour to put her off life in this idyllic spot at this stage!

CHAPTER THREE

AFTER lunch Claudia went back to her room and began to unpack, laying her underwear neatly in the carved black chest of drawers and hanging up her dresses and skirts in the wardrobe. The door stood ajar, and from time to time she glanced over her shoulder towards it, fairly sure she was being watched. She hummed softly to herself as she put out her make-up and perfume on the dressing table, pausing to sniff the roses, only to find them scentless, to her disappointment. When she came to her final suitcase she positioned it carefully so that its contents were invisible from the door, drew a large parcel from it and put it on the bed, relocking the suitcase and putting the keys in her handbag. As Claudia stood at the dressing table mirror to brush her hair she could see the reflected door open a little wider and a small face peer round it cautiously. Very slowly she laid down her hairbrush and turned to look at the little girl staring at her from the doorway.

'Hello,' Claudia smiled, her face friendly, but made no move towards the child. 'Would you like to come in?'

Becky shook her head and stayed where she was, her face suspicious.

'O.K.,' said Claudia carelessly, and turned back to the mirror, spraying on a little perfume. Reflected in the glass she could see the little girl's eyes riveted on the parcel on the bed. The wrapping paper had a pattern of black and red golliwogs, the whole thing finished off with a big red ribbon bow. Very slowly Claudia turned to look at the little figure hovering in the doorway, halfpoised for flight, even though obviously ensnared by the lure of the tempting parcel on the bed. Pale gold curling hair tied in bunches framed an oval face with sunflushed peach-textured skin, the dark Prussian-blue eyes the only reminder of her father. Her over-elaborate

38

white eyelet cotton dress was crumpled and soiled, and there were tearstains on the hectically flushed cheeks. Becky eyed Claudia with suspicion, then spun round and ran down the corridor, presumably to the kitchen, judging by the voices upraised above the clatter of dishes.

Claudia shrugged and made a little face, then closed her door and returned to the verandah. Bea looked up from her letter-writing with a smile.

'Finished your unpacking? One of the girls could have helped you.'

'I'm so used to looking after myself I find the thought of maids a little hard to get used to as yet. At least this way I shall know where everything is.'

From the sundial standing near the house the garden descended the slope in front of her in gentle tiers, each level bright with flowering shrubs and beds of tall, brilliantly-coloured roses accenting the manicured sweep of lawn. The bottom tier of grass levelled out gradually, merging into a belt of tall trees.

Claudia's eyes shone as she gazed at the panorama of colour spread out before her, drinking in the atmosphere of this new, exotic location that was to be her home for quite some time—barring accident. In spite of Becky's resentment, and the forbidding personality of the child's father, Claudia felt optimistic. She was drawn to the entire place irresistibly. She liked it here, and decided that if she couldn't manage to teach one small girl, however rebellious and difficult, after the numbers coped with at Highdean, she would willingly eat the white cricket hat brought in anticipation of this new, blazing sun.

'That's rather a fierce little smile,' remarked Bea with amusement.

'I've just arrived at the conclusion that this is a very picturesque place, and I know I'm going to like it here.' Claudia flung out a hand to include the whole of Campo d'Ouro as she turned to Bea with a sigh of pleasure, then remembered Becky. 'By the way, I've met my little charge. She kept me under surveillance at a discreet distance from the doorway of my bedroom.'

'I expect she wanted a good look at you.'

'Wondering what the ogre was like, no doubt! Though I rather suspect her main interest was in a parcel on the bed, gift-wrapped in golliwog paper with a lot of eye-catching red ribbon.'

'Did you hand it over?' asked Bea curiously.

'No. She turned tail and ran before I could make any real overtures. Don't worry—sheer curiosity will probably win in the end. Best to let her come round in her own time—the last thing any of us wants is a relationship founded on unwilling obedience.'

'I do hope you're right.' Bea sighed anxiously. 'I've had very little experience of children at all, myself, and at my age it's difficult to start learning to cope. I love Becky dearly, but at times I admit she exhausts me!'

Claudia's smile was warmly sympathetic.

'No doubt I'll feel the same on times.' Suddenly the light of battle shone in her eyes. 'But it will work both ways, I promise you. I'm used to children, girls and boys—little ones at the Home, then older girls at Highdean. I intend to earn every penny of my salary.'

'Well, there's no need to make a start at this very minute,' said Bea, her eyes twinkling. 'Let me show you round the house.'

She led the way through the glass doors at the right of the verandah into a long dining-room, its three windows protected with venetian blinds against the afternoon sun. It was furnished with modern jacaranda furniture, the effect uncluttered, the only ornaments plaques in beaten copper on the walls.

'Most of the furniture in the house is fairly old-fashioned,' said Bea, 'bought from the previous occupant, as in your room, but in here it's new. Saul bought it when he was expecting Elaine to join him.'

Claudia was silent, admiring her employer's taste, surprised to feel a pang of sympathy for him as she followed Bea through a pantry lined with china cupboards into a large, marble-floored kitchen where, though the appliances were fairly modern, the white cupboards had obviously come with the house.

Maria was standing at one end of a scrubbed wooden

table chopping vegetables while another younger girl was vigorously polishing cutlery at the other. A third girl sat on the doorstep with the hunched little figure of Becky alongside her pointedly ignoring the newcomers, boredom and hostility in every line of the small body.

'You've already met Maria,' said Bea, ignoring the little girl blandly as Becky gave a furtive peep over her shoulder. 'The girl polishing is Maria de Lourdes, but is referred to merely as "Lourdes", a very popular name in this country. The young one on the step is Afra.'

The girls were both dark-hued, slender young things with long braids, dressed in blue print and white aprons like Maria, the cook. They smiled diffidently at Claudia, who smiled back and ventured "*Como vai?*" to them, hoping it meant more or less "How are you?" As Bea ushered her back into the main central corridor there was a buzz of excitement the moment the door shut behind them.

'I think that went very well.' Bea chuckled softly. 'Did you see the look of indignation on Becky's face!'

Claudia nodded ruefully.

'I think she was all geared up to refuse to have anything to do with me, then we took the wind out of her sails. Poor little mite!'

'Don't weaken. I really believe you're on the right tack, to keep to the nautical. Now; the bedrooms you've already seen, but here on the left is Saul's study.' Bea opened a door and Claudia peered into a room lined with bookshelves holding rows of heavy technical books and periodicals and numbers of paperbacks. The furniture was basic and functional, a large, battered desk with a goose-neck lamp and a telephone, a scuffed leather armchair and sofa, a worn rug on the floor. The entire room had a strong, men-only atmosphere.

'The doors from this room to the verandah are kept closed,' explained Bea. 'Saul does rather consider his retreat off limits, apart from a little necessary dusting and polishing.'

Claudia nodded, Bea's tactful little message received and understood instantly.

Bea threw open the next door and motioned her

inside. To her surprise it was quite small, virtually empty except for the packing case of books shipped from England for Becky's education. 'I fancy Saul has this in mind for your schoolroom.'

Claudia viewed it without enthusiasm. The only light came from the French doors leading to the verandah, and there was an air of gloom and disuse about the room she disliked instantly. 'I see,' she said noncommittally, and followed Bea into the hall.

'There are three rooms left—well, five, if you include bathrooms.' Bea opened the door ahead of her to show a room furnished in similar style to Claudia's. 'This is mine, and the door on the far side leads to what was once a dressing-room and is now a bathroom—Saul had it done for me before I came.'

As Claudia followed Bea into the next room she experienced an immediate sense of intrusion. This was the master bedroom, aptly named to house the autocratic Mr Treharne, she thought. The furniture was in jacaranda, like the dining-room, a woven cane headboard backing the huge double bed with its spartan brown linen cover. Curtains of the same material hung at the two mesh-screened windows, which looked out on a terraced section of the garden at the side of the house. One wall consisted of matching jacaranda built-in wardrobes and dressing-table, with an extra door leading to a bathroom.

Bea withdrew.

'Originally the room had a silk spread and curtains and vicuña rugs, in readiness for Elaine, but as I said, she never arrived.'

Claudia felt as though she were trespassing in some private, vulnerable corner of Saul Treharne's life, and was relieved to follow Bea into the final room, the drawing room. Light and airy, it was the only one fitted with a carpet, in a warm shade of rust-red as a glowing contrast for the comfortable couch and chairs with their covers of oatmeal cotton tweed. There was even a fireplace with a carved ironwood mantel, and jacaranda tables bore big alabaster lamps with rust silk shades, while cream and russet printed curtains moved gently in the slight breeze coming through the open windows.

'This is lovely,' said Claudia without reservation. 'To which category does it belong?'

'The B. Treharne style of furnishing,' said Bea with a smile. 'Saul never used this room until I came. He took the furniture and carpet with the house, but I had new covers and curtains made, bought a table or two, added the lamps and the result is as you see. And now I think we deserve some tea, after which we'll explore outside.'

As they sat chatting over the tea-tray delicious smells floated out from the kitchen as Maria began preparations for dinner.

'Do your maids live in?' asked Claudia.

'Maria and Lourdes, but Afra and José the gardener come in daily.'

'Where do the girls sleep?'

'They have their own quarters behind the house, with a bedroom and shower. It means they can retire in there for a couple of hours in the afternoon after lunch, and Maria does the ironing in there, too.' Bea laughed. 'On Mondays we have a general reshuffle. Maria does the laundry and I do the cooking. She's a superb laundress—I'm sure you've noticed the whiteness of the aprons.'

Claudia nodded, a wry smile on her face.

'Crackling with starch—I noticed too. I wouldn't know what to do with a packet of starch if you gave it to me. To be honest I'm not all that domesticated. I keep my flat tidy due to rigid early training at the Home, but I'm not all that marvellous in the kitchen. I confess it freely—I'm a true convenience-food freak!'

'You'll find life here very different. When do you intend to introduce yourself to Becky officially, my dear?'

'Tomorrow, some time, when the occasion presents itself spontaneously. Perhaps you could arrange for her to stay close to the house so that I can choose my moment.'

'Yes, of course, let's go outside now it's cooler.'

Claudia wandered round the garden with Bea as the

sun was about to set, admiring the flowering shrubs in the cooler atmosphere just before the sun slid below the horizon and the day was gone. In an instant, without the intermediary of twilight, darkness was upon them; a warm, blue-velvet darkness ablaze with stars.

'Glory!' Claudia stared in fascinated awe at the sky. 'I never really believed it happened like that. "At one stride comes the dark", well and truly. And just a couple of days or so ago I was fighting my way through the rain and wind, not to mention the odd snow shower!' She pushed her hair away from her neck and yawned suddenly.

Bea laughed.

'Come along—I think jet-lag is beginning to catch up with you. Have a rest before dinner. Saul will be home shortly and we eat about seven. Then you can go to bed early to prepare yourself for getting to grips with Becky.'

Claudia was grateful to obey, and retired to her cool bedroom to lie down on the bed with a sigh. It seemed only seconds before she woke to discreet knocking on the door.

'Come in,' she mumbled hazily, to find Bea bending over the bed ready for the evening in a navy silk dress, pearl studs in her ears.

'Nearly dinner-time, Claudia.'

Claudia shot up, blinking, and thrust a hand through her hair. She swung her legs guiltily to the ground.

'I'm sorry, you should have chased me up earlier. I'll be five minutes. Where's Becky?'

'In bed and asleep, worn out by the varying emotions of her day, I think.' Bea smiled encouragingly. 'Drinks on the verandah in ten minutes, then.'

Claudia stripped off her crumpled dress and slid into her kimono to dash to the bathroom to brush her teeth and splash her face with cold water. Within minutes her face was made up, hair neatly brushed, and she was zipping herself into a dress of maize-coloured linen piped in white. She left her room as quietly as possible to avoid disturbing Becky and went noiselessly through

the hall to the verandah, dismayed to find Saul
Treharne there alone at the rail, staring out at the night
in moody abstraction, a long, ice-clinking glass in his
hand.

'Good evening,' said Claudia quietly.

He lounged away from the rail and turned at the
sound of her voice.

'Good evening. Do you feel better now?' He stood
surveying her as if she were some miscreant up before
the bench.

'It was only jet-lag. I had a little rest and now I'm
fine.' Claudia felt immediately on the defensive.

'I was referring to your—er—stomach disorder.'

It would obviously be some time before she would be
allowed to forget her unfortunate travel-sickness.
Claudia inclined her head coolly, as unsmiling as her
host.

'What will you drink?' he asked, taking a swallow
from his glass.

'If that's a gin and tonic I'd like the same, please.'

In silence Saul moved to a bottle-laden trolley and
filled a tall glass with gin, tonic water, several ice-cubes
and slices of lime.

'Thank you.' Claudia took a sip, enjoying the icy,
bitter taste, praying that Bea would put in an
appearance as soon as possible.

'Sit down, please.' He gestured to one of the chairs
and Claudia sat obediently, putting her drink down on
a wooden coaster on the table. Saul continued to stand
at the rail, his face invisible in the dim light of the glass-
shaded candle that flickered in a copper holder beside
Claudia. It was just possible to see that his cotton shirt
was white and thin, and his beige cotton trousers had
obviously been made for him, to judge from the way
they fitted his surprisingly slim waist and hips below the
Herculean spread of his shoulders.

'I gather you made no attempt to make friends with
my daughter today,' he observed flatly.

Claudia was deeply grateful for the dim light, which
hid the quick, angry flare of colour that flamed along
her cheekbones.

'On the contrary,' she said with care, striving for calm, 'I feel I've made some progress on that score.'

Even though his face was invisible, the very angle of his head proclaimed his opinion of her answer.

'But you made no attempt to introduce yourself to the child. Becky says you haven't spoken to her.'

Claudia swallowed some of her drink before answering.

'I did say "hello" at one stage, but she ran off like a startled fawn, so I just left it. She was making rather a fuss when she thought she was being dragged home expressly to meet me, so I followed my instinct and left her severely alone.'

'Is this the general method applied to all children these days?' His derisive tone was beginning to get on Claudia's nerves.

'One doesn't apply just one rule to "all" children, Mr Treharne.' Her voice was a little more acid than she would have wished, and she made it deliberately colourless as she went on. 'I believe that each child is an individual, and one must find a separate approach for each one, according to personality.'

'Very high-principled, but hardly practicable for teaching in a large school, surely!'

'Oh, but I'm not,' said Claudia instantly. 'You're paying me very generously to concentrate all my professional skill on just one child.'

Her tiny triumph was shortlived.

'I'm very much aware of the expense, Miss March. Very much,' he drawled, draining his glass. 'The professional skill remains to be proved, of course.'

'Of course.' Claudia was definitely unhappy about his first sentence, but decided to ignore it. 'But don't worry, Mr Treharne, I'm sure Rebecca's natural curiosity will prompt her to make the next move tomorrow.'

Saul moved to mix himself another drink, frowning.

'Aren't you assuming rather too much that she *will* feel any interest in you?'

'I did say curiosity, not interest,' she said gently. 'And I'm not flattering myself that it's directed solely at me, more at the parcel she's already seen on my bed. She has a suspicion it might be for her.'

'So you're relying on bribery?'

'No,' said Claudia with dignity. 'I merely wanted to make Becky well-disposed towards me, and if she is it will halve the difficulties of teaching her, Mr Treharne.'

'I thought we were all going to be on first name terms!' Bea emerged suddenly from the dining-room and sat down near Claudia with a sigh. 'Sherry, thank you, Saul.'

'We obviously need time to accustom ourselves to the idea, Aunt Bea.' Saul looked across challengingly as he poured out a sherry and handed it to his aunt. 'May I top up your glass—Claudia?'

She refused, her colour high, as Bea asked Saul about his day.

'Slight hiccup with the crusher in Reduction, which was my reason for rushing you back this morning.' From his stance at the rail he looked down on Claudia with a sudden glint of white teeth.

'You should have sent someone else to meet me,' said Claudia uncomfortably.

'By the time Becky had finally been located behind the bananas it was too late to organise another willing English-speaking volunteer.' Saul looked at her steadily. 'No doubt you've heard about our little drama this morning. Naughty child, cruel father, etc.'

'That wasn't precisely how I heard it, but yes, I did hear Becky went missing.'

'She wasn't crying for fear of punishment because she was hiding,' put in Bea quickly. 'When she was calmer she confessed to eating several of the bananas, which she obviously considered a far greater crime than the scare she gave us.'

Dim light notwithstanding Saul's scowl was black enough to be plainly visible.

'What the hell do I care for a few bananas?' he said with violence.

'You know that, I know that,' said Bea soothingly, 'but Becky quite plainly regarded her theft as a deadly sin.'

Happily Lourdes came to announce dinner at that moment, and the tension dispelled somewhat as they went in to enjoy the first course of chilled melon and grapefruit balls.

'Maria did something rather special in honour of your first meal with us,' said Bea as the first course was cleared away. 'I hope you'll enjoy Brazilian cooking.'

'If the wonderful smell is anything to go by I can't fail,' said Claudia, her eyes sparkling as Lourdes pushed in the trolley and set down a platter of meat and several dishes of vegetables on the table.

'Does your impressive list of qualifications include cooking?'' Saul's eyes were a shade more friendly as he looked in query at Claudia. 'Try your wine, by the way, it's local and very good.'

'I'm a hopeless cook,' said Claudia frankly, and sipped her wine, impressed by its quality. 'I agree, the wine *is* good, and so is this meat, by the look of it. What exactly is the dish?'

'Pork fillet stuffed with apricots and flavoured with garlic,' said Bea.

It melted in the mouth and was utterly delicious, as were the glazed whole carrots, courgettes in a spicy tomato sauce and tiny, deep-fried potato balls, crisp and golden.

'I shall have to watch my weight!' Claudia smiled as she accepted a second helping of meat.

'Your weight's a problem?' asked Saul blandly.

'When I'm doing the cooking, no. But with food like this I might have to resort to self-control!' The laughter in Claudia's eyes died as she met the saturnine gleam in Saul's across the table.

'That's an additional problem?' he enquired sauvely.

Bea interposed hastily, frowning at her nephew. She offered more vegetables, which Claudia refused politely, her enthusiasm for her meal entirely gone.

'I shall have to make sure we have something special for Christmas Day.' Bea plainly considered it time for a change of subject. 'I believe they generally eat pork here, not turkey. What are you in the habit of doing at Christmas, Claudia?'

Claudia laid down her knife and fork.

'It's a time of the year I don't relish too much,' she said quietly. 'It was fun in some ways at the Home when I was young. But when I went to college I always worked in a hotel over the holiday, and lately I stay at hotels instead of working in them.'

Saul looked at her searchingly.

'No friends to invite you to stay?'

'Oh yes. One very good friend in particular.' Claudia's face softened as she thought of Liz. 'But one can't be a perpetual responsibility to someone else. I choose to be independent.'

'Spoken like a true feminist,' he stated dryly.

Claudia's curving mouth compressed, but she resisted the temptation to cut back with a tart answer in deference to Bea.

'I think a hotel at Christmas sounds very dreary,' declared Bea. 'Pass your plate, dear, if you've finished, and I'll stack them on the trolley.'

Claudia jumped up from force of habit.

'Please let me.' She took Saul's plate and put it on the trolley with the rest.

'You needn't act as waitress here,' said Saul flatly. 'God knows there are enough servants for the purpose.'

'Saul!' Bea regarded him with deep disapproval. 'Claudia was just being helpful. Thank you, dear.'

Claudia was annoyed. She returned to her seat with a suspicion of a flounce.

'Forgive me.' Her smile was over-sweet. 'I need time to accustom myself to the idea of being waited on rather than doing the waiting myself.'

Saul's smile was quizzical.

'Are you a Socialist, by any chance?'

Claudia's eyes glittered.

'Now that *is* against the rules, surely. I was under the impression that politics and religion were never discussed at the dinner-table.'

'And you were right.' Bea paused, looking significantly at Saul. 'Aren't you being just a trifle over-abrasive this evening, Saul?' She turned with relief as Lourdes arrived with a tray bearing a crystal bowl of trifle and a cheeseboard.

The rest of the meal passed fairly amicably, Saul apparently realising that his aunt's remark had been made in earnest. Conscious that Bea was genuinely distressed by the atmosphere of cut and thrust, Claudia turned the conversation to her own first highly favourable impressions of Brazil. They settled themselves in the drawing-room for coffee and Claudia was able to appreciate her second taste of the local coffee at more leisure than the one gulped down at Boa Vista airport. She refused Saul's offer of a liqueur coolly.

'I really was joking when I mentioned dietary problems,' he said surprisingly.

'Were you?' Claudia smiled politely. 'It isn't that. I'm just a little tired.'

'No wonder,' said Bea with sympathy. 'It's something like one in the morning by your own personal clock.'

'I'll be right as rain tomorrow,' said Claudia cheerfully. 'I really do have a constitution like an ox and——' she held up a hand, 'before we hark back to my experience of this morning I must reiterate that it was an isolated occurrence.'

Saul unbent sufficiently to smile slightly at her for the first time.

'We'll take your word for it,' he said. 'Have some more coffee.'

'Thank you.'

'Incidentally, Aunt Bea,' Saul remarked, 'no need to worry about Christmas Day, as it happens. As usual it slipped my mind. Luc had a word with me today, and it seems Emily would like us all to have dinner there.'

Bea was obviously delighted.

'How lovely! We are, of course, related, Claudia.'

Saul handed Claudia her coffee cup and sat beside his aunt, lighting a cigarillo. 'Luc and I are second cousins, and Aunt Bea is old Mrs Fonseca's niece.'

Claudia was little the wiser at this and Bea looked at Saul in affectionate exasperation.

'Really, Saul, I'm sure the poor girl hasn't an idea what you mean. Let me explain.'

Claudia listened, feeling pleasantly comfortable and

relaxed as Bea related how Thurza Treharne had married Jaime Fonseca sixty years before and come to make her home in Casa d'Ouro, where she survived both her husband and her son, and now lived with her grandson Luc, his English wife Emily and their three children, Jamie, Mark and Lucy.'

'Thurza is my aunt, my father's sister,' finished Bea, 'and I've spent several holidays here when I was young. Which is why I needed very little persuasion to come out and live with Saul.' She broke off. 'My poor child, your eyes are beginning to glaze! Off to bed with you, and only get up tomorrow when you feel like it.'

Claudia got wearily to her feet, Saul following suit.

'I trust you'll sleep well in your strange bed, Miss— Claudia,' he said.

'No problem there—I've slept in a lot of different beds in my time,' she said unthinkingly, then could have bitten her tongue out at the expression in the cynical blue eyes looking down into hers.

Bea, fortunately, seemed to read nothing amiss into Claudia's ambiguous statement, and wished her goodnight pleasantly.

'I'll see you to your room,' said Saul unexpectedly, grinding out his cigarillo.

'I can find my way, thank you.' Claudia suddenly wanted to get away from his overbearing presence as fast as she could, and turned away, but he followed her through the hall with that oddly catlike silent tread. She retreated down the corridor at speed, feeling as if she were being stalked by some predator, but to her relief he paused at his daughter's door and wished her goodnight impersonally as he went in, closing it softly behind him.

CHAPTER FOUR

CLAUDIA was pensive as she prepared for bed. Behind that sardonic mask of his Saul Treharne obviously cared for his little daughter deeply, and was prepared to go to great lengths to ensure the best possible for her welfare, including an expensive governess. After going to such expense it was a pity that he disliked his aunt's choice, though. Well, maybe dislike was the wrong word—disapproved was possibly more accurate. She creamed her face absently as she stared unseeingly in the mirror. His disapproval must be a purely personal thing, as surely her qualifications were good enough.

Claudia sighed. She was not naïve enough to expect everyone she met to like her, of course, but the fact remained that most people did. But not Saul Treharne, it seemed, and with father and daughter two to one against Bea life could prove a trifle difficult. Yet even taking dislike or disapproval into account, there was something else in Saul Treharne's attitude that troubled her, like a grain of sand in an oyster shell, grinding away beneath his impassive exterior. Claudia had a nagging feeling she failed to meet with his gold seal of approval in more ways than the mere drawback of relative youth. Maybe it was her rather spectacular lack of pedigree that stuck in his throat. Whatever it was, he had clearly been predisposed against her long before their first encounter today. Her clear grey eyes narrowed as she tissued her face clean with energy. His little dig on the subject of self-control had rankled, too. Was he implying she handed out her favours with indiscriminate enthusiasm? The men she'd known would be surprised to hear it. None of them had ever managed to persuade her to more than a few affectionate kisses which left her senses completely unstirred—the result of channelling all her excess energies into squash and aerobics, as one of them had once commented acidly.

Once in bed Claudia stared out at the starlit sky, unwilling to hide it from view behind the curtains. I *will* make a success of the job, she vowed fiercely. Becky needed love and attention, Bea was patently glad of congenial female company and Saul—well, Saul's battle-cry was value for money, by the look of it, and she would soon show him he had no cause for complaint. This comforting thought was enough to relax her tired mind, and she slept.

When Claudia opened her eyes again the room was bathed in light. Blinking sleepily she glanced at the watch on her wrist to find half the morning was gone. She frowned in dismay and sat up, then stilled, aware that the bedroom door was ajar, and she was being subjected to the scrutiny of a large pair of blue eyes. Claudia watched with interest as Becky, her hair in pigtails this morning, advanced a very small distance into the room, staring at Claudia with rather unnerving intensity.

'Good morning.' Claudia smiled encouragingly, wishing she were less at a disadvantage with her hair in an uncombed tangle. Becky cast a covert glance at the familiar parcel, which now sat, conspicuous and tempting, on the chest of drawers.

' 'Morning,' she muttered ungraciously. She thrust her hands into the gathered pockets of her embroidered pink cotton dress and stared at her white sandals, then out of the window, anywhere but directly into Claudia's face.

'I think I saw you yesterday, didn't I?' said Claudia casually. 'Do you live here?'

The child nodded, her face scornful, disdaining to reply.

'It must be time for me to get up,' said Claudia briskly, and swung her feet out of bed to stand on the fluffy white rug beside it. She thrust her arms into her kimono and searched for her towelling mules, then gathered up her toilet bag. 'Would you excuse me for a moment? I'm off for a shower.'

There was no response.

'Perhaps you'd like to wait here until I get back?'

Claudia left the child and went next door, hurrying through her morning ritual, protecting her hair from the shower spray with a plastic cap. When she returned to her room Becky appeared to be in exactly the same place, but Claudia's observant eye noted that the parcel was in a slightly different position.

'Oh good, you're still here,' she said cheerfully. 'Now what shall I wear?'

With a lack of selfconsciousness due to much community living she rapidly put on fresh underwear and took a sleeveless white shirt and thin jade green cotton trousers from the wardrobe. The little girl watched in silence as Claudia tied the white rope slotted through the waistband of the slacks and slid her feet into white sandals.

'I'll just brush my hair, then perhaps you could show me where Miss Treharne is so that I can apologise for being so late.'

Becky frowned, puzzled.

'She's in bed.'

'Is she unwell, then?' Claudia felt concern. She had banked on a little friendly support on her first actual day in her new job. Her only reply was a blank stare from Becky, who stood planted in the middle of the room, obviously determined not to budge. Her eyes flicked up at the parcel, then back to Claudia.

'Whose parcel is that?' The question finally burst from her, her silky brown eyebrows drawn together in a ferocious frown as she began to shift from one foot to the other.

Claudia began to make her bed.

'I brought it all the way from England on the plane to give to a little girl called Rebecca, but she doesn't seem to be here. At least, she hasn't spoken to me yet.' Claudia glanced casually over her shoulder at Becky's face, which was scarlet with suppressed emotion.

'*I'm* Rebecca!'

Claudia solemnly removed one of the small clenched hands from the frilled pocket and shook it formally.

'Hello, Rebecca. I'm Claudia.'

Some deep-down instinct of good manners prompted

the child to say 'hello', reluctantly to be sure, but deciding the initial hurdle had been taken moderately well Claudia put an end to the child's frustration.

'If you're Rebecca, then this parcel is for you.' She placed the large package carefully in the child's hands. Becky fiercely clutched it to her chest and turned to go, but halted as Claudia said gently,

'What does one say when one receives a present, Rebecca?'

For several moments blue eyes clashed with the steady clear grey of this new presence in Becky's young life. Young as she was, something told the child surrender was inevitable.

'Thank you,' she mumbled sullenly, then whirled in a flurry of pink skirt as a knock came on the half-open door and Lourdes's apologetic face appeared hesitantly round it.

'*Olha,* Lourdes, *ten' presente!*' the child cried, then stopped dead at the girl's smile, her face a picture of guilt.

'*Bom dia,*' said Claudia before the maid could say anything, and Lourdes recollected herself hurriedly.

'*Bom dia, senhora. Cafe de manhã esta pronto na varanda.*'

Claudia's sketchy course in Portuguese had been sufficient for her to understand this perfectly well, but she shrugged regretfully and appealed to Becky.

'What did Lourdes say? I'm afraid I don't know much Portuguese.' Which was only the truth.

If it had been less touching it would have been amusing to watch the struggle taking place in the child's mind, and Claudia exchanged a look of smiling comprehension with Lourdes over Becky's bowed head.

'She said breakfast is ready on the verandah,' said Becky at last, with the air of one admitting to a crime.

'Oh, good—though it seems late for breakfast. Have you had yours?'

Becky shook her head and meekly allowed Claudia to take one hand while the other held on possessively to the red ribbon binding her parcel, even managing an unwilling smile as Lourdes threw up her hands and said,

'*Que presente lindo.* Becky *tem sorte, não e?*'

The child nodded in unselfconscious agreement, and asked Claudia quite politely if she could open her present after breakfast.

Surprised by this unlooked-for forbearance, Claudia praised Becky for her patience and followed the child to the verandah to find Bea, crisp and fresh in white-striped grey cotton shirt and grey linen skirt, enthroned behind an array of china at the table, which was set for three. Becky ran to her, suddenly a normal, noisy five-year-old.

'Aunt Bea! Aunt Bea! Look at my present!'

'Good morning, darling, aren't you the lucky girl!' Bea turned to Claudia with a smile of welcome. 'And good morning to you, Claudia. Fresh as a daisy today, I see.'

'And so I should be.' Claudia smiled guiltily. 'Forgive me for being so late. Good morning anyway, even if it is good afternoon.'

Bea consulted her watch, puzzled.

'It's only just past eight, my dear. I thought you were remarkably early under the circumstances.'

Claudia gave her own watch a shake, frowning, then realisation dawned.

'I'm an idiot! I forgot to put my watch back—I'm still functioning on U.K. time.' She turned to Becky. 'Shall we put your parcel on one of the chairs, Becky, then you can open it the minute you've eaten breakfast.'

Reluctantly the little girl allowed Claudia to relieve her of the box and put it on the chair next to her, beginning to eat a slice of melon-like fruit very rapidly, her eyes returning repeatedly to her fascinating gift.

'Will you try some fruit too, Claudia?' asked Bea. 'In this country the name is *mamão*, but you probably know them as papaya.'

'Only from books!' Claudia savoured the unfamiliar, delicious flavour of the peach-textured flesh and smiled appreciatively. 'Heavenly!'

'There are trees full of them in the upper back section of the garden. We must show you everything properly today.' Bea indicated the two china pots alongside her. 'Tea or coffee?'

'Tea, please.' Claudia exchanged a look with Bea above Becky's head. 'Perhaps Becky will come along too, and tell me the names of all the plants.'

Suspicious blue eyes turned on Claudia.

'Don't know all the names,' said Becky ungraciously.

'Well, you must know more than me.' Claudia helped herself to a boiled egg. 'Are you having an egg, Becky?'

Bea watched in fascination as Becky instinctively began to refuse, then wavered and let Claudia neatly slice the top off an egg set in a yellow pottery chicken. Claudia quickly cut a slice of bread and butter into fingers and popped them on Becky's plate, then left her alone and turned her attention first to her own egg, then to the toast and marmalade that followed it.

Becky drained her beaker of milk and, with the air of one who could endure no more, asked Bea,

'*Now* can I open the present?'

'Yes, darling. Shall I cut the string?'

Becky shook her head.

'My fingers are stiff. Ask Claudia.'

Becky's eyes turned on Claudia with mute appeal and, unable to prolong the child's agony of impatience any longer, Claudia untied the bow and unravelled the knots of ribbon, carefully re-rolling it as Becky tore off the paper and lifted the lid from the box underneath. The pink mouth opened in an O of surprise as she discovered numbers of other boxes and packages inside.

'My goodness,' said Bea, laughing, 'I think you'd best get down on the floor, Becky, then you can undo all the boxes one by one.'

Eagerly the child squatted on the floor, her fingers trembling with excitement as she unwrapped a small box of paints, a painting book, two jigsaw puzzles, a drawing book, a huge packet of felt-tipped pens, a tiny blackboard and chalks, erasers and pencil-sharpeners shaped like fruit, several little jotting pads, a small, furry koala bear, and a wooden pencil-box full of pencils, its sliding lid containing the name 'Rebecca' stencilled on it in large gilt letters.

'That's my name!' squealed the child, her cheeks bright crimson with excitement.

'What a lot of lovely things,' said Bea indulgently. 'Are you pleased?'

Becky nodded absently, busily going over her hoard of loot and smoothing the fur of the little koala with delight.

'Who gave you all these things?' persisted Bea.

'*She* did,' said Becky, waving a careless hand in Claudia's direction.

Claudia hid a smile. Obviously now the present was safely in her grasp Becky felt she could dispense with any soft-soap towards the donor.

Bea frowned, sighing.

'I think you should say thank you, don't you?'

'I already did,' said Becky mutinously, then looked up to meet the unwavering look in Bea's eye, hastily directing a perfunctory 'thank you' at Claudia.

'Thank you what?' said Bea inexorably.

'Thank you very much?' said Becky hopefully.

'Thank you very much, *Claudia*,' amended Bea.

Becky considered this with disfavour, obviously.

'Don't worry, Becky,' said Claudia briskly. 'It's a bit hard for you to say, I expect.'

Bea busied herself in collecting the breakfast things together to hide the smile twitching the corners of her mouth.

'Of course I can say it,' said Becky scornfully, then with an air of weary boredom, 'Thank you Claudia.'

'A pleasure, Becky,' said Claudia gravely. 'I hope you enjoy using all the things.'

To her surprise Becky began to stack all the presents very neatly in the big box.

'Where are you taking them, Becky?' asked Bea. 'To your room?'

'Show Afra and Lourdes and Maria—and José,' panted the child, staggering slightly as she got to her feet with her burden, and bore it off through the dining-room doors.

'You must forgive her lack of grace,' said Bea apologetically. 'Her upbringing was an uncertain, patchy affair, and the few months here with us hasn't been sufficient to give her any real feeling of belonging yet.'

'It's been quite sufficient for one thing, though!' Claudia's eyes twinkled. 'That young lady very definitely speaks a fair bit of Portuguese. I more or less forced her into translating what Lourdes said this morning.'

'I know she does. But for some reason she won't admit she can communicate. Of course you heard just then how accurately she pronounced the servants' names.' Bea looked troubled. 'It's with Saul she's at her worst, unfortunately. He's really very patient and forbearing, but insists on a certain amount of discipline, which I suspect was a commodity totally lacking in Elaine's ménage. When Becky first came here she barely had any manners at all. Another thing Saul insisted on was that presents for her were out for a while. He felt there'd been far too many material things and not enough care and love.'

'Oh dear!' Claudia made a face. 'I've really put my foot in it with my little peace-offering, then. No wonder Mr Treharne was rather acid about it last night.'

Bea shrugged.

'Pay no attention, dear. Saul suffered some very disillusioning treatment at the hands of Elaine. I'm not revealing anything that isn't common knowledge I assure you. She was the most beautiful young woman I ever saw, but unfortunately her soul didn't match. Elaine was selfish, cold. I don't mean physically—naturally I know nothing about that. To be old-fashioned, I think I mean her heart.'

Claudia felt uneasy, disturbed by this unsought glimpse into Saul Treharne's past.

'Do you think he would wish me to know all this?' she ventured.

'You mean I'm a garrulous old woman who shouldn't be telling my nephew's secrets to a complete stranger,' said Bea frankly. 'I've never spoken of it to anyone before, except to Henry, Saul's father. However, you have come to live with us, part of our household with all its problems, and without some idea of Saul's background you might wonder at times why he's—well, somewhat distant.'

'I just assumed he had some personal antipathy towards me,' said Claudia, embarrassed.

'I don't think it's you in particular, Claudia, just women in general.' Bea looked up as Lourdes appeared. '*Obrigada*, Lourdes.'

As the girl cleared away the breakfast things the telephone rang and Claudia got up to stand looking down on the town while Bea went off to answer the shrill summons. The red roofs and white walls of the houses clustering far below were bathed in glittering sunshine, and Claudia marvelled that just a short time before she had been shivering in the British winter. Bea popped her head through the hall door, interrupting her reverie.

'Saul would like a word with you, Claudia.'

Surprised, Claudia hurried to pick up the receiver, Bea retreating discreetly to her bedroom as Claudia said 'hello' cautiously.

'Good morning. I gather you slept well.' Saul sounded positively human, thought Claudia.

'Yes, thank you, I did.'

'You were too tired last night to discuss any details,' he went on. 'But I should have mentioned that any actual lessons won't be necessary until after Christmas. Perhaps you could utilise the time in settling down and getting to know Becky before making a start on the harsh realities of school.'

'As you wish, Mr Treharne.'

There was a pause.

'Perhaps we could persevere with the suggested use of first names,' he said expressionlessly.

'Very well.' Claudia wrinkled her nose at the receiver.

'Good. I'll leave you to get on with the task of thawing Becky, then. Tell Aunt Bea I won't be home for lunch, will you? Goodbye.'

'Goodbye.'

Claudia went off to knock on Bea's door to give her

Saul's message. Bea opened it, smiling at the look on Claudia's face.

'Received your orders for today?'

'Yes. I'm to put off lessons until after Christmas, apparently, so perhaps I can prevail upon you to show me the rest of the garden.' Claudia checked on the time. 'It's still only nine—you start the day early here. What time does Mr Treharne leave the house?'

'Just after six, usually.' Bea looked at her consideringly. 'Are you wondering what on earth you'll do with yourself?'

Claudia shrugged, smiling, as they went along to the kitchen.

'Life was fairly busy when I was teaching. Things seem a lot more peaceful here.'

'You'll soon get used to it.'

The kitchen was entirely disorganised, with the three maids and an older man, presumably the gardener, all exclaiming over Becky's box of treasures. Becky sat in the middle like a little queen bee, and was by no means pleased when Bea suggested she help show Claudia the back garden.

'Perhaps you could let the maids get on with their jobs now,' said Claudia reasonably, 'and after you've toured the garden with me you could come back and sit at the kitchen table to show them how well you can colour one of the pictures in your book with the felt-tip pens.'

It was apparent that Becky badly wanted to refuse, but as the maids guiltily began to resume their interrupted tasks at that moment she gave in with reluctance.

'You go on,' suggested Bea. 'I need a word with Maria about dinner.'

The garden rose steeply behind the house, a grassy slope bordered by tall trees bearing clusters of large, melon-like fruit, a tall privet hedge marking the boundary of the grounds.

Becky waved a hand at the trees.

'*Mamão*,' she said laconically. 'We had some for breakfast.'

Claudia followed her up the rise, her long legs making it difficult not to outdistance her small companion, who toiled on at a great rate until they reached the top of the rise to look down on a series of vegetable beds, which progressed in terraced layers down past the far side of the house containing the bedrooms belonging to Bea and Saul. José was digging in the red earth among rows of rustling corn, the only other vegetables Claudia was able to identify being French beans, lettuce, and what looked like celery, each plant wrapped to blanch it white.

Without a word Becky went doggedly on down the wide concrete path, which descended in broad, shallow steps to the paved patio in front of the house. She led the way to a small gate, which opened into a veritable forest of bananas.

'The *bananeira*,' she announced. 'Mustn't go in. Snakes.'

Claudia looked sharply at Becky's challenging little face and decided to take her word for it, keeping to the lawns that descended the front slopes gently, as she stopped to sniff roses which, although brilliantly coloured, were entirely scentless. One large flowerbed situated directly below the house in the comparative shade was devoted entirely to tall white lilies, stiff and melancholy in their isolation, like mourners waiting for a funeral. Claudia shivered and turned away to peep through the small windows visible through the trellis masking the basement wall.

'The *porão*,' announced Becky. 'Maria hangs the clothes in there to dry when it rains. The jeep's kept there too.'

'Thank you, Becky, you've been a big help.' Claudia felt decidedly hot and sticky. 'Let's go inside and see if you can colour a picture.'

Becky cast her a look of supreme disdain.

'Of course I can!'

She rushed up the verandah steps, almost coming to grief as one of her pockets caught on a protruding nail and tore with a rending sound. She fell on her knees but picked herself up stoically, swallowing hard and brushing at herself angrily.

'Did you hurt yourself?' Claudia examined the knees, but apart from dust there seemed little wrong.

'Stupid pocket,' blurted Becky, scowling. 'Stupid dress! I want shorts like Jamie.'

'Don't you have any?'

Becky shook her head crossly and went on up to the verandah, running through the dining room to the kitchen. Claudia followed more slowly, her eyes dreamy on the view as she lingered on the steps. When she reached the kitchen herself there was a stormy scene in progress. Becky had found Maria making bread on the table, and there was no room for the proposed colouring session.

'*Boba!*' she screamed, tears of rage running down her scarlet cheeks. '*Não deixou lugar para mim. Eu quero pintar!*'

Bea arrived in a hurry to find out what the noise was about and stood aghast at the sight of Becky, her dress torn, screaming abuse at Maria in a language she normally refused to speak.

Claudia decided it was high time for her to start earning her money. She had understood sufficient to know Becky was calling Maria a fool for not leaving enough space for her to paint. Her face was stern as she drew herself up to her full height, looking down calmly on the furious child.

'Please apologise to Maria, Becky.' There was a note in her voice many a young lady at Highdean would have recognised. 'There are other places to do your colouring.'

'Shan't!' The child rubbed dirty knuckles in her eyes. 'Want to do it here.'

'I see.' Claudia took up the box and deliberately replaced the lid. She turned to the distressed Maria and said haltingly,

'*Eu minha culpa,* Maria, *disculpe-me.*'

'*De nada, senhora,*' the gentle black face lit with its usual white smile.

'It certainly is *not* your fault, Claudia.' Bea put a weary hand to her forehead with a helpless little gesture.

'I did say she could come back here to colour, and of

course I should have realised it would be inconvenient,'
said Claudia reasonably. However, there was certainly
no need for all that shouting.'

'What's happened to her dress?' said Bea with
disapproval. 'The dressmaker spent a lot of time on that
embroidery.'

'She caught the pocket on a nail.' Claudia glanced
round at the interested faces of the other maids, who
had both run to see what was happening.

Bea followed her look and said immediately,

'Lourdes, *café, por favor.* Afra, *lava* Becky *e trouça o
vestido d'ela.* Come, Claudia.'

Having sorted out everything and given instructions
for Becky to be fetched to the verandah when she was
clean and her dress was changed, Bea swept out.
Claudia followed, carrying the box.

'My box!' howled Becky, as she was borne away in
Afra's arms.

'I'll keep it safe for you,' promised Claudia, and
hurried through the dining-room—to cannon blindly
into the large, solid figure of Saul Treharne, who
steadied her by the upper arms, frowning blackly into
her startled face.

'What the devil's going on?' he ground out. 'I
thought the idea was to make friends with Becky, not
reduce her to hysteria.'

Bea was behind him, her face creased with distress.

'It's all easily explained, Saul,' she began uneasily.

'Then by all means let Claudia do so,' he said,
releasing Claudia's arms, which were still clutched
around the cause of all the trouble, Becky's box.

'Perhaps I could do so out of earshot of the maids,'
she said quietly.

Saul gave her a frosty look, then waved her in front
of him.

'Very well.'

Claudia marched out to the verandah with her head
held high, and sat down on one of the upright chairs at
the table. Bea followed her and began pouring coffee.
She handed a cup to Saul, who stood leaning against
the verandah rail to drink it, the mere size of him

seeming more daunting than usual as he waited for Claudia's explanation. She related the incident in a few brief words, hoping she appeared relaxed as she drank her coffee. Something in her casual attitude seemed to annoy Saul. He raked a hand through his thick black hair, his mouth compressed.

'It would seem, then, that your present was the root of the trouble—which rather underlines my theory that gifts for no particular reason do more harm than good for small children.'

'Had I been aware of your veto on presents,' answered Claudia, an icy glitter in her eyes, 'I would naturally not have gone against your wishes. I merely thought a few pens and pencils and colouring books might trigger off an interest which would pave the way for lessons.'

Bea intervened in an attempt to lighten the atmosphere.

'What are you doing at home this time of the day, Saul? Claudia said you would be out for lunch.'

'I just called in for some cigars on the way to the Dam.' Saul stood upright, his face grim. 'I'd have done better to go without——'

He broke off as a small figure came hesitantly through the door in a fresh blue dress, her face shining and apprehensive, the silver-gilt hair re-braided.

'Hello, Becky.'

'Hello.' She eyed him warily, then gave him an uncertain smile. 'Want to see my present?'

Claudia felt an ignoble flush of triumph as Becky took her father's hand and led him to the box, showing him each inexpensive item with guileless enthusiasm, all traces of her tantrum disappeared. Saul examined all the bits and pieces with due interest and pronounced the present very thoughtful, asking his daughter if Claudia had been thanked properly.

'I said thank you—didn't I, Claudia?' She gave a swift look over her shoulder in appeal.

'Indeed you did, Becky, very nicely.' Claudia felt a little exaggeration would do no harm under the circumstances.

'Shall I do a picture for you?' Becky asked her father. His face held an unreadable expression as he looked down into the enquiring little face.

'Could you do it by the time I come home this evening? I have to get back to work now.'

'O.K.,' she said airily, and with a brush of his hand over her head Saul stood up.

'Would you walk to the jeep with me, Claudia?' he asked civilly, and bent to kiss his aunt. 'See you this evening, Aunt Bea.'

His aunt watched him with troubled eyes as he descended the verandah steps with Claudia reluctantly following him. She shook her head and turned back to Becky, who was demanding advice as to which picture 'he' would like.

Certain she was in for another lecture, Claudia was surprised when they reached the jeep without Saul saying a word. She stood looking up into his dark, withdrawn face, her hands in the pockets of the green trousers, the sunshine pinpointing fiery glints in her rather untidy hair.

'That was a storm in a teacup,' said Saul finally. He leaned against the dusty bonnet of the jeep, staring morosely down at his even dustier boots. 'I apologise. You were, of course, very kind to buy Becky a present.'

'The entire incident sounded a lot worse than it really was,' said Claudia, in what she hoped was a conciliating tone. 'I promised Becky that she could paint a picture after she'd shown me round the garden and she was, not unnaturally, incensed when she found she couldn't.'

Saul sighed.

'I'm afraid Becky reacts adversely to discipline.' He shot a sudden look at her attentive face. 'I depend on you to accustom her to it gradually. One day she'll have to go to school in the U.K., and life will be pretty hard for her if she can't conform to some extent.'

Claudia nodded.

'I agree.' She hesitated, then looked at him squarely. 'Am I to be given a free hand with how I deal with Becky, or do you have some modus operandi you wish me to follow? It will avoid problems if I know precisely where I am from the start.'

Saul pushed his large frame upright and opened the door of the jeep, his face remote and impersonal.

'Becky's education and behaviour are your department entirely. I shall only intervene if I find myself in total disagreement.' With a curt nod he got in the driver's seat and started the engine, backing the vehicle up the steep drive with the speed of long practice, José appearing instantly to close the gates behind the jeep as it swung out and disappeared rapidly down the hill.

Claudia was thoughtful as she mounted the verandah steps. Saul's answer had been very ambiguous, leaving her none the wiser. She could pursue her own course with the child, apparently, as long as it never ran contrary to Saul Treharne's. Indian giver! she thought crossly, the smiled at the peaceful scene that met her eyes. Bea was sitting in one of the easy chairs knitting, and Becky was installed at the table colouring in her new book with her felt-tip pens, the tip of her tongue between her teeth and a look of furious concentration on the flawless little face. She tore her eyes away from the page for an instant as Claudia appeared, then resumed her labours with painstaking care.

Bea's eyes twinkled over her gold-rimmed spectacles as she laid down her knitting.

'Hauled over the coals?'

Claudia sat down at the table to inspect the artist's progress.

'No. I'm not sure, but I rather think it was more of an apology, really.' She smiled mischievously. 'It was rather difficult to tell.'

'It quite often is.' Bea shook her head regretfully and returned to the small white cardigan she was making for Becky.

It was no surprise to Claudia to see that the picture Becky was patiently colouring was done with accuracy, the various colours kept within the outlines with precision. She was applying herself to an illustration from *Pinocchio* with a great regard for harmony and contrast in her choice of colour, and with a final careful shading in of blue sky as background she finished the scene and sat up straight with a look of satisfaction on her face.

'There!' Her blue eyes blazed with triumph. 'Finished. Look!' She pushed it across the table for Claudia to see, her face expectant as she waited for the verdict.

Claudia examined the finished work with due care, then nodded with approval.

'Very good indeed, Becky. I like your choice of colours very much. Well done!'

The look of unguarded delight on the child's face was infinitely rewarding as Becky slid off her chair and ran to Bea with her work of art.

'Look, Aunt Bea, look at my picture!'

Bea joined in the compliments and gave permission for the little girl to run off and show her masterpiece to the maids, smiling fondly as the small figure in the frilly blue dress dashed off to the kitchen, calling to Maria as she went.

'She really did well with that, Claudia. I think her main problem is boredom; she just needs something to occupy her fully.'

'All children do,' agreed Claudia. 'A case of channelling their energies, that's all. I think Becky will be quite happy to start lessons.'

An atmosphere of cordiality prevailed over the lunch table, with Becky eating everything put in front of her as she listened to the conversation of the two grown-ups, Bea naturally being deeply interested in the latest news from England.

'I miss a great many things, of course,' she admitted. 'Television, friends, and my visits to the local library. Books are in short supply here.'

'When my trunk arrives you can have your pick of any of mine,' Claudia offered instantly, glad she had something of some use to the other woman.

After lunch Afra appeared to take Becky off for a while, and with her artist's equipment in hand she skipped off happily with the maid to do another picture out in the garden in the shade of the trees.

Claudia looked at Bea searchingly when they were alone.

'Are you feeling quite well? You ate very little.'

'To be honest I'm not.' Bea brushed a hand over her forehead, wincing. 'I think I have a migraine coming on—I get them rather often, I'm afraid.'

'Did the rumpus with Becky this morning start it off?'

'Not so much the fuss itself, but Saul walking in on it, I think.'

Claudia felt stricken.

'I'm very sorry—it was all my fault. What can I do for you?'

Bea rose to her feet with care, giving Claudia a wan smile.

'Not very much; no one can. And it certainly wasn't your fault. We've had much worse scenes than that during these past few months.' She patted Claudia's hand. 'I shall take two of my pills, lie down on my bed and sleep it off behind drawn curtains. That usually does the trick.'

Possessing excellent health herself, Claudia felt a little helpless in the face of Bea's obvious distress.

'You get into bed,' she suggested, 'and I'll bring you a cold drink to take with your tablets.'

She saw Bea to her room, then went into the kitchen and asked Maria haltingly for iced orange juice for Dona Bea. She took it along to Bea's room and saw her settled down in the cool gloom of the curtained room, then wandered back to the verandah feeling at a decidedly loose end. Reading seemed the answer, but where to find a book. She went on tiptoe through the hall and approached Saul's study, opening the door hesitantly, remembering only too well that Saul disliked anyone trespassing on his private domain, but with no idea where else to look for something to read. Among the hundreds of volumes on the shelves there was very little fiction, and furtively, like an intruder, Claudia glanced quickly along the titles, most of which were not to her taste. Right at the end of one shelf she found several books by Daphne du Maurier, and chose two, *Rebecca* and *Frenchman's Creek*, first read when she was a teenager. Claudia hastily left the shadowy room and went back to her own. She sat down on the bed, wondering which to read first. As she opened the copy of *Rebecca* she saw on the flyleaf the inscription 'Elaine, from Saul, Happy Birthday'. Claudia snapped the book shut, breathing quickly, conscious of a feeling of intrusion.

Something fluttered to the floor—a snapshot. Almost unwillingly Claudia bent to retrieve it. It was the photograph of a young girl in a brief bathing suit leaning against rocks on a beach. Golden hair streamed away from the pure oval of her face and she was laughing, invitation in every perfect line of the slender body. So that's Elaine, thought Claudia. Saul had no need of photographs to recall his wife's face to mind; Becky was the image of her mother, her face a perfect facsimile except for its youth and her father's dark blue eyes. The eyes of the girl in the photograph were half closed against the sun, their colour impossible to make out. Very carefully Claudia replaced the snapshot in the book, then went quietly back to the study and replaced both books exactly where they were on the shelf.

CHAPTER FIVE

As Claudia left the room Becky came running towards her with her colouring book. She stopped short as she saw Claudia, her eyes bright and curious.

'We mustn't go in there—he doesn't like it.'

'I know, Becky. I just wanted to borrow a book, but your daddy doesn't have any I like.'

Becky lost interest.

'Where's Aunt Bea?' she demanded. 'On the verandah?'

Claudia shook her head and put a finger to her lips, taking Becky's hand.

'She's lying down with a headache, so let's go out this way not to disturb her.'

Claudia and Becky went out to the shady verandah, where Becky looked in her magic box and came up with a carton containing a hundred pieces of jigsaw puzzle that made up a scene from *Snow White and the Seven Dwarfs*. Claudia sent the little girl to beg a tray from Maria, then they both set to with a will to fit the sturdy pieces together once Claudia had established a little of the border. After a while she left Becky and went very quietly to check up on Bea, glad to find her deeply asleep.

When she got back to the verandah Claudia laughed as she saw Becky's progress.

'You've done jigsaws before, young lady, you're too fast for words!'

Becky nodded, her face shadowed.

'But it's no fun doing them on my own.'

'No, Becky, I know.' Claudia was touched. 'Never mind, I'm here now—not that you need much help from me.'

With Claudia to look on and encourage Becky finished the puzzle in record time, a look of such pure glee on her face when she regarded the finished picture Claudia had to resist the impulse to hug her. Softly, softly, catchee monkey, she reminded herself and confined herself to praise on Becky's skill. Soon afterwards Lourdes came to collect Becky for her bath, Claudia promising faithfully to take care of the puzzle for display to Bea and her father later.

As she let herself quietly into the hall Lourdes informed her that Becky had finished her bath and was on the verandah. Claudia went quickly to join her, hesitating a little as a tall, dusty figure rose from one of the long chairs at her approach.

'Good evening, Claudia.' Saul looked tired, the lines pronounced at the corners of his mouth, the cleft in his chin deeply shadowed. 'Please forgive my unprepossessing state. One of the great advantages of a verandah like this is that it allows me to have a drink as soon as I get in, without changing first.'

'Good evening. Where's Becky?'

'Fetching the picture she coloured this afternoon.'

His face relaxed a little. 'I've already admired the puzzle. Have a drink.' He gestured towards the tray on the table.

'Thank you. Gin and tonic, please.' Claudia sat down on an upright chair at the table, accepting the long, frosty glass he handed her and smiled as Becky, looking like a Pre-Raphaelite angel in a white cotton nightgown, ran in with her colouring book open at the picture of Pinocchio.

'See,' she said proudly, as Saul sat down and took the book, 'I did it all by myself! Claudia only watched.'

It was absurd how gratified Claudia felt to hear her name come naturally to the child's lips, though she had as yet to hear Becky refer to Saul in any way but 'he' or 'him'.

Saul inspected the picture with solemn attention before giving his verdict. Becky waited anxiously, studying his face expectantly.

'I should say that's the best painted picture of Pinocchio I've ever seen,' he said gravely, then looked at Becky with a smile, his teeth white in his dark face, transforming it completely from its usual expressionless mask. Instantly an answering smile lit his daughter's more volatile countenance.

'I'll do another one tomorrow—if you like,' she offered, elaborately off-hand.

'I would like—very much,' her father assured her. 'Do one after breakfast and show me at lunch time, but for the moment I rather think it's time for bed, young lady.'

'Aunt Bea always tucks me in,' mumbled Becky, casting a look of appeal in Claudia's direction.

'As she's not well tonight, would I do instead?' said Claudia promptly.

Her only answer was a careless nod, and with another goodnight in Saul's direction Becky went off through the dining room with Claudia following behind.

In the pretty little bedroom Claudia popped the child into bed and tucked the sheet around her, her eyes lingering on the lovely little face in its frame of shining gilt hair.

'Goodnight, God bless, Becky,' she said quietly.

' 'Night.' Becky's eyes followed Claudia's figure out of the room. On impulse Claudia popped her head back round the door and blew a kiss to the surprised child, then rejoined Saul on the verandah.

'How is my aunt?' he asked, as Claudia sat down.

'Her migraine came on rather badly after lunch, so she went to lie down, I think she's probably asleep. I'll check again when I've changed.' Claudia drank the remaining liquid in her glass and smiled politely at the long, relaxed figure in the reclining chair. 'Have you had a hectic day?'

'Very.' His eyes narrowed in amusement. 'How domesticated we sound!'

Claudia was glad the darkness hid the colour in her cheeks.

'I was just making conversation.' Her voice was tart.

'You don't have to. After running after Becky all day long I assure you the evenings are your own. There's no obligation to entertain me.'

Offended, Claudia said nothing after that, for several minutes they sat in silence, Saul apparently perfectly relaxed, while the sounds and perfumes of evening rose up from the garden below.

'What's that sound I can hear?' asked Claudia after a while, her curiosity getting the better of her.

'Which? Maria's clattering of pans in the kitchen, or music coming up from the town below——'

'No, I mean that constant sort of chirruping coming from the garden. Is it some kind of night bird?'

'You mean the *grilos*—crickets. One gets so used to the sound it's just part of life in Brazil, like the smell of the *dama da noite*.' Saul ground out his cigarillo in an ashtray, his head outlined by the light filtering through the doors to the dining room.

'At the risk of being tiresome—what is *dama da noite*?'

'Have you noticed the purple and white flowering tree not far from the gates? It's scentless by day, but once darkness falls it gives out the perfume you can smell—unless the aroma of tobacco is defeating it.' Saul

sounded tired, admittedly, but much less distant than
Claudia had expected after the unfortunate incident of
the morning.

'I quite like the smell of your cheroot. Combined
with the flowers and the earth it typifies Brazil to me
already; exotic, different.' Claudia stood up, Saul
automatically doing the same.

'And do you think you can settle to life here?'

Claudia was almost persuaded her answer was
important to him. No doubt it was after all the money
invested in getting her here, she thought prosaically.

'Yes. Very easily,' she said positively. 'I think Becky
will knuckle down to her lessons very well once we
start, and as for myself, I would have to be very hard to
please if I couldn't enjoy living in a beautiful house like
this.'

'Even though it's so quiet here?'

'Ah, but then there's quiet and quiet.' Claudia cast a
sparkling glance up at the dimly-seen face of her
employer. 'The variety you have here could easily be
addictive, I think.'

Almost sure he smiled involuntarily in response,
Claudia excused herself and went off to bath and change
for dinner, a little uneasy at the prospect of dining alone
with her formidable host despite his slightly warmer
manner towards her. Some perverse instinct made her
choose her plainest dress, a shirtwaister in cinnamon
shantung, cut like a man's shirt, it's only gesture towards
frivolity the two gold tassels that swung at the end of the
hip-level sash. She brushed her hair back from her face
relentlessly, securing it in a knot on top of her head, made
up her face with a sparing hand, then hesitated and
weakened, choosing a pair of gold hoops to thread
through her earlobes rather than the tiny gold studs she
habitually wore.

When she was ready Claudia went quietly to look at
Becky, who lay on her back, arms outstretched, with all
the vulnerable beauty of a sleeping cherub. Claudia
gazed at the slumbering face for quite some time. If the
dead Elaine had been as lovely as her little daughter it
was hardly surprising Saul had become so embittered

when she left him for another man. Gently Claudia drew the sheet over Becky and tiptoed noiselessly from the room, hesitating in the corridor, wondering about Bea. Silently she crossed the polished expanse of the dark hall and very carefully opened Bea's door. The room was in darkness and quiet, even breathing seemed to indicate that the invalid was sleeping peacefully, so with no desire to disturb her Claudia backed out of the room and closed the door.

All at once Claudia was aware she was hungry. Lunch had been a long time ago, and her athletic, healthy body was in need of refuelling. Delicious smells came from the kitchen as she opened the door to find Maria busily occupied with preparations for dinner, with Lourdes in attendance.

'*O patrão está na varanda*, Dona Claudia,' said Lourdes shyly, and Claudia smiled her thanks, indicating how heavenly the food smelt, to Maria's obvious pleasure. Claudia would have much preferred to stay in the kitchen and watch operations, but realised her presence would only hinder, and went through the brightly lit dining room, with its attractively laid table, and joined Saul, who was leaning in his favourite place against the rail, glass in hand as he stared down at the lights of the town. A fat candle in the glass-shaped copper holder on the table gave a faint illumination, augmented by the light of the moon just rising over the peak of Morro d'Ouro, with its lighted cross at the summit.

Saul turned as Claudia joined him.

'You were remarkably swift,' he said dryly. 'I thought women generally took a fair time over their toilette, or whatever one calls it, so I told Maria to hold dinner for another fifteen minutes or so.'

'I can't answer for other women,' she retorted, 'but half an hour is positively lingering as far as I'm concerned.'

Saul moved over to the tray on the table.

'Gin and tonic?'

Claudia felt doubtful.

'I don't know that I should. I feel a bit empty, to

be truthful, and more gin might have a disastrous effect.'

He laughed, a sound as attractive as it was unfamiliar, and insisted on a small drink, handing her a dish of peanuts.

'Have some of these to keep the hunger pangs at bay,' he suggested. 'There are some olives here too, if you care for them.'

Claudia accepted the nuts with enthusiasm, but refused the olives.

'I've heard they're an acquired taste, but I've never had enough of them to acquire it.' She wandered over to the rail and looked out on the moonlit scene, shaking her head in wonder. 'This is unreal. It looks like a film set.'

Saul resumed his place beside her, and to her dismay Claudia found herself overreacting to the accidental touch of his arm against hers. Suddenly aware in every nerve of the large, lounging presence beside her, she began to eat peanuts with nervous speed, with the aim of keeping herself occupied.

'One gets used to it.' Saul's profile was clearly limned against the night sky as he looked down on the lights of the town. 'It looks unearthly from up here at this time of night, especially when there's a moon, I grant you, but in reality everyone down there is occupied with the serious business of the evening meal, eating enormous quantities of beans and rice, pork or *carne seca*, a type of salted, dried meat, and all kinds of dishes I can't begin to describe. I'll take you out to one of the sub-stations one day and have the wife of the Power Engineer cook you a meal. An experience you won't forget, I assure you—the table literally groans!'

Claudia laughed, then looked down guiltily at the dish she held, realising all the peanuts were gone.

'Sounds like my idea of fun,' she said, glad of the excuse to move away to replace the dish on the tray. 'My appetite was famous in college.'

She turned to find Saul giving her a very deliberate appraisal, his eyes leisurely in their examination of her graceful, slim-hipped figure.

'It's hard to credit,' he said mockingly. 'You look as if you live on leafy green vegetables and yoghourt.'

'I do,' said Claudia, with a smile up at his definitely friendlier face, feeling reassured and more relaxed in the appreciably warmer atmosphere between them. 'But I eat stacks of other things as well. I'm lucky, I suppose, it's just metabolism.'

Lourdes's appearance signalled the arrival of dinner, and despite the warmth of the evening Claudia sat down to steaming julienne soup with gusto, aware of Saul's amused eyes on her, but in no way put out as she enjoyed the spicy, vegetable-filled liquid. There was little conversation while Claudia blunted the first edge of her hunger, but when the *camaroes baiana* appeared the dish itself was a conversation piece. King-sized prawns, cooked in a hot peppery tomato sauce, were served on a bed of fried rice and accompanied by runner beans, okra and marrow, or *quiabo* and *xu-xu*, as the latter were known as locally. Claudia was almost lost for words.

'This is absolutely fantastic—I've never tasted anything more delicious!'

Saul laughed outright, neglecting his own meal to watch the relish with which Claudia attacked hers. She looked up at him, her long grey eyes sparkling.

'You should laugh more often,' she said bluntly.

He went on with his dinner, the laughter fading from his strongly-marked face immediately, the dark blue eyes shuttered. Claudia cursed herself silently for a tactless idiot and searched for a neutral topic of conversation.

'Does Becky see much of the Fonseca children?' she asked in desperation.

'No, not all that much. She and Jamie are inclined to clash if too long in each other's company.' He clicked his fingers impatiently. 'A good thing you mentioned them. Luc said Emily would like you to go over there to visit. She's given you a day's grace to settle in, but will probably ring tomorrow. I'm sorry, it went clean out of my head.'

'Not to worry.' Claudia felt curious about the wife of

Luc Fonseca. 'What age-group are the Fonsecas? They have young children, I know, but I assume that if he's the owner Senhor Fonseca is an older man.'

There was a delay while Lourdes removed their plates and put the cheeseboard and a compote of fresh figs on the table.

Saul helped himself to cheese, his face wooden again.

'Why are you interested in Luc Fonseca?'

Claudia blinked. What had she said now?

'I'm not particularly, at least only in relation to Senhora Fonseca,' she said carefully. 'I was interested in her because she's British, I suppose.' Forget about making conversation, Claudia, she told herself grimly. Just get on with your dinner.

There was silence for a while as Claudia kept her eyes on the fruit in her crystal dish, refusing to look up. For once her pleasure in her food was impaired, and she was obliged to abandon her dessert after only a mouthful or two, deeply resentful that her appetite had taken any notice of Saul's censorious attitude.

'Shall we drink coffee in the drawing room?' said Saul, rising to his feet.

Claudia followed suit with reluctance. She had little desire to sit à deux with him, even for the short time it would take to dispose of a *cafezinho*.

'If you don't mind . . .' she began stiffly, but he cut her short and held open the verandah door peremptorily.

'Oh, but I do,' he said with emphasis. 'Lourdes will have checked on Bea and Becky, so there's no reason why you can't spend a peaceful half-hour or so talking, or listening to records if you prefer.'

Claudia stalked across the verandah and through the open doors of the drawing-room, settling herself on the comfortable couch as Saul entered the room. She ignored the coffee-tray on the table in front of her and took the bull by the horns.

'Before I pour out I must be honest and say a peaceful half-hour, as you put it, would be very pleasant. But, Mr Treharne—Saul,' she amended hastily in response to his wagging finger, 'I don't care much for conversations where I appear obliged to guard

constantly against putting my foot in it. It's wearing.'
Her grey eyes were bright and stormy as she locked
glances with the man who stood rock-still with surprise,
looming over her like a lighthouse.

'Is that how you feel?' His thick black brows rose
almost to the equally thick hair beginning to stray
across his forehead as he ran his fingers through it,
some of his imperturbability lost at her sudden attack.

Claudia nodded and poured out two cups of coffee,
rather triumphant to see how steady her hand remained
as it handed Saul's to him. He took it absently, and
drank it down in one swallow, apparently careless of
scalding his throat.

'Liqueur?' he asked.

She shook her head and sipped her own coffee with
more caution. I suppose that's torn it, she thought
despondently. Just as things were beginning to relax a
bit too. Oh well, in for a penny, in for a pound. 'There's
something else,' she added.

'Perhaps I'd better sit down,' he murmured, his blue
eyes expressionless as he sat opposite, his face all polite
attention. 'Do go on.'

'When I was at a loose end this afternoon I had
nothing to read. Bea had shown me your study briefly,
and as it was the only place where there seemed to be
any books I borrowed one.' Claudia paused, but he said
nothing, merely looking at her steadily. 'A snapshot fell
out of the book; someone so like Becky it must have
been your wife. I felt as though I'd trespassed, so I put
the book back without reading it. I'm sorry—I won't go
in your study again.'

'What was the book?'

Claudia looked at him uncertainly.

'Daphne du Maurier's *Rebecca*.'

Saul nodded, and held out his cup for more coffee.

'It would have been—it was her favourite. You might
say Elaine was obsessed by it; she even called our
daughter Rebecca.'

Claudia gave him his coffee and leaned back against
the sofa cushions, not sure if he was annoyed or merely
indifferent.

'You have absolutely no need for embarrassment, or sympathy,' he said, a sardonic twist to his mouth. 'I've no objection to your frequenting the study—borrow what you like. If you're concerned about my—er—feelings, for want of a better word, don't be. Any I had for Elaine underwent rather a violent metamorphosis when she left me for a wealthier man and took my child with her. And please don't imagine I'm nursing any secret sorrow,' he added. 'Elaine taught me a very valuable lesson. All women have a price. Someone else offered her a higher price than I could pay, and off she went.'

'It's surely not possible to generalise to that extent,' objected Claudia.

'The price varies, Claudia, that's all. Elaine's was a luxury life style, Becky was won over today by a present. You——' he paused, a mocking smile on his lips as she started, sitting bolt upright. 'You, Claudia, stood out for more money before you'd take the job. Admittedly it was in the name of security, a condition beloved by you above all else, as I heard it, nevertheless it was a price. Only the degree is different—the principle is more or less the same.'

Claudia sat very still for a moment or two.

'Miss Treharne said the extra sum would be something private, an agreement purely between herself and me,' she said quietly. All was now revealed, she thought fatalistically. At least she now had the key to Saul Treharne's attitude towards her.

'Unfortunately both my aunt and myself are B.S. Treharne. I opened her bank statement by mistake and the sum in question was large enough to be conspicuous before I realised my error.' Saul poured himself a brandy and sat down again, his eyes sombre on the liquid in his glass. 'I was worried, naturally, about Aunt Bea's need to spend such an amount, and asked about it when I apologised for opening the wrong letter. She was obliged to tell me how she prevailed upon you to leave England.'

There was nothing in the least condemnatory in his deep voice, yet Claudia felt guilty, degraded, like a criminal caught redhanded. There seemed no point in trying to vindicate herself, so she kept quiet, her cheeks burning.

'You don't spring to your own defence?' He sat relaxed, quite obviously enjoying her discomfiture.

Claudia raised her head and looked at him levelly.

'I don't have one. With no family behind me I needed the security a lump sum in the bank would represent before leaving not just England, but the very good job I had there. If there is any defence, as you put it,' she added, 'I would stress that I made this very clear when I turned down the post in the first place. There were, after all, several other applicants your aunt could have chosen.'

His answering look was saturnine.

'Yes, indeed. Any one of whom was older, more suitable, in my estimation, and had the advantage of being a damned sight cheaper!'

Claudia was stung.

'I may be younger than you wished, Mr Treharne,' she said tightly, 'but my teaching abilities are proven and above question. My qualifications aren't so bad, either. I intend to make a good job of Becky's education, in all departments; even my so-called youth is an advantage, surely, when it comes to games and swimming.'

'Oh, I grant you all the attributes,' said Saul mockingly. 'It's such a shame you happen to be so mercenary as well, don't you agree?'

'You can hardly expect me to agree to that!' Claudia's nostrils flared as she took a deep breath to steady herself. 'The extra money was a great incentive. I grant you that. Even so it wasn't the deciding factor. Apart from the instant rapport I felt with your aunt she said the one thing, quite unknowingly, which made her offer irresistible; the bit about being welcomed into your family in your home. You already know about the orphanage. I've lived in institutions of one kind or another for most of my life. My price, if you must think of it in that way, wasn't only the money, generous and tempting though it was. It was the idea of being accepted in someone's home as part of their family.' Her eyes were clear and cold on his. 'I'm sorry you consider me an unsuitable addition to your household, Mr Treharne.'

'I don't consider you unsuitable in the least,' Saul said surprisingly.

Claudia managed a crooked little smile.

'Just expensive! Don't worry—I'll do my utmost to prove worthy of my hire, Mr Treharne.'

'I'm relieved to hear it.' He rose to his full, towering height and drained his glass, then crossed to pour himself another brandy. 'Sure I can't persuade you to a liqueur?'

Claudia shook her head.

'No, thank you.'

' "Saul",' he prompted.

This seemed a night for clearing the air. Claudia looked up at him with an odd little smile.

'I'm afraid it doesn't come easily. In my mind you've been "Mr Rochester" from the beginning—my literary hang-up was *Jane Eyre*, not *Rebecca*.'

Saul stiffened and turned on her with an air of menace only half-feigned.

'Spare me any more unhealthy fixations on fictional characters, for God's sake—I've had enough of that sort of thing to last a lifetime!'

Something suddenly occurred to Claudia.

'If you knew about the money before I came why didn't you stop me coming? There would have been time—you could have engaged one of the others.'

Saul turned away to the open doorway, leaning against the lintel to look out into the night.

'Too many wheels had been set in motion by then,' he said. 'Besides, if Aunt Bea was sufficiently determined you were the only one possible, to the point of paying the added inducement out of her own pocket, who was I to go against her wishes?'

'I see.' Claudia looked thoughtfully at his broad back.

Saul swung round to look at her with a disturbing gleam in his eyes.

'Not quite, Claudia. You had your price, but I felt it was up to me to pay it, as Becky's father. So I reimbursed Aunt Bea for every penny. Contractually, at least, you are now my property.'

A trickle of cold apprehension ran down Claudia's spine, but her eyes met his unflinchingly, as clear and expressionless as panes of glass. The abrading quality of his tone flayed the outer skin of her composure badly, and she rose to her feet without hurry, even managing the suggestion of a yawn to mask her erratic pulse.

'There's really not a lot to say in answer to that, Mr Treharne,' she said evenly. 'Goodnight.'

'Goodnight, Claudia.' Saul was swift to open the door for her, his eyes hard and mocking on her face. 'By the way, if scraping your hair back like that is a gesture towards the Jane Eyre image, it doesn't really work—you're a damned sight too down-to-earth and contemporary to sustain the effect!'

Claudia glared at him for an instant, abandoning her careful inscrutability, then walked quietly away through the hall, her head in the air as she forced herself to walk slowly in the direction of her bedroom.

CHAPTER SIX

CLAUDIA was up by seven next morning, guiltily aware that in her vexation the night before she had quite forgotten to look in on either Bea or Becky before falling into her bed. After a speedy shower she dressed in black cotton slacks and a long sleeveless white tunic with a white-dotted black scarf tied at the waist.

A peep into Becky's room showed the child still fast asleep, and Claudia hurried along to Bea's room to find the door ajar and Bea sitting up in bed drinking a cup of tea and looking a great deal better. She smiled at Claudia in welcome.

'Good morning, you're an early riser. How are you today?'

'I'm fine, but how are you?' Claudia went in, her face

apologetic. 'I was so—tired—last night I forgot to come
and see you before I went to bed.'

'That's all right, my dear. Saul brought me some fruit
juice last thing, but my headache had almost gone by
then, and with the aid of yet more pills I had quite a
good night. He mentioned you were very tired. One's
inclined to forget about the altitude, but it makes a
tremendous difference, you know. You must be
careful.'

'I will. I'll just see if Becky has surfaced yet. She was
still sleeping a moment ago.' Claudia felt very guilty at
Bea's solicitude.

'I'll be with you for breakfast in half an hour.' Bea
smiled briskly. 'One day in bed in this heat is quite
enough!'

Claudia went back to Becky's room to find that
young lady sitting on the floor in her nightdress poring
over the contents of her beloved box.

'Hello. You're starting early this morning!'

'Hello.'

There was a marked lack of enthusiasm in the child's
greeting as she cast a careless look up at Claudia, but at
least she was not precisely hostile. Lourdes arrived to
dress Becky, so Claudia wandered off to walk round the
garden in the early morning sunshine, surprised to find
how warm it was even at that hour. She said good
morning to Afra, who was sweeping out the servants'
quarters, and strolled down the terraced lawns to look
past red roofs and clusters of greenery to the white
supports of the flume far below. The thought of
breakfast drew her back to the house, which she entered
through the kitchen, greeting the smiling Maria, who
told her the meal was waiting on the verandah.

Becky was already there, in a pale yellow muslin
dress, yellow ribbons at the end of her pigtails.

'Do I have to do lessons today?' she demanded, her
face belligerent.

'No.' Claudia sat down at the table, motioning Becky
to take her place. 'Your father says after Christmas is
soon enough.'

'When's Christmas?'

'In a week or so—not long.'

Bea came out to join them and poured tea while Claudia and Becky began their meal. She passed Claudia's cup and asked how they were going to spend the day, her eyes bright and clear, all traces of her migraine disappeared.

'I'm going to do more pictures,' announced Becky instantly, with a challenging look at both women to see if there was any opposition.

'Fine,' said Claudia casually, and helped herself to scrambled eggs and toast, hungry despite the excellent dinner consumed the evening before. She looked up at Bea enquiringly. 'Is this the hottest part of the year? It's very warm outside even at this hour.'

'No. January and February, even March, can be quite a lot hotter than this, and of course we get quite a lot of rain, too.' Bea looked at Claudia curiously. 'I hope your evening passed fairly amicably, my dear?'

'Yes, thank you. Reasonably so.'

'I'm glad.' Bea coughed delicately. 'You seem to— well, affect each other a little adversely. Saul really can be quite charming.'

Claudia smiled, shrugging.

'I'm sure a big part of the fault is mine.'

'You ring the little bell for Lourdes to clear away, Becky,' said Bea, avoiding Claudia's eye, 'and then you can start on your colouring.'

For an hour peace reigned on the verandah while Bea returned to her knitting and Claudia just lay relaxed in a long chair, chatting desultorily while Becky brought the full force of her attention to bear on a picture of Hansel and Gretel. The sound of the telephone eventually disturbed the quiet and Claudia got up to examine Becky's picture while Bea answered the phone.

'Is it nice?' asked Becky, her tongue curling out over her upper lip in her concentration on the tiles of the gingerbread house.

'I prefer to use the word "nice" for things to eat,' said Claudia. 'Your picture is very attractive, Becky.' She looked down on the bright gold head, wondering if the child still missed her mother. There had been tears of temper since Claudia's arrival, admittedly, but not of grief, though it was difficult to tell what went on in that complicated little brain.

Bea came back with a wide smile on her face.

'That was Emily. She announced that her curiosity has been contained long enough, and could Saul drop us off at Casa d'Ouro after lunch to spend the afternoon there.'

Becky looked up sharply.

'Can I take my box?'

'It might be a good idea to take just one or two things,' suggested Claudia. 'Otherwise there might be problems.'

'No,' said Becky instantly, an ominous frown darkening her face.

'Well, you could stay here with Lourdes and Maria, of course,' said Claudia reasonably. Something in her manner plainly told Becky discretion was necessary, and with a pout she returned to her painting.

Bea watched with admiration and patted Claudia's hand silently.

'Coffee-time, I think,' she announced. 'Becky, would you be kind enough to ask Maria to make coffee and tell her what you want; that is if you can?'

' 'Course I can,' said Becky loftily, and slid off her chair to run to the kitchen.

'I thought I'd take a leaf out of your book,' said Bea with a smile.

'I'm used to children,' said Claudia practically. 'By the way, it's kind of Mrs Fonseca to invite us over.'

'She would have sooner, she said, but she thought it best to let you get your bearings first.' Bea's eyes twinkled. 'Don't forget, we lead a quiet life here. Any diversion is welcome.'

'Thank you! I've never thought of myself in the light of a diversion.' Claudia laughed, then looked down at herself. 'Should I change?'

'Not unless you want to. You look very elegant as you are. How I wish trousers had been worn when I was your age!'

Saul was home to lunch promptly, Claudia feeling distinctly apprehensive as she heard his jeep arrive outside, but one look at his face as he ran up the steps lightly gave her reassurance. The forbidding manner was absent, and he smiled in a friendly fashion as he greeted all three, kissing his aunt, acknowledging Claudia casually and demanding to see the latest masterpiece from his artistic daughter. The agreeable change in his attitude made lunch a pleasant meal, at which Claudia had her first taste of brown Brazilian beans cooked with garlic and butter, and served with rice, a minute steak and salad. Becky, obviously fond of beans and rice, ate her portion with gusto, also the fruit salad that followed.

'Luc tells me I'm commanded to take you all over to Casa d'Ouro on my way back to the mine,' said Saul, glancing at his watch. 'I trust all you ladies are ready, as I need to be off in ten minutes minimum.'

There was instant activity as Bea and Claudia went to make necessary repairs, and Becky flew to her box to choose which trophies to take on her visit, and shortly afterwards they were all installed in the jeep and on their way down the hill towards the town, veering away from it to skirt the foot of Morro d'Ouro and follow the winding road that brought them eventually through open gates into a garden filled with poinsettias and bougainvillaea, the curving drive coming to an end in front of another square house, bigger this time, virtually nestling among palms, with a verandah running almost the entire length of the front of it. Saul sounded the horn, then jumped from the jeep to lift down his aunt before receiving his daughter from Claudia, finally holding up his arms to swing her to the ground in turn, his hard hands warm through the thin cotton of her tunic.

'Tell Emily I'm in a hurry,' he said, and leapt back into the jeep. 'I'm meeting someone in two minutes.' With a squeal of tyres he waved and turned the vehicle in a circle to shoot back down the drive out of sight.

A small, elderly lady with snow white hair came to meet them, her carriage imposing despite the stick she leaned on slightly. Sharp dark eyes gave Claudia an all-encompassing look even as she kissed Bea on the cheek and patted Becky's head. Bea drew Claudia forward.

'Thurza, this is Claudia March, Becky's new governess. Claudia, this is my aunt, Thurza Treharne Fonseca.'

'How do you do, Miss March. Welcome to Casa d'Ouro.'

Claudia smiled politely.

'How do you do, Senhora Fonseca. Thank you for inviting me.'

'To be accurate,' said Thurza Fonseca, with a slight smile, 'it was Emily who invited you, but at this moment she's involved in a minor crisis in the nursery. These crises happen several times a day, so it's not remarkable that one should occur just as you arrive. Do come in.'

Thurza led the way to a group of cushioned bamboo furniture very similar to those at Saul's house. She sat on a straight-backed chair and waved Bea and Claudia to the more comfortable seats, beckoning the little girl to her.

'And how are you today, Rebecca?'

Becky dropped her head and murmured, 'Very well, thank you,' obviously ill at ease with the old lady.

Thurza inclined her rigidly coifured head and told the child to run into the garden to look for Jamie, if she wished. Becky was off like a shot, only pausing long enough to give her painting book and pens to Claudia, with anxious instructions to take care of them.

Thurza turned her attention to Claudia, who was drinking in her surroundings with pleasure.

'And what are your first impressions of Brazil, Miss March?' The old eyes were observant, missing no detail of the slim figure sitting relaxed in the long chair.

Claudia decided the old lady possessed a far more astringent personality then her niece, and returned her assessing look with a direct gaze in her clear grey eyes that appeared to meet with Thurza's approval.

'Colour, light and warmth, Senhora Fonseca. I love England very much, but it was very cold and grey when I left Heathrow. This sunshine is a welcome contrast.'

'You were fortunate to arrive during a clear spell. At this time of the year one must expect frequent storms and heavy rain.' Thurza gave Claudia a shrewd look. 'I gather you taught at a girls' school. You'll find it different to concentrate all your energies on one small five-year-old, even one with as forceful a personality as Rebecca.'

'A great change,' agreed Claudia pleasantly. 'I shall enjoy the challenge.'

'She copes with Becky very well,' said Bea with satisfaction. 'My life is already becoming more relaxed.'

The sudden, ear-splitting cacophony of the macaws put an end to the exchange as a young girl emerged from the far wing, hand in hand with two small children. She came quickly along the verandah, light of step, her long, sun-streaked fair hair tied back with a red ribbon, the children breaking into a trot beside her. Blue eyes smiled in glad welcome at Claudia and Bea as the girl called.

'Hello, sorry I wasn't on hand to meet you.' She released the children and stooped to kiss Bea, looking up with undisguised curiosity at Claudia, who had risen to her feet. 'You must be Claudia. Welcome. I'm Emily Fonseca.'

Claudia smiled at her, somewhat at a loss. This serene, happy creature in the plain white sundress, though older than she had first thought, was still a far cry from the mature, sophisticated woman pictured as the mother of· three children and chatelaine of this large, imposing house.

'How do you do,' said Claudia, her smiling eyes dropping to the two children. One was a boy of about four with a mop of dark curls and big dark eyes, in a tanned face with features already dominantly male. The other child was a girl, a year or two younger, with lint-white hair and her mother's blue eyes. They stared inquisitively at the newcomer, smiling shyly in response to Claudia's greeting.

'These are Mark and Lucy,' said Emily, and shooed her offspring away. 'Go and find Dirce, you two monsters, and ask her for a drink, then tell her to fetch a tray for us.' She turned to her guests. 'Where's Becky?'

'She went to find Jamie,' said Bea.

'And of course there'll be squabbling very soon as a result,' said Thurza dryly, 'so let us enjoy our peace and quiet while we can.'

Emily laughed and sat beside Claudia on the settee.

'We don't get too much peace here in the daytime. They all sleep well at night, thank God.'

There was a natural friendliness about Emily Fonseca that captivated Claudia instantly, and when a maid arrived with a tray of cold drinks the group split quite naturally into two parts, the older women enjoying a chat together while Emily unashamedly bombarded Claudia with questions about herself and her life in England, jumping to her feet after a while with the suggestion that the two of them took a stroll in the garden to find the children. She turned to Thurza and Bea with a smile of apology.

'You will excuse us, won't you, but I'm sure Claudia would like to see round the grounds.'

Thurza waved them off indulgently, presumably glad to indulge in a tête-à-tête with her niece.

Claudia followed the slim, white-clad figure down a flight of steps into the patio, past the aviary and out into the garden beyond, where clusters of palms and poinsettias gave pools of shade at intervals. For a while she and Emily wandered over the lawns, talking amicably on general subjects, eventually reaching a tall gate in the thick green foliage of a hibiscus hedge starred with brilliant coral-pink blossoms. Emily unlocked the imposing padlock on the gate and ushered Claudia through to look at a turquoise blue pool of impressive demensions, complete with diving boards and paved surround, sunbeds and garden chairs drawn up alongside it.

Mystified Claudia followed Emily to some white-painted chairs grouped around a table with a gay umbrella, out of sight of the verandah where the older women sat. Emily sat down, waving Claudia to another chair, a purposeful expression on the delicately-marked features of her attractive face.

'I want a private chat,' she said bluntly. 'I'm very fond of Thurza, but just this once I'd like to talk to you alone and sound you out.'

Claudia was intrigued.

'Fire away, Mrs Fonseca——' she stopped short as Emily shook her head.

'Thurza is Mrs Fonseca. I'm plain Emily.' She leaned her elbows on the table and said without preamble, 'I know it's a terrible cheek to ask, but I'm wondering if you'd consider teaching three children instead of one.'

Claudia drew in her breath, blinking, her first thought more concerned with Saul's reaction rather than her own.

'It's really not for me to answer that one,' she said frankly. 'Mr Treharne has put out a lot of money to get me over here to teach his daughter. I'm not sure how he'd feel about the idea.'

Emily nodded understandingly.

'I thought you might worry about Saul. Let's leave that side of it for a moment. The thing is, Claudia, how would *you* feel?'

Claudia thought it over carefully, watched anxiously by the other girl.

'Competition is good for children, of course. All three would probably do better academically with the stimulus of company.' She hesitated, her light eyes questioning. 'Correct me if I'm wrong, but do I gather Becky and Jamie don't get on too well?'

Emily smiled.

'Becky is a defensive, insecure child, and my elder son is a budding M.C.P.! He's never known anything but love and attention and behaves accordingly. The Latin in him takes over sometimes, even at his tender years. Becky secretly adores him, but he's at the age where girls are a nuisance, and orders her about, which she doesn't take very kindly to at all.' She made a face. 'I'm being honest, because there's no point in pulling the wool over your eyes. But from the point of view of lessons I sincerely believe they'd try harder together, and Mark could possibly do some simpler things too.'

'How old is Jamie?' asked Claudia, still somewhat taken aback by this new proposition.

'Six. So it means they are all different ages, but—not that I know anything about it, of course—I thought that might be an advantage. They could be doing three different things, but doing them together.' Emily's eyes were bright and persuasive, and Claudia knew perfectly well that were it left to herself to decide she would say yes on the spot.

'The numbers don't matter,' she said slowly. 'I'm obviously used to teaching fairly large classes. In some ways three would be better than one, in others I'm not sure. In any event it would up to Mr Treharne—I'm his employee.'

'Yes, I understand that,' persisted Emily, 'but if Saul's agreeable you wouldn't object?'

'No. No, I wouldn't.'

'Don't think we're trying to angle in on a good thing financially, of course,' Emily assured her. 'We're not trying to get something for nothing. We'd naturally pay two-thirds of your salary and give you an extra bonus on top.'

'My God, no!' Claudia looked at Emily aghast. 'No, please. Even if Saul does consent I don't *want* any more money. What I receive now is more than generous. Don't add to it. Your arrangements with Saul are naturally your own affair, but as far as I'm concerned I can't accept any additional payment.'

Emily stared at her in concern.

'I've obviously touched on a nerve.' She jumped up. 'Come on, let's find the children.'

They set off through the garden, Emily telling how Luc's idea had been to hire a tutor, but that Emily kept putting it off, not caring for the idea of a strange young man living with them. When Saul had announced Claudia's arrival as governess to Becky it had seemed like a splendid solution to everyone's problem. Emily cast a glance at the co-ordinated walk of the tall girl beside her and said frankly,

'With that figure you must be good at sport, which would be great, as I'm afraid I'm about to resign from the football team for the time being.'

Claudia halted, wondering if she'd received the right message.

'You mean——?'

Emily nodded, smiling serenely.

'I'm pregnant again. I had a miscarriage last year, so I shall have to watch my step this time.' She began to laugh softly at Claudia's expression. 'You look a bit stunned. Does my talent for reproduction embarrass you?'

Claudia found that it did, for some reason. As she looked at Emily she was beset by all sorts of feelings—wonder, anxiety, even envy. Envy? She caught herself up short. That was surely taking things a bit far!

'You seem very young to be the mother of several children, that's all,' she said. 'I thought you were a schoolgirl when I first caught sight of you.'

'I'm twenty-five.' Emily cast her a sidelong glance and said deliberately, 'Would it shock you if I said that my husband and I are highly compatible—in every way?' She laughed softly as the colour rose in Claudia's cheeks. 'Obviously it does. I'm sorry. How do you get on with Saul?'

Her sudden change of subject was a relief, though the question was a little difficult to answer, and Claudia had an uneasy feeling it was hardly the non sequitur it seemed.

'He was a little unbending at first,' she said carefully, almost tempted to confide in this charming, utterly natural creature. 'In fact I thought he actively disliked me on sight, but I gather it's not so much me personally, but his general attitude to most of the female sex.'

Emily looked at Claudia in astonishment.

'He's not in the least like that with me!'

Probably no one was like that with Emily Fonseca, thought Claudia sadly, following Emily to the source of noise near the servants' quarters at the back of the house, where the four children were milling round a perch, their voices raised in excitement.

When they all trooped up on to the verandah a long table was laid with a snowy embroidered cloth and set with dishes of dainty crustless sandwiches and tempting small cakes and cookies. Tall pitchers of lemonade and a silver tea service stood waiting on the trolley beside it. Thurza and Bea looked up smiling as the warm, perspiring group arrived.

'Say goodbye to peace and quiet now for a bit, Thurza,' said Emily cheerfully.

'And very thankful I am to do so,' said the old lady emphatically, to Claudia's surprise. 'The house had far too much quiet for too many years. This is the way it was intended to be.'

'I'd like to wash my hands,' said Claudia to Becky. 'I wonder if you could show me the way to the bathroom?'

The child nodded importantly and, with an apology to the others, Claudia followed her to the bedroom wing, where Becky showed her into a large bathroom and even volunteered to wash her own hands without being told. When they rejoined the others everyone was settling down to a tea-party which had a decidedly festive atmosphere.

Claudia was amused to notice Jamie's eyes on her a great deal, also to find that Becky sat beside her behaving with model propriety, a fact appreciated by Bea, as she caught Claudia's eye in silent congratulation.

Tea-time was a prolonged, noisy affair, after which the two smaller children were taken off for their baths, while Becky and Jamie sat at the cleared table and became silently absorbed as they each coloured a picture from Becky's book. The afternoon had grown oppressively hot and humid, and Claudia was glad to sit chatting with the other three women, smiling inwardly as she looked at her watch and remembered what her occupation had been a week or so ago at this time. Trying to inject some enthusiasm for poetry into the Lower Fifth, probably, she thought, then looked up at the sound of the noisy arrival outside of two vehicles.

'Luc!' Emily sprang to her feet expectantly. At the same moment Jamie cried 'Papae!' and slid off his chair to run towards the two tall figures approaching from the hall. Luc Fonseca was a little shorter than Saul, and built on slightly less massive lines, but instantly recognisable from his startling resemblance to his sons, despite the grey streaks in his thick black hair. He swept Jamie up and kissed him, before setting him down in order to kiss his wife with the same lack of selfconsciousness. Claudia watched, fascinated, as he kept his arm close round Emily even while greeting his grandmother and Bea.

'And this is Claudia March, Luc,' said Emily, smiling warmly.

Luc bent and took Claudia's hand, raising it to his lips with a smile of great charm on his handsome, strong-featured face.

'*Muito prazer,*' he said.

Becky sat very still at the table, her eyes wistful on Jamie and his parents, and Claudia's heart was wrung as she saw the look on the child's face. Saul turned from greeting Thurza and Bea, acknowledging Claudia with a casual nod, his eyes narrowing as she tried to convey a silent message in her own. She gave an almost imperceptible turn of her head in Becky's direction, and relaxed as he interpreted it correctly and strolled over to his daughter, ruffling a hand over her head as he bent to examine what she was doing. Claudia met Emily's comprehending blue eye as she turned to Luc Fonseca.

'What do you think of Campo d'Ouro, Miss March?' he asked, sitting on the settee alongside her, his arm around Jamie.

Thurza laughed and wagged her stick in Claudia's direction.

'Your ingenuity will be taxed to find different polite answers, Miss March, as everyone will ask the same thing for the time being.'

Claudia smiled politely.

'I haven't actually seen Campo d'Ouro itself yet, unless one counts the view of it from the house. It looks very picturesque, Senhor Fonseca.'

Luc called over to Saul.

'When are you going to take Miss March on a tour, Saul——'

'We're going to use first names,' interrupted Emily

firmly. 'None of this "Miss" and "Senhor", if you don't mind!'

'One asks permission first, *carinha*,' said her husband reprovingly, then turned his smile on Claudia. 'You permit?'

She nodded, smiling warmly, responding automatically to his friendly charm. 'Of course.' She looked up to find Saul's eyes on her with a cold expression in them, and looked away hurriedly.

'Luc, you may offer our guests drinks while I take Saul away in private and have a little chat with him,' announced Emily, a statement which plainly surprised everyone present. Luc rose to his feet, frowning doubtfully at his wife.

'*Carinha*, don't you think I——' he began, but was silenced by the smile in the lambent blue of Emily's eyes. He shrugged gracefully. 'Very well. Saul, I apologise for my wife. She wishes to ask you a favour and firmly believes you will not refuse her.'

'She's probably right,' said Saul laconically, and followed Emily's small figure along the verandah.

'What is Emily up to, Luc?' demanded Thurza suspiciously.

'She will tell you herself in due course,' answered her grandson. 'May I give both you ladies your customary dry sherry, after which I shall attend to the requirements of Senhorita Becky and Senhorita Claudia.'

'And me!' said Jamie indignantly.

'And you,' amended his father indulgently.

Becky slid off her chair and came to stand silent at Claudia's side, her face brightening as Jamie jumped to his feet restlessly.

'Come on, Becky, let's play in the garden. You can have a turn on my bike.'

'Can I, Claudia?'

'Yes, of course.' Claudia was gratified Becky even remembered to consult her. 'Can you ride a bike?'

'She can with the balancing wheels on,' said Jamie with slight condescension. 'Come on, Becky, or it'll be time for you to go home.'

The children ran off together as Luc handed Claudia her gin and tonic, then two pyjamaed little figures appeared and hurled themselves, shrieking, at their father, who sat down with one in the crook of each arm and proceeded to devote himself to Mark and Lucy, while Bea drew Claudia into conversation with Thurza.

'Thurza's having a bridge evening tonight, Claudia, and to be honest it had slipped my mind. Would you think me utterly barbarous if I abandon you yet again?' Bea looked anxiously at Claudia, who was able to assure her quite honestly that she had no objection in the slightest.

'I'm sure a dinner alone with Saul holds no terrors for you, Miss—Claudia,' said Thurza, with a twinkle in her eye.

'None at all, Senhora Fonseca,' answered Claudia quietly. 'How could it?' She finished her drink slowly, wondering what Emily was saying to Saul, just as the two of them came back to join them, Emily's face triumphant, and Saul's wooden as his eyes met Claudia's.

Luc got to his feet, a child held in each arm.

'Who won?'

'I did,' said Emily, and relieved him of her small daughter.

'Saul, had you forgotten that I'm making up a bridge four with Thurza this evening?' asked Bea apologetically.

The navy-blue eyes of her nephew flickered for an instant, but he merely shrugged. 'I had, of course, but no problem. Have a pleasant evening.'

'You and Claudia stay, too,' said Emily immediately. 'Becky could sleep here.'

'That's kind of you Emily, but I need to get back— things to see to at home.' He raised an eyebrow at Luc. 'I'll have a word with you tomorrow.'

Luc put down his small son and shook Saul's hand, suddenly very formal.

'My grateful thanks, Saul. As you say, we will talk tomorrow.'

There was a flurry of leave-taking, a reluctant Becky

was fetched from her cycling, her belongings collected, and eventually Claudia was in the jeep with Becky on her lap as Saul reversed at speed all the way down the tortuous drive until they were outside the gates and headed in the direction of home. Becky lay sleepy against Claudia's shoulder and Saul was silent, giving Claudia time to think about the afternoon. Emily had presumably made her request, and obviously it had been granted, but it was hard to judge from Saul's withdrawn face whether the suggestion had met with his approval. He spoke once to ask Claudia how she had enjoyed her afternoon, but otherwise the drive was completed in silence.

When they reached the house Becky was surrendered to Lourdes for her bath and Claudia stood irresolute in the kitchen for a moment, wondering what to do next. The sky was overcast and heavy, the air warm and thick with no trace of breeze. It seemed fairly likely a storm was brewing—in more ways than one, and Claudia's heart sank as Saul came in from garaging the jeep and asked coldly if she would spare him a few moments on the verandah.

CHAPTER SEVEN

CLAUDIA followed the tall figure through the dining-room out on to the verandah where the air was, if anything, warmer than inside the house. She sat on one of the upright chairs and refused Saul's offer of a drink, her tension increased by the sound of thunder rumbling in the distance.

Saul leaned against the rail, glass in hand, his back to the lights of the town below, his face impossible to see in the darkness.

'Emily said you approved the idea of teaching her children along with Becky,' he began abruptly, his voice as impersonal as an answering machine, and considerably less friendly.

'Yes.' There seemed little else to say. Claudia sat quietly, one leg crossed over the other, and waited for him to continue.

'My idea in hiring you was as a personal preceptress for my daughter, not as a teacher for half the children in Campo d'Ouro.' Now his tone was biting.

'It was difficult to dismiss Senhora Fonseca's idea out of hand,' began Claudia carefully, looking down at her clasped hands.

'It would surely have been more politic to consult me first!' Saul tossed back his drink and crossed to pour himself another, dropping in ice with a force that threatened the safety of the glass.

'When she filled me in on the circumstances it would have been very unfeeling to voice my disapproval, surely,' she retorted, stung. 'Besides, I made it quite plain my consent was entirely subject to yours, naturally, when you'd gone to the expense of bringing me out here. As you so aptly put it, contractually I'm in your hands. You pay me.'

'And there, of course, we come to the crux of the matter,' he said bitterly. 'Finance. I gather Emily offered you a substantial reward.' The icy flash of her eyes must have got through to him even through the gloom as he quickly amended, 'Yes. I know you refused it, but can you deny that in your mind there is just the hint of a "great expectation" at some time or other?'

'Yes.'

Saul moved over to the table and lit the candle in the copper holder. He replaced the glass shade and sat opposite her, staring at her face in the soft glow. 'Yes what?' His voice was flat and hard, like a piece of slate.

'Yes, I deny it, of course.' This was impossible in Claudia's view. 'I said I wasn't concerned with the financial arrangements, that would be up to you and the Fonsecas. I, personally, have no wish for anything more than the substantial remuneration you already pay me. What else can I say?' Mutinously she threw back her head and stared into his face, more mask-like than ever in the light thrown up by the candle. For a moment or two she thought he would speak, but he kept silent. Claudia decided to have one last shot at appealing to him. 'I genuinely feel it might be the best thing for Becky if she did have company and competition at lessons. Most children do better this way. I gather Senhora Fonseca has been doing lessons with her children herself, but of course, now that she's pregnant again——'

'What!' He stared at her, eyes narrowed. 'Emily's expecting another baby?'

'Oh dear.' Claudia pushed her hair behind her ears uncomfortably. 'I thought she would tell you that as a means of persuasion. I'm sorry; I had no idea I was betraying a confidence.'

Saul got slowly to his feet and stood, rubbing his chin.

'I see. She could hardly have said anything more likely to enlist your sympathies. You know she lost a baby not too long ago? I see now why you agreed.'

'That was only part of the reason. I also genuinely happen to think it's a good idea. But if you wash out the whole arrangement I couldn't blame you after all. I am *your* employee,' pointed out Claudia. She was beginning to feel tired again and stood, facing him, squaring her shoulders unconsciously as she looked very directly into the dark, deep-set eyes above her. 'Mr Treharne, do you really consider there is much point in continuing with this arrangement? From my own point of view I firmly believe I could very soon establish a reasonable relationship with Becky. But, living as I do, as part of your household, life will be grim if you—well, if you find me unacceptable. Perhaps you should find someone else.'

Saul made a chopping motion of his arm in negation.

'How the hell am I to do that? I can't just take off for the U.K., and there's no way of engaging a person for this type of job without a personal interview. Besides, as you say, I've already spent a fair amount of money merely in getting you here—it goes against the grain to waste it.' He drew in a deep breath. 'Will it be of any use if I apologise? I had a tricky day in work, then when I got to Casa d'Ouro I found you and Emily airily disposing of my arrangements without a thought about my views on the subject, or at least, that was how it seemed.'

'Ah, but you were wrong,' said Claudia insistently. 'Believe me, they were my first thought! If the idea makes you unhappy, teaching the others, I mean, naturally it's your wishes that count.'

Saul sighed irritably.

'I can't go back on my agreement with Emily, even if I wanted to. As I may have said before, although Luc is my second cousin I never for an instant lose sight of the fact that he's also my employer. Besides,' he added, a softer note in his voice, 'I could hardly hurt Emily.'

Her own feelings, apparently, could go hang, thought Claudia acidly, then came to with a jolt as she realised she was listening to an apology.

'I'm sorry, Claudia,' said Saul shortly. 'Personal considerations apart, I have never been in any doubt about your ability to handle Becky, and to teach her, which is, after all, the important factor. Perhaps we could make more of an effort to understand each other's point of view.'

We, thought Claudia indignantly, but aware that this was the biggest olive branch she was ever likely to be offered she hastily opted for magnanimity.

'Very well, Mr Treharne.'

'Saul,' he said quietly.

'Saul,' she repeated with docility. 'I'll just go and see what Becky's doing. I'll read her a story after her meal.'

'I'll see you at dinner, then.' Saul sounded almost awkward, and Claudia gave him an uncertain glance as she passed him and retreated into the house in search of Becky.

That young lady was seated at the kitchen table, eating her supper and telling the maids about her afternoon, with much knife and fork waving. Claudia told Maria that Bea would not be in for dinner, and was surprised to see a look of dismay on the broad, genial face.

'*Tem problema*, Maria?'

It took a lot of hand-waving, plus the occasional

rough translation from the helpful Becky, before Claudia was finally given to understand that Maria and Lourdes would like the night off to attend a *festa*, an anniversary party, at Maria's home. A cold meal had been prepared in expectation of this, the food ready in the refrigerator, and Maria would be grateful if Dona Claudia would ask the *Chefe* for permission in Dona Bea's absence.

Claudia went off to look for Saul, not over-disposed towards asking the 'Chefe' for anything, despite his apology earlier. The verandah was deserted, so was the hall, and Claudia hesitated outside the door of his room, not relishing the prospect of bearding the lion in his den. As she stood, undecided, his voice could be heard coming from the study, and she went towards the half open door along the corridor, rather daunted by the intense irritation only too plain in his raised voice, even though his staccato, rapid Portuguese was unintelligible. Claudia bit her lip and decided to retreat and choose a moment slightly more propitious, but as she turned away Saul strode through the door, almost colliding with her.

'Ah, Claudia—good. I'm going out.' His face was abstracted as he made rapidly for the kitchen. 'Don't wait dinner, I'm needed at the mine.'

'Oh, but hang on a minute,' Claudia ran after him. 'There was something I wanted to ask—Maria . . .'

'Save it till I get back,' he interrupted impatiently, and bent to kiss his daughter's cheek. 'Goodnight, Becky.' Then he was gone within seconds, his jeep roaring up the driveway and out on to the road.

Claudia spread her hands in apology and smiled ruefully at the maids.

'*Disculpe-me*, Maria. *O Chefe tem problema na mina.*' She searched desperately for the words, then appealed to Becky, who was watching her struggles clinically. 'How do I say your daddy had no time to listen to me?'

Becky obligingly translated, then looked at Claudia with a scowl.

'Can't Maria 'n Lourdes go, then?'

Both maids broke into voluble speech, the gist of

which seemed to be how early they would return in the morning, the word '*aniversário*' repeated continually. Claudia was torn. There was surely no harm in letting them go. They seemed to think Bea's permission would have been automatic, so eventually she shrugged and nodded her head, rewarded with wide, white smiles of joy as the two girls flew off to get ready, apparently quite undisturbed by the menacing rumbles of thunder, which Claudia noted uneasily were getting distinctly nearer.

A wide yawn from Becky recalled Claudia to her responsibilities.

'Bedtime,' she said firmly.

'I want to do more colouring.' Becky's face was as stormy as the atmosphere, and she was plainly prepared to do battle to stay up a little longer.

'Not tonight.' Claudia was immovable. It had been a full day, and it was already some time past Becky's normal hour.

With her father out of the way, and no one else to intervene, Becky gave way to a regrettable temper tantrum, pushing Claudia's patience to the limits.

'*Won't* go to bed!' She stamped a small bare foot, wincing as it made painful contact with the hard marble floor, tears starting in the great blue eyes. Claudia was unimpressed, knowing full well they were tears of rage, her own stomach contracting sickly as a roll of thunder boomed with sudden violence, making the kitchen windows rattle. Ashamed of her own cowardice, especially in the face of Becky's apparent unconcern, she spoke sternly to the sobbing child.

'If you stop that rather babyish display, Becky, I'll read you a story, if not you can go to bed and settle down straight away to sleep. I don't mind which you choose, but either way you're off to bed right now.'

Becky rubbed her knuckles into her eyes, her tears dying away almost at once as she gave Claudia a wary look from behind her fingers, obviously deciding Claudia meant what she said. She nodded, pouting, a hiccup shaking the small body as she trudged along the corridor to her room, making no objection when

Claudia suggested a detour to the bathroom to brush her teeth. The thunder was beginning to crash and crack around the house with growing ferocity by this time, and lightning flashed through Becky's room as Claudia drew the curtains, heroically suppressing her instinctive flinch away from it as she lit the little oil lamp which served as a nightlight..

Becky climbed into bed and submitted to being tucked in, her rebellion over for the time being.

'I like storms,' she said surprisingly. 'Sometimes the house jumps up and down when the thunder's loud.'

This piece of news brought no pleasure to the listener. Claudia loathed and feared thunderstorms, a weakness wild horses would never succeed in making her admit, and with iron control she fought a regrettable tendency to jump out of her skin at each clap of thunder, asking Becky which story she preferred.

Her own little storm forgotten, Becky sat up in bed, eager and bright-eyed.

'*Sleeping Beauty*—please. My books are in the toybox.'

Claudia began to read, acting out all the characters and bringing the story to life as much as she could, both to capture Becky's interest and to take her own mind off the ear-splitting elements outside. The child listened enthralled, sliding lower and lower in the bed as she fought against sleep. By the time Claudia reached the 'happy ever after' stage Becky was almost too drowsy to say goodnight. as the sheet was tucked round her again and she snuggled contentedly into her pillow.

As Claudia closed the door behind her the whole house seemed to shake on its foundations as lightning flashed end to end through the dark hall, the sky overhead simultaneously rent by a peal of thunder whose reverberations seemed to boom on and on for ever. Claudia stood flattened against the wall, her hands over her ears, her body vibrating with fright. After a moment she pulled herself together and made for the kitchen just as the whole house was plunged abruptly into darkness. She breathed hard, fighting for control of her stomach, which was displaying an annoying tendency to heave, and tried to remember where exactly the switch was she was supposed to turn off. Without light she had problems. Eventually her brain began to function again, despite the constant flashes of lightning and the almost continuous barrage of thunder. She remembered the candle on the verandah, and she had a book of matches from some restaurant in her handbag. The rain was sheeting down outside as Claudia dived through the dining room doors on to the verandah, which was lit brilliantly by the lightning as she retrieved the candlestick with a shaking hand and scuttled back into the house, bolting the glass doors and hurrying into her bedroom. She flung a hand in front of her eyes as a great fork of lightning seemed to earth just outside the open window, and, teeth chattering, she drew the curtains, and rummaged blindly in her bag on the dressing table, almost sobbing with relief as her fingers closed over the small matchbook.

Claudia managed to light the candle at the third attempt and immediately felt better, guilty at her panic. She took a cautious peep at Becky, who, amazingly, lay fast asleep, oblivious to the storm, the sight of the peaceful child making Claudia ashamed of her own shortcomings.

After locating the main switch and turning it off Claudia felt a little safer and found that by closing the door at each end she could make the bedroom corridor into a windowless tunnel where the lightning was shut out, if not the noise. She crouched on the floor with her candle, her clothes damp with perspiration, her hands over her ears, and prepared to sit out the storm. She lost count of the time as she sat there, moving only to check on Becky now and then, until the storm began to lessen and move away into the distance. Claudia was forced to leave her post finally by the sound of the telephone ringing she went to the instrument, picking it up with extreme care, her hand unsteady.

Emily's voice came unmistakeably through the static on the line.

'Everything all right, Claudia?'

'Fine,' croaked Claudia, and cleared her throat. 'Fine, thanks, Emily.'

'Look, the storm has brought Aunt Bea's migraine on again, so we've put her to bed here . . .'

The rest of her sentence was lost in atmospherics, and Claudia bit her lip.

'Yes, of course, Emily. I understand,' she said loudly.

'Crackle, crackle . . . so you'll be all right in any case. Goodnight.'

'Yes, thank you for ringing. Goodnight.'

Claudia was thoughtful as she returned through the house, the pitch darkness emphasised by the dim glow of the candle in her hand. Her whole instinct was to bolt to bed like a coward before Saul came home, but she had a feeling he would regard this in a worse light than waiting up to face the music. Her reflection looked eery and disembodied in the mirror as she brushed her hair by candlelight. The shadows emphasised her cheekbones, and miniature candle-flames danced in her eyes, their normal pale gleam obscured by the darkness of pupils still dilated by tension and fear. Claudia turned away in distaste, deciding her main problem was hunger. In the kitchen the refrigerator was still cold enough to preserve the food Maria had left for her dinner. There was even ice in the freezer compartment, which seemed to augur well, so Claudia made a sparing selection from cold chicken, some kind of fish mousse and a salad of red peppers and tomatoes. She found some bread in the big bin in the pantry and had a picnic on the kitchen table, washed down by milk, after which she felt a great deal better, though very weary. She washed her plates, then sat at the kitchen table, squinting at her watch in the gloom, noticing uneasily that the candle was burning down rapidly. It was almost ten. How long would it be before Saul came back, she wondered. She laid her head on her arms on the table. Just for a moment or two, she thought drowsily, and drifted off into sleep, worn out by the varying experiences of the day. She was rocketed to consciousness again by hard hands which shook her relentlessly, an all to familiar voice repeating her name loudly.

'All right, all right!' she mumbled crossly, then came back to earth with a bump as she realised the room was in darkness and only his voice made it possible to identify Saul.

'What the hell are you doing in the kitchen in the dark?' he demanded irately. 'The lights have been back on everywhere else for a couple of hours. Why didn't you ring the mine and tell me you had no power here?'

Claudia licked her dry lips, glad she couldn't see Saul's face.

'The switch,' she said huskily.

'What switch?'

'The main one you showed me. I turned it off.'

With a muffled curse Saul swung away from her and crossed the room, crashing into something in the dark before he found the master switch, most of the lights in the house springing to life as he turned it on. Irritably he went round switching them off, while Claudia ran silently on bare feet to Becky's room, relieved to find the child fast asleep by the light of her little lamp. Claudia covered her gently and went back to the kitchen to face the music.

'Are you hungry?' she asked politely. 'Maria left cold food before she went.'

Saul turned from the refrigerator with a bottle of beer in his hand, his eyebrows almost meeting his untidy black hair. The look in his eyes was enough to make Claudia quail.

'Maria isn't here? Lourdes?'

'She—she went with Maria.'

'Would it be too much to enquire where?'

Claudia leaned against the table, pushing her hair nervously behind her ears.

'They went to some kind of party at Maria's home. They'll be back first thing in the morning.'

'Aunt Bea gave permission, of course?'

Claudia looked at him with the calm of desperation.

'No. She wasn't here. If you remember, you were in too much of a hurry to listen when I tried to ask you earlier.'

'And what did she say when she came home?' Saul's

face held a look of polite enquiry, which chilled Claudia more than his anger.

'She didn't—come home, I mean. She's staying the night at Casa d'Ouro. The storm brought on her migraine again and they put her to bed there, as far as I can gather. The line was crakling so badly it was difficult to hear what Emily was saying.'

'Why didn't you tell Emily you were alone?'

'The line was very bad, and I couldn't see what could have been done about it. Becky was asleep by that time, and I knew you'd be home eventually, anyway.'

'That, Miss Claudia March, is the whole damned point. I *am* now home—virtually alone in the house with you. And in Campo d'Ouro this is just not permissible, strictly against the rules—contrary to what you might consider normal in England.'

Claudia glared at him with dislike.

'How do you know what's normal behaviour for me? Besides, the whole idea's archaic, apart from the fact that no one will know!'

He gave her a look of such contempt Claudia felt a streak of red-hot rage pierce her.

'Use your much-vaunted brain, girl! The servants, of course.'

'I'm sorry,' she said stiffly. 'When I gave them permission I had no idea your aunt would stay at Casa d'Ouro, and I never gave a thought to the fact of being alone here with you. To be honest, even if I had it wouldn't have disturbed me at all.'

'Why not?' There was a disturbing change in Saul's tone as he moved slowly towards her, finishing the beer in his glass without taking his eyes from her pale face.

Claudia frowned up at him resentfully.

'Well, you don't think of me like that—nor I you.' She leaned her hands on the table, secretly longing to make her escape, and turned her eyes away from the unsettling look in his. Saul put out a long hand and picked up a lock of her hair, sliding it idly through his fingers, a faint, cold smile playing at the corners of his mouth and deepening the cleft in his chin. He sighed.

'Surely, Claudia, with all those qualifications of

yours, you must have learned that if a man is alone in the middle of the night with a woman who's even halfway attractive, it's ten to one he *will* start thinking like that if he's normal.' He put out a finger to jerk her face up to his. 'And, believe me, I'm very normal.' He stood overpoweringly close, staring down into her stormy eyes.

'I think it's time I went to bed now,' said Claudia hurriedly. 'I'm sorry to have caused such trouble——'

'I had a feeling you were trouble the moment I laid eyes on you,' he muttered to her consternation, and pounced, backing her up against the kitchen table, held fast against him, holding her off balance so that her bare toes dangled just free of the floor. His mouth was so close to hers she felt, rather than heard, him murmur,

'After all, we might as well have the game as well as the candle.'

Something seemed to have robbed Claudia of all power of movement, even thought, as his mouth made contact with hers, not hard and punishing as expected, but subtle and persuasive, and infinitely more danger-ous. It generated a trembling deep down inside her that increased as one of the arms holding her slackened its hold to allow a hand to slide rhythmically up and down her spine, slithering over the silk of her shirt in a lulling, hypnotic motion, relaxing her body, curving it against his as a little warm, sighing breath entered his mouth from lips she had opened in surprise as he seized her, remaining open in hesitant response to the insistent, demanding pressure of his.

Claudia forgot she hardly knew this difficult, disturbing man; no conscience prodded her to erect defences against the strong arms that held her in a security she dimly recognised to be almost sheer unalloyed comfort, save for an underlying warmth of some other, sensuous feeling, a flicker that grew and grew as his mouth became increasingly insistent, igniting to a flame as the stroking hand moved in a faster rhythm, accelerating the beat of her heart and taking away her breath as her head bent back beneath the pressure of his, her hair streaming down her back like a banner as his lips left hers to follow an inflammatory path down her arched throat to the point where the buttons of her shirt presented an obstacle to his progress. His stroking hand ceased its activity, only to find a new one as his fingers flicked the buttons from their moorings, her high, pointed breasts springing into ivory-white relief between the parted black silk, vulnerable and defenceless against his lips and fingertips.

Her feet still clear of the floor, Claudia's body arched like a bow, her arms held to her sides in the vice-like embrace of one of Saul's powerful arms, for the first time in her life utterly helpless before the dominance of male physical superiority, her own bemused senses his powerful ally as her erect, sensitised nipples experienced the onslaught of subtle, seeking lips and flicking tongue that sent streaks of fire much lower, to add fuel to the fire already raging where her hips were thrust against the unmistakable arousal of Saul's body as it ground against her own.

At this some half-buried instinct of common sense woke up in Claudia's brain. She gave a hoarse little sound of protest and shook her head, fighting suddenly to free her hands. Her whole body became a writhing, wriggling opposition to the lips and hands and rock-like frame, but Saul's only response was a laugh deep in his chest, vibrating against her, making her shiver. Abruptly she was free. Her eyes glittering like rock crystals with self-disgust and banked-down emotion, Claudia shook back her hair and frantically tried to match buttons to buttonholes, avoiding Saul's knowing eyes, furious with him, furious with herself. Raging inwardly at her spineless lack of opposition to his unexpected attack, she lashed herself unsparingly for behaving like a sex-starved fool. With cold distaste she realised the back of her thighs hurt from their contact with the edge of the kitchen table—the kitchen table, for heaven's sake! Like all the lewd, crude jokes she'd ever heard.

Saul stood, arms folded, not in the least disturbed and watched her disarray with apparent enjoyment.

'Why?' she spat at him, her voice unsteady.

He shrugged, 'You were so sure there was no harm in remaining alone in a house with a man at night, or indeed at any time. I decided to demonstrate how wrong you were.'

'There was no necessity for—for all that, surely!'

'All what?'

Claudia thrust her shirt into her slacks and looked at him with distaste.

'I would have preferred the point made verbally, not—not in a practical demonstration, like a cookery lesson!'

Saul threw back his head in a spontaneous laugh that altered his face so completely she stared at him with rancour at his lack of timing; hardly the moment to demonstrate that he was capable of mirth like any other mortal!

'I assume you were more annoyed by the motive than the deed?' He was obviously having trouble in recovering his gravity.

'I wasn't precisely thrilled by either of them,' she snapped, with a fine disregard for the truth, and made for the door with as much dignity as bare feet allowed.

'Claudia, Claudia, tell the truth!'

Unwilling she turned to look at him, her eyes icy.

'What do you mean?'

'Can you really place your hand on your heart and swear you experienced not one glimmer of response during our little—er—interchange?' Saul strolled towards the outer door of the kitchen, turning to look at Claudia's incensed face with a look in his eyes that made her drop sharply, the telltale colour tinting the taut skin along her cheekbones. 'Are you implying I was mistaken?'

'You took me by surprise,' she said woodenly. 'No one does that twice.'

'Always supposing they felt inclined!' Saul gave her a mocking little bow. 'Goodnight, Claudia, pleasant dreams.'

She stared at him blankly, her antagonism forgotten.

'Where on earth are you going at this time of night?'

'Back to my office to a hard, uncomfortable couch, where I shall ostentatiously remain until roused in the morning. Being last to leave tonight I might, with luck, get back without being seen. You won't be nervous on your own?'

'Less than if you stayed.' Claudia's chin went up defiantly.

Saul stood looking at her with infuriating indulgence, as if she were Becky in one of her tantrums.

'Not the nervous type, I gather?'

'No.' Claudia was back in possession of her much-tried composure.

'I'll wish you goodnight, then.' Saul sauntered through the door and Claudia crossed the room to lock it behind him, relieved to be alone again, leaning against it for several troubled minutes.

She had lied to Saul. She *was* nervous. The storm had moved away, and the thought of an intruder held no fears, but at the thought of what had happened a few moments earlier chills of apprehension chased up her spine. Her own emotions scared her to death. Or was emotion a rather fancy word for the feelings experienced by both of them a short while earlier? Claudia pushed a clenched fist against her mouth, mentally flaying herself for behaving like a—like a what? Alley-cat, or just woman? Claudia pulled herself together with an effort, turning out lights and checking on doors. Becky lay deeply asleep, arms outflung, the purity of her face so enchanting in the dim light that Claudia stayed, arrested, looking at her for quite some time. Elaine must have looked like that when she was asleep. The thought of Saul in bed with his wife sent Claudia off to her own room at the double. She stripped off her clothes and slid into bed, burying her face in the pillow in an attempt to blank out the memory of those few self-revelatory moments in Saul's arms; moments of discovery about herself that shook her to the very core.

There was only one course to adopt. No more thoughts of Saul Treharne in any way except as her employer; otherwise he meant nothing to her. Nothing.

Over and over again the words went round in her brain,
nothing, nothing, like some hypnotic mantra that
eventually had the desired effect and she slept.

CHAPTER EIGHT

AFTER her disturbed night Claudia woke only when
Becky ran in to say someone was clapping their hands
outside the kitchen door.

'I think it's Maria, Claudia!'

'Hang on a minute, Becky, I'm coming.' She pulled
on her kimono and pushed her hair away from her face
as she hurried to unlock the kitchen door and admit
Maria and Lourdes, who both looked heavy-eyed and
apologetic.

'*Bom dia*, Dona Claudia.' They both bade her good
morning and Maria began preparing coffee at once
while Becky ran off to dress, chattering with Lourdes,
full of curiosity about the previous evening's festivities.
Claudia decided to have a shot at explaining about the
night before.

'Dona Bea *passou a noite na* Casa d'Ouro,' she began,
her sleepy brain having trouble in finding the right
words to tell the maid Bea wasn't in the house.

'*Donde?*'

Claudia nodded.

'*Com dor de——*' she hesitated and tapped her
forehead. Maria nodded, her kind face creased with
sympathy, obviously familiar with Bea's headaches.

Claudia went on doggedly, bent on establishing
Saul's absence as soon as possible.

'*O Chefe ficou na mina.*' She knew very well Saul
would have slept in his office, not the mine, but her
vocabulary was limited at the best of times, and this
morning it was nearly non-existent. She pointed to the
light. '*Falta de luz.*'

Maria nodded vigorously.

'*E sempre assim em caso de relampago.*'

This was too much for Claudia's Portuguese, and the girl made a sizzling noise to indicate lightning.

Smiling in rueful agreement Claudia went off to dress, wondering how Bea was feeling this morning, and what sort of night Saul had spent in his office. She hurried into pink denims and a matching sleeveless shirt, and was tying her hair at the nape of her neck with a pink cord when Becky burst in, dressed in frilly blue organdie, her hair in a pigtail of rippling gold.

'It was Maria's birthday yesterday, Claudia,' she said excitedly. 'That's what "*anniversario*" means—"birthday". It was her party they went to.'

'What a pity we didn't know, Becky, we could have given her a present!'

'Oh yes, and cake and candles, like Jamie.' Becky was downcast.

Claudia thought for a moment, then rummaged in the suitcase that still remained unpacked. She drew out a smart box containing French soap and dusting powder, a parting gift from the Lower Fourths at Highdean.

'Do you think she'd like this, Becky?'

The little girl agreed with enthusiasm.

'But there isn't any wrapping paper, Claudia. Presents must have fancy paper.'

A further search produced a pretty paper bag which was pronounced suitable, and Becky tugged at Claudia's hand impatiently.

'Come on, let's give it to her!'

Claudia followed the flying figure into the kitchen, where the gift was received with rapture by Maria as Becky cried '*Feliz aniversário*, Maria,' turning with comic condescension to explain to Claudia that it meant 'happy birthday'. Claudia thanked her solemnly, then looked up sharply, her bonhomie evaporating as Saul appeared in the doorway, yawning, looking haggard and hollow-eyed from lack of sleep, a villainous growth of stubble on his chin.

'Good morning,' she said quietly.

'Good morning.' He peered at the package in Maria's hand. 'More presents? Quite a lady for handing out largesse, aren't you, Claudia?'

'No, not lar—not what you said,' said Becky
earnestly. 'Soap and powder for Maria's birthday.'

'I stand corrected. *Parabéms*, Maria.'

His sudden appearance threw Lourdes and Maria
into a frenzy of activity, and any awkwardness Claudia
felt at encountering him in the cold light of day was lost
in the barrage of instructions as Saul requested
breakfast as soon as he'd showered and changed and
sent Lourdes to ask José to clean some of the mud off
the jeep before it went back to the mine. Even breakfast
in Saul's company proved to be uneventful, as Becky
was unusually talkative, giving details of Maria's party,
and her father took full advantage of her uncharacteristic chattiness, leaving Claudia to hand round
food and pour coffee and juice without having to
contribute much herself.

The fleeting glimpse of her own face in the
bathroom mirror had shown shadows under her own
eyes equal to Saul's, and she stifled a secret giggle at
the thought that anyone watching would think they
had been engaged in an entire night of mutual
debauchery, instead of the short, sharp little episode
that actually took place.

'That was an odd little smile, Claudia.' Saul drained
the last of his coffee and stood up, stretching. 'It's just
possible I might manage to face the day now, thank
God—what did you find amusing?'

Claudia shook her head.

'Nothing of any interest. How soon do you think I
can ring to see how Bea is feeling?'

'Leave it an hour or so.' Saul stood at the top of the
verandah steps looking at her appraisingly. 'Did you
sleep well?'

She nodded coolly, busying herself by pouring more
tea.

'Once the storm died down I slept like a top. How
was your night?' Her eyes were unwavering on his,
pellucid with innocence.

'I spent the night on a three-foot sofa of leather as
slippery as glass. For one reason and another I've slept
better.' His own eyes returned her look with a

significant gleam. 'I won't be home for lunch, by the way.' He waved to Becky and ran down the steps, leaving Claudia to finish her breakfast in relative peace, quite satisfied with her own aplomb.

'Where's Aunt Bea?' demanded Becky suddenly. 'She's late.'

'Still at Casa d'Ouro. She had a headache, so she slept there.'

'Is she coming home this morning?'

'We'll ring and find out in a while.'

Becky showed no signs of animosity this morning, and after breakfast Claudia spent an hour helping her to use water paints to make a more ambitious picture, leaving the child deeply engrossed while she went off to look up the Casa d'Ouro number in the book beside the telephone. Emily answered and told her Bea was better, but was staying in bed a little longer, and would come home after lunch.

The rest of the morning passed without incident. Becky behaved like a normal child, with no tantrums to mar the oddly peaceful morning, with only two of them for lunch. Afterwards she even consented to lie on one of the long verandah chairs for a rest, cuddling the little koala bear somnolently while Claudia leafed through a couple of glossy American magazines.

The Fonseca chauffeur brought Bea back in the middle of the afternoon, while Becky and Claudia were engaged in a more complicated jigsaw puzzle. She apologised profusely for her absence overnight and kissed Becky fondly, giving Claudia a guilty smile.

'Advanced hypochondria, you'll be thinking, I know, and no wonder!'

'Nonsense! I know migraine is a terrible thing.' Claudia gave a conspiratorial wink at Becky. 'We managed, in any case, didn't we, Becky?'

The little girl nodded absently.

'Aunt Bea, it was Maria's birthday yesterday. She had a party.'

Bea looked stricken, gazing at Claudia in dismay.

'Oh dear! She mentioned it to me last week and I forgot—in fact I think she said something yesterday morning too, but it went clean out of my head. Age has an eroding effect on the memory!' She glanced at Claudia questioningly. 'Did you let her go?'

'Yes. Lourdes too.' Claudia smiled wryly. 'That was before I knew you weren't coming home last night.'

Bea collected herself visibly and asked Becky if she would order tea from Maria. When the child was out of earshot she turned to Claudia in agitation.

'Was Saul angry?'

'He wasn't pleased.' Claudia saw no point in dissembling. 'When he came home, which was in the early hours of the morning, he turned round and went back again when he found I was alone in the house with Becky. He slept, or rather didn't sleep, on a couch in his office.'

Bea groaned, then smiled brightly as Lourdes appeared with a tea-tray. Lourdes asked Bea something in rapid Portuguese, and Bea consented, with various instructions, telling Claudia Becky was going down to the village store with Afra to buy coffee.

'She loves it there—they generally give her a sweetmeat of some kind, and I need to talk to you, Claudia.' Bea's handsome face took on a look of resolution as she poured out tea and offered Claudia a piece of coffee-cake. 'I know you will probably find things a little behind the times here, my dear, but it wouldn't do for you to spend the night here alone with Saul. Oh dear, that sounds wrong! I mean merely under the same roof is sufficient. Normally the circumstances would never arise because the maids are usually here and I'm always here—last night was an unfortunate coincidence.'

'Please don't worry.' Claudia leaned over and patted the other woman's hand reassuringly. 'Saul turned up for breakfast after Maria and Lourdes arrived. They think he spent the entire night at the mine.'

Bea sighed with relief. 'Thank heavens for that!'

No more was said on the subject, and they talked of other things while they finished tea, after which Bea took Claudia to her room and gave her a choice of reading matter from a shelf of American paperbacks.

'I hope my trunk arrives before Christmas,' said Claudia with a frown. 'Becky's presents are in it.'

'I'm sure it will. It may even have arrived already; we must ask Saul this evening.'

Saul was late, arriving home long after his daughter was in bed and looking gaunt with fatigue. Both women had bathed and changed for the evening, and Claudia felt at a decided advantage in her cool beige dress as he came wearily up the steps and stood for a moment leaning against the rail at the top as he greeted them both and asked Bea if she were better.

'Yes, dear. Let me get you a drink——'

'For once I need a bath before I do anything,' he said wearily, and rubbed a hand over his eyes. 'I'll only be a few minutes.'

Claudia watched Saul leave with a more sympathetic eye than usual.

'It's been a long day for him,' she remarked. 'Especially after that disastrous night.'

'Yes,' said Bea with feeling. She hesitated delicately. 'Perhaps we could keep the dinner-time conversation to neutral subjects this evening.'

'Claudia laughed, her eyes dancing.

'I'm sorry. I hope our tendency to argue isn't causing indigestion as well as migraine!'

Bea laughed with her and turned the conversation to Christmas and the fourthcoming festivities at the Fonseca household, assuring Claudia it would not be necessary to take gifts. An early light lunch would be eaten at home, then they would all arrive at Casa d'Ouro well before dinner, Becky going with them and sleeping with the Fonseca children.

'I understand Emily intends gathering up a few lone bachelors for the occasion,' explained Bea. 'Tom Enys, one-time Drill Doctor at the mine, and John Trelaur, the retired Mine Captain. Both Truro men and bachelors, so when they retired they decided to share the next house down the hill from here. Oh, and Bob McClure, the geologist, will be there too.'

Claudia was surprised. 'Sounds quite a party,' she commented.

Bea looked round as Maria came to the dining room door with a question, and rose to her feet.

'Some problem about the main course; I'll just investigate.' She looked at her watch with a frown. 'Saul's a long time. Just knock on his door and hurry him along, will you, dear?'

Claudia went through the hall with a marked lack of enthusiasm. She tapped on Saul's door and waited. Silence. She knocked louder and heard a muffled 'Come in.' She stood, undecided.

'Dinnertime!' she called.

'Come in, for God's sake!'

Startled, she obeyed, to find Saul lying face down on the bed, his magnificent body bare except for the towel tucked round his hips.

'Sorry!' Claudia backed away in dismay. 'I thought you told me to come in——'

'I did.' He twisted round and lay sideways, propped up on his elbow as he looked at her, examining her flushed face with clinical detachment.

'Your aunt sent me,' Claudia sidled nearer the door. 'Dinner's ready.'

Saul stood up and stretched, threatening the security of the towel.

'Don't be nervous,' he said lazily. 'I'm a damned sight too tired to be much danger at the moment. I merely wanted to know what you told Aunt Bea about last night.'

'The truth,' said Claudia succinctly, and turned on her heel.

'All of it?'

She halted in the doorway.

'Obviously not. I left out the worrying bit.'

'It worried you?' he asked, with exaggerated concern.

'No.' She stared up at him blankly. 'But I rather felt it might worry Bea.' She walked out and closed the door quietly, then went to Becky's room, standing for several minutes watching the sleeping child while she recovered her self-possession.

This was unshakeable during dinner while she complied with Bea's request and kept the conversation to neutral subjects, refusing to rise even when Saul's intention to aggravate was obvious. Only once her feelings threatened to get the better of her. When Bea asked Saul if Claudia's trunk was likely to arrive in time for Christmas his impassive face registered faint apology for once as he confessed it had arrived before Claudia, and only needed transporting from the company stores to the house. It gave Claudia enormous satisfaction to behave with saccharine magnanimity and display none of the irritation she felt inside. Saul could have saved her a great deal of anxiety if she'd known sooner. Claudia was allowed only a short time in the role of Pollyanna before Saul excused himself and went to bed immediately after coffee, and Claudia was quite glad when Bea suggested that an early night was a good idea all around.

Armed with a borrowed copy of *Princess Daisy*, Claudia read for an hour propped against her pillows, then settled down to a rather disturbed sleep. At some stage during the night she shot upright in bed, aware that something had woken her. There was no thunder, and after a while she realised that the sound she could hear was sitfled weeping coming from Becky's room. Claudia shot out of bed and into the child's room, to find the little girl burrowing her hot, sodden face into her pillow, her little body convulsed with sobs.

Claudia's heart was wrung. The child was probably having one of her periodic fits of longing for her dead mother. She sat on the bed and gently drew Becky on to her lap, cradling the feverish fair head against her shoulder, stroking the little girl until she quietened.

'What is it, poppet?' she asked gently.

A convulsive shudder racked the little body.

'B-bad dream.' Becky sniffed hard and pushed herself closer.

Claudia braced herself mentally.

'Can you tell me about it?'

Becky nodded blindly.

'I dreamed Father Christmas didn't bring me a bike

like Jamie's.' She hiccuped, and turned drowned blue eyes up to Claudia, her face blotched and swollen.

Oh boy! thought Claudia, blinking.

'Well, it's not Christmas yet,' she said soothingly. 'I expect he's waiting to see what a good girl you are.' God forgive me, she added silently.

'I'm a *bit* better, Claudia, aren't I?'

The appeal in the drowned blue eyes was irresistible. Claudia hugged her, hard.

'Yes, Becky today you've been great. But I think the idea is to go on trying hard pretty much all the time.'

'I will,' said Becky passionately, a stray sob shaking her hot little body.

'Then the first step is to go back to sleep now—only your pillows are sodden. Hang on——'

'Can I help?' Saul stood in the doorway in his dressing gown, watching them both.

Claudia got to her feet with care and handed her burden to him.

'Perhaps you'll cuddle Becky for a moment while I change her bed; it's a bit sweaty.' She gave an embarrassed glance down at her green nightie, which happily was a modest white-dotted cotton, nevertheless she ran to her own room for her kimono. Saul watched in silence, cradling his child closely as Claudia took fresh linen from the chest of drawers and remade the bed rapidly. Becky was fast asleep by the time she had finished, and Saul gently lowered her into the bed, tucking the sheet loosely round her with hands which looked incongruously large for the task.

Claudia smiled briefly and whispered goodnight, but before she could slip into her own room he said softly, 'Was she crying for Elaine?'

'No. She had a bad dream. Father Christmas came and didn't bring her a bike like Jamie's.'

He stifled a laugh, then whispered, 'Come into the study a moment, Claudia, please.'

Claudia followed him, standing just inside the closed door of the study as he switched on the desk lamp.

'Was that really the cause of all that sorrow?' Saul propped himself against the edge of the desk, his long brown legs stretched out in front of him, his long feet bare.

Nice toenails, thought Claudia irrelevantly, then recollected herself hurriedly, nodding in answer to his question. Saul frowned, scratching his chin thoughtfully.

'Tricky,' he said slowly. 'Bea bought a doll for her when she was over in the U.K., plus a typewriter as my present to her.'

'Oh dear,' Claudia bit her lip. 'I just brought various books for her. Without knowing the child beforehand it was a bit difficult to know what would appeal.'

'There's only one thing for it.' Saul looked at her questioningly. 'How do you feel about braving the road to Boa Vista one day next week?'

Claudia's face lit up. 'That would be marvellous!'

He raised his eyebrows. 'Tired of Campo d'Ouro already?'

She shook her head impatiently.

'No, of course not, but I couldn't think how to get the present for her I really know she'll like—apart from the bike. And please don't start on the subject of bribery!'

'Never entered my mind. Come on, it's late, let's go to bed.' He reached past her to open the door. 'Perhaps you'd prefer me to re-phrase that.'

She wasn't going to rise to that one. With an impersonal little smile Claudia wished him goodnight and left the room as he switched out the light. She listened to his almost soundless retreating footsteps as she did her best to get to sleep again, which was rather difficult after the disrupting little scene with Becky. The word to describe life here so far was leisurely, rather than quiet was her last thought. Even the nights were proving fairly eventful.

Events proved her wrong. For the next few days life went along serenely enough, with Becky trying hard to behave well enough to merit her much-coveted bicycle, and in the process finding she quite liked having Claudia around after all. Bea's migranes kept away in the absence of tension and upsets and Claudia settled into her new life with ease, writing to Liz on the subject at length. One of the reasons for all the serenity admittedly, was the absence of Saul for a few days over Claudia's first weekend. He and Luc went off on an inspection tour of some outlying sub-stations, and Bea took the opportunity of inviting Thurza, Emily and the children for the day on the Sunday they were away. Both ladies remarked on the difference in Becky, congratulating Claudia on her success with the child. Claudia disclaimed it, smiling, explaining that the angelic behaviour was merely advance payment on Becky's behalf for the hotly desired bicycle. Whatever the reason for Becky's reform, the result made life a great deal more pleasant for everyone in her vicinity, including herself.

When Saul came home he was unable to take a working day for the proposed trip to Boa Vista, and the following Saturday was settled on for the shopping expedition.

Boa Vista proved to be a modern city, its tall white buildings and wide streets raying out from a main tree-lined avenida. *Lotações*, the small local buses, scurried along crammed with people alongside big American limousines and dusty jeeps in an atmosphere of petrol fumes, roasting peanuts, coffee and cooking food, all blended together into a hot, foreign aroma by the fierce afternoon sun. Claudia breathed it in deeply, her eyes sparkling behind dark, white-framed lenses as she tried to take in everything around her at once. Advised by Bea to wear something on her head, Claudia had tied a white-spotted yellow kerchief over her hair, and chosen a double-breasted white overblouse and swinging pleated yellow skirt as both cool and suitable for the city.

Saul kept tight hold of her elbow as he steered her through the crowds thronging the wide pavements and pointed out various buildings of interest. A large department store was their goal, where they took the lift to the toy department and purchased the desired bicycle without fuss, leaving it to be picked up later.

'Would you give me a few moments to make a purchase of my own?' asked Claudia. 'I promise to be quick.'

Saul shrugged.

'No rush. I'll have a beer in the bar next door. Turn left as you leave the store, and join me when you've finished. Are you all right for currency?'

'Yes. Thanks a lot—I shan't be long.'

She watched his tall figure out of sight, then haltingly asked an assiatant for directions to the department selling children's clothes. Shaking her head at the enchanting frilly concoctions on display, Claudia eventually managed to make herself clear to the courteous, patient young man who served her, and bought three pairs of small jeans, the same quantity of shorts in vivid colours, plus half a dozen tee-shirts in every colour imaginable. A secret inspection of Becky's wardrobe had given her the right shoe size for two pairs of sneakers, and the final touch was several headbands in brightly coloured stretch-towelling.

Claudia had bought gifts in England for Saul and Bea, but when she left the elevator at the ground floor she noticed a kiosk selling cigarettes and saw the brand of cheroot Saul smoked and bought a large box to add to the framed antique map of Cornwall already chosen as suitable for an employer. It had taken quite an effort of armwaving and miming to buy the cigarillos, which she now knew was the Portuguese word, and feeling very pleased with her shopping spree Claudia left the air-conditioned store to emerge into the glaring heat outside, blinking in the brilliant light despite her sunglasses. She turned in the direction Saul had instructed and saw him immediately at one of the pavement tables just outside a small bar, his long legs stretched out under the table, his face absorbed as he read a newspaper, a half empty glass of beer in front of him.

Claudia stood silent, smiling down at his unconscious profile for a moment before Saul realised she was there and shot to his feet, a look of surprise on his face.

'My God, you were quick! I was all set for at least another half-hour's wait.'

'I said I wouldn't be long.' She grinned at him in such a friendly fashion he grinned back spontaneously and indicated a chair.

'Fancy a beer?'

'Not really.' Claudia eyed him hopefully. 'What I'd really sell my soul for is a cup of tea!'

'Why not?' Saul drained the beer in his glass and took her parcels, putting a hand under her elbow. 'If your soul can survive two blocks' walk in the sun it shall have its wish.'

He led her through the colourful crowd, past exciting shops selling tempting leather goods and jewellery, where Claudia would have given much to linger, privately promising herself a browse on some future occasion, until they reached a large, multi-storied building, the Hotel Paranà. Saul conducted her to the restaurant on the first floor, where half the tables were outside on a shaded balcony overlooking the Avenida. Claudia was delighted when Saul led her to one of these, able to gaze at the passing show to her heart's content while enjoying the tea Saul ordered, though rather wary of the plate of very ornate sweetmeats served with it.

Saul accepted a cup of tea but refused a pastry, urging Claudia to try one in her aim to experience the true flavour of everything Brazilian. She accepted one of the smallest, not because it was much to her taste but to please Saul, whose face today was without its habitual withdrawn expression. She disposed of the delicacy, a date embedded in a nest of marzipan, finding it over-sweet for her taste.

'Do these things have names?' she asked, wiping her fingers on her napkin.

'The one you ate is known as *Olha da Sogra*,' he said, with a sly grin. ' "Mother-in-law's eye" to you!'

Claudia's recoil was patently rewarding as he bent towards her with a mollifying look in his eye.

'Never mind, have some more tea, then we have one more call to make before we get the jeep and call back for the bike.'

'Where else are we going?'

'Just around the corner to a delicatessen where they stock imported products as well as very good food. Aunt Bea gave me a list of odds and ends.'

The delicatessen was a fragrant, dark Aladdin's cave of a place, where Saul was obviously well known, and the proprietor, a rotund personage in a white apron, greeted him like a long-lost son, sending minions scurrying in all directions while he himself presented Claudia with titbits of ham and cheese to taste, all of which were delicious. She watched, fascinated, as a box gradully filled with various delicacies, a kilo of hand-carved ham, another of Queijo Estepe, a superb local cheese, together with a slab of moist Mozzarella, special coffee from the city of Sao Paulo, jars of fat green olives, tins of anchovies, cashew nuts, walnuts, almonds, small biscuits like ratafias, and finally, carefully wrapped against the heat, some enormous chocolates were tenderly arranged before the lid was tied on the box surrendered to Saul with much quick-fire Portuguese, the gist of which Claudia understood to be Christmas wishes.

Soon after they were on their way back to Campo d'Ouro with the bicycle safely stowed beneath a tarpaulin with the other parcels in the back of the jeep. Saul drove at a less headlong rate than on Claudia's first, disastrous introduction to the scenic grandeur of the route to Campo d'Ouro.

'No troubles with your digestive system today?' he asked, with a gleaming sidelong glance.

'Nary a one,' she answered firmly, turning her mind away from thoughts of "mother-in-law's eye".

'I thought you were relaxed on the way in; you must be getting used to my driving.'

Even the scent of his cigarillo had no effect on Claudia this time, and she sat enjoying the breathtaking panorama of mountain peaks, her body swaying with the vehicle as it wound along the undulating route.

'You were in a towering hurry that first day,' she said. 'I was uncomfortably aware that you were hellbent on getting back, fast, and that fetching me from the airport was about the last on your list of priorities.

Today I'm getting different vibes. You don't seem in as much of a hurry.'

'I'm not.' Saul's eyes narrowed in concentration on a sharp bend ahead. 'I enjoyed our little excursion.'

'So did I.'

'Find everything you wanted? The shops here must be a bit different from the ones in England.'

'Very good, though. Figuring out the money was a bit tricky, but the shop assistant was patience itself with my fractured Portuguese and had just what I wanted, which is a relief.'

'Relief'?'

Claudia nodded with satisfaction.

'Becky has done her utmost to be good lately and I wanted to buy her something I know she'll like—apart from the bicycle, of course. I've hit on the right thing, I think.'

Saul gave her a sharp glance.

'So your purchases were for Becky, not you? How do you know what she wants—another dream?'

'No. But I know she'd like shorts, jeans—things she can play in without messing up all those rather elaborate dresses she wears.' Claudia eyed him warily, unwilling to have anything spoil this pleasant outing, which had been notable for its lack of disagreement.

'I'm afraid my aunt just called in the village dressmaker, and she provided what she thought suitable for a little girl.' His face was bleak. 'I brought as little as possible from England when I collected Becky from Elaine's ménage.'

Claudia said nothing, inwardly sad for the child uprooted from everything familiar, not even her own possessions to cushion the strangeness of her new life in a foreign country with this unfamiliar father of hers.

'Thank God you heard Becky crying the other night,' Saul went on. 'Otherwise we would have had a very disappointed child on our hands on Christmas Day. What exactly had you in mind for me to do about the typewriter?'

A slight dryness in the last words made her smile.

'At the risk of being considered bossy, could I suggest

that you save it for her birthday, or some other appropriate time?'

'But of course, Claudia. I hired you for your educational qualities—I can hardly complain when you bring your talents to bear on the rest of the household as well.' This time the dryness was more marked.

'Just comfort yourself with the thought that you're getting your money's worth,' said Claudia tartly.

'That I intend to do, never fear.' Saul's teeth showed white in a grin that made Claudia uneasy and for the remainder of the journey she steered the conversation to more neutral topics until the conical peak of Morro d'Ouro came into sight, its cross already alight in preparation for the abrupt drama of sunset.

As the jeep came to a halt in the drive of the house a small figure danced up and down at the top of the verandah steps, the frills on her short pink lawn nightdress bobbing up and down as Claudia ran up the steps towards her.

'Clauida! Your box came. José put it in the *porao*.'

'Hollow, Becky, that's good news. Good evening, Bea.'

Bea Treharne was sitting near a drinks-laden tray on the table, an open picture book on her lap. She smiled as Claudia sank down on the settee beside her.

'How did you enjoy your afternoon, Claudia? What did you think of Boa Vista?'

'Very spectacular. The town itself was such a visual surprise. For some reason I never expected something so sophisticated and modern, and yet so very attractive. I think it's the contrast of the great interleaved double row of trees making an avenue of green shade in the middle of all that bright whiteness created by the buildings.'

Bea nodded, handing Claudia a long glass of gin and tonic.

'I find it utterly exhausting myself. It's the combination of the journey in, plus the impact of all that colour and noise, not to mention the different smells. I feel Boa Vista is a city for the young.'

'Nonsense!' Saul came springing up the steps with the

box from the delicatessen. 'Here are all your goodies, you poor ancient thing!'

'Splendid, dear. Now we can have a rather more special cold lunch tomorrow.'

Becky was examining the box Saul held, her curiosity plain to see, but with admirable self-control she forbore to enquire about its contents, to her father's amusement. He held out his hand.

'Come on, Becky, let's take this out to Maria to unpack, and see if we can find something in it for you.'

Joyously the child jumped up and took her father's hand without hesitation, chattering to him spontaneously as she skipped along at his side, watched with surprise and approval by Bea.

'You know, Claudia, I think you must be a catalyst. Since your arrival on the scene both Becky and Saul seem to be thawing.' She smiled kindly at Claudia, who shook her head instantly.

'It's early days yet. Perhaps the novelty of having someone come all the way from England for her sole benefit will wear off once lessons start in earnest. Perhaps she'll be more on her mettle with Jamie and Mark joining in.'

'Yes.' Bea gave a little cough. 'Has Saul recovered from his initial disapproval on that score?'

'I think so. Learning about Emily's pregnancy changed his attitude very quickly, anyway.'

Bea shook her head in vague disapproval.

'Personally I think it's too much for her—three children and a miscarriage already, and she's not even twenty-six yet. They should have waited a while before starting another.'

'Gossiping, Aunt Bea?' There was a slight warning note in Saul's voice as he reappeared suddenly from the hall, followed by Becky, busily engaged in removing the paper from an outsize chocolate.

'Thurza and I merely feel——'

'Surely it's more a case of what Luc and Emily feel!' His voice was crisp and dismissive as he helped himself to a drink.

Claudia jumped up and prepared to depart, reluctant

to listen in on any family disagreements, especially on this particular subject.

'If you'll excuse me, I must have a bath. The road wasn't nearly as dusty today after the rain we've had, but I feel a little scruffy, just the same.'

Saul looked her up and down with veiled amusement from his usual post at the verandah rail, but said nothing, downing the contents of his glass with enjoyment.

'Won't you feel like reading to me tonight, Claudia?' Becky's chocolate-daubed face was crestfallen.

'Becky!' Bea was indignant. 'I've already read you one story tonight—Claudia must be tired, after all.'

'Are you, Claudia?' Becky frowned earnestly as she turned apologetically to Bea. 'You see, Aunt Bea, Claudia makes different voices—like a really truly story!'

Bea held up her hands goodnaturedly, defeated.

'Oh well, in that case, how can I compete?'

'It comes of long practice in keeping young girls awake while I tried to cram some literature into their unwilling heads,' smiled Claudia. 'Come on, then, Becky, choose a dress for me while I shower, then I'll read you your story.'

All smiles, Becky ran to her great-aunt and her father, kissing them both goodnight without any prompting before dancing off with Claudia to her bedroom. Saul's eyes were thoughtful as they rested on the two departing figures, a fact secretly noted by his watchful aunt.

Dinner was ready by the time Claudia had showered, dressed and unleashed her talent for the dramatic on 'Red Riding Hood', to Becky's immense satisfaction. When Claudia said goodnight Becky opened her big eyes and stared up at her with anxious intensity.

'I've been a *very* good girl today, Claudia.'

'Well done!'

'Even though you weren't here, I mean. Cross my heart!'

Claudia smiled at her, touched.

'That's good news. Quite easy, really, isn't it?'

Becky nodded drowsily, the very picture of cherubic innocence. Claudia let herself out of the room quietly, smiling to herself, not a little doubtful about the ethics of good behaviour merely as a sprat to catch a mackerel, or bicycle in Becky's case. With luck Becky might adopt reasonable conduct as a life-style if practised long enough, bike or no bike. Aware that she was indulging in sophistry, Claudia joined Bea and Saul in the dining room, seating herself with anticipation before a tempting glass goblet containing large prawns in a sauce of delicious piquancy.

'Maria adds a dash of cream and brandy before serving,' explained Bea in response to Claudia's rapturous praise of the sauce.

'Did you come up to scratch with your rendition of Becky's bedtime opus?' Saul smiled blandly and leaned over to fill her wine glass.

'Red Riding Hood tonight.' Claudia gave him a mischievous smile. 'It's really quite difficult to read that one without histrionics anyway. It's quite surprising how children enjoy the ghoulish stories the best—they always did at the Home. I read somewhere that Eleanor Roosevelt was renowned for the drama of her bedtime stories and her family refused to allow anyone else to read to them.'

Bea shook her head regretfully.

'Definitely not a talent I posses. *And* I tend to stick to Cinderella and the prettier stories. No wonder Becky was bored—I honestly thought the more violent ones would frighten her.'

'Children are barbarians on the whole,' said Saul dryly. 'The fortunate grow up to be more civilised, but a great many never manage it, even in maturity.'

Bea looked rather smug. 'Claudia certainly seems to be civilising Becky—you must admit that, Saul.'

'Let's not get over-optimistic, Aunt Bea, perhaps we should wait a while before awarding accolades.' Saul gave Claudia a look that said quite plainly she had no reason to rest on her laurels.

Unperturbed, Claudia began on her Beef Stroganoff. Saul could put away his goad. She had no intention of allowing herself to relax her vigilance with either father or child. Her confidence in winning Becky over was unshaken, but as far as Saul was concerned there seemed little point in trying. Her mercenary proclivities plainly had the upper hand in his opinion of her. Yet the trip to Boa Vista had been pleasant, surprisingly so. Her musings were interrupted by a question from Bea on Claudia's opinion of the shops in Boa Vista, and for the rest of the meal the conversation centred on shopping and Christmas.

'I believe you drive,' remarked Saul later when they were lingering over coffee in the drawing-room.

Claudia nodded, pleasantly tired after the strenuous afternoon.

'Will she have to take another test, Saul?' asked Bea.

Claudia's sleepiness vanished.

'Another test?'

'I'm afraid so.' Saul's smile had a wolfish quality. 'No problem to an efficient lady like you.' He drank his brandy, obviously relishing something more than just the flavour of the spirit. 'They test several people, one at a time down on the Praca, the square in the town. It's a bit different from in the U.K. A fair crowd usually turn out to watch.'

Claudia set down her coffee cup with care.

'It sounds more like an *auto-da-fé*,' she said acidly. 'What would I have to do?'

'The only thing that differs very much is the *balisa*. This consists of reversing and backing acurately through a pair of posts without touching them— something like football posts, only a little closer together.' Saul was clearly enjoying himself.

'Do I have to?' demanded Claudia.

'Well, you can't drive here without a Brazilian licence, and it would certainly be a help for Bea and Rebecca if you could act as chauffeur when I'm not around.' Saul lit a cigarillo and watched Claudia's face through the smoke with patient pleasure.

Defeated, Claudia said nothing, but gave him a look that spoke volumes.

'Well,' he persisted, 'shall I put in an application?'

'I suppose so,' she agreed reluctantly.

'Cheer up, it won't be so bad,' he said patronisingly. 'Now, have some more coffee.'

With a sympathetic look Bea changed the subject and asked Claudia if there was anything she urgently required from her trunk, or could it wait until the following day.

'Having waited this long,' said Claudia sweetly, her eyes sending a barbed glance in Saul's direction, 'I'm sure I can hang on until the morning.'

Bea hid a smile as Saul looked defensive for once.

'I'm afraid it slipped my mind before I went away—you could have reminded me, you know.'

'I wouldn't have dreamed of bothering you with something so unimportant!' It gave Claudia great self-satisfaction to see the mighty Saul put out for a change. Her eyes were crystal-bright with conscious virtue as she watched him stub out his cigarillo with rather unnecessary force.

'Is your tennis gear in the trunk?' he asked surprisingly.

'Yes—the racquets anyway.'

'Fancy a game of tennis tomorrow?'

'With you?' asked Claudia, her eyes startled.

'Yes. I enjoy a game now and then, usually with Bob McClure, the geologist. Becky and Bea can watch.' The challenge in the dark blue eyes made it impossible to do anything other than agree.

'Fine,' said Claudia brightly. 'I'll look forward to it. In that case, though, perhaps I'd better get a good night's sleep in to prepare myself for the fray!'

CHAPTER NINE

CLAUDIA was awake next morning at the crack of dawn with the thought of the ensuing game hanging over her like a cloud. Worry about Saul's standard of tennis had made sleep harder to achieve than usual, and Claudia grew quite irritable with herself, knowing very well that she played a strong, workmanlike game, not brilliant, but certainly good enough to give Saul a run for his money, any day.

She dressed silently, putting an old denims and an elderly rugby shirt in preparation for tackling her trunk. It was very early, not long after six, and she made herself some tea in the kitchen, taking it on the verandah to lean against the rail, drinking in the scene below her, the colours crystalline in the early light. Gradually her sense of proportion was restored. Back in England Sunday was a lonely day to pass as well as she could, which at this time of the year meant a long lie-in, a browse through the Sunday papers while her solitary lunch cooked, then an afternoon in front of the television with a pile of marking, and if the quiet became too intense sometimes an evening trip to the cinema. Whereas here she had sunshine, company, the prospect of tennis at the club, conversation and good food—in fact, Claudia, she told herself impatiently, count your blessings. She remained counting them for some time, enjoying the relative coolness of early morning and her moment of peace.

'You look happy this morning!'

Claudia turned to Saul standing behind her in the dining-room doorway in jeans and sweatshirt, looking more rested than at any time since her arrival.

'I was laughing at myself,' she said with complete truth.

'What was so funny?' He strolled across and leaned on the rail beside her. Claudia pushed her hair behind her ears. 'Something bothering you?' asked Saul casually. 'You do that when you're nervous.'

'Do what?'

'Push your hair behind your ears.'

'Do I? Great! Must be a dead give-away.'

'So what are you uptight about?' he persisted.

Claudia looked up at him for a moment, head on one side, then opted for frankness.

'I was nervous about playing tennis with you.'

It was his turn to stare.

'Why, for God's sake?'

She shrugged. 'I have this insane feeling that if I don't measure up to your requirements in every department—give you value for your money, as it were—you'll pack me back to England at the first opportunity.'

'And you don't want that?' There was no mockery in his dark blue scrutiny for once.

Claudia shook her head and looked away.

'Your idea's nonsense anyway,' he said. 'I engaged you to teach my daughter, not entertain me. I merely thought you might enjoy some tennis today—it's the only one I have free.'

She smiled sheepishly.

'And you're perfectly right—I will enjoy it. I was being rather immature for a while, but at least I paid you the compliment of honesty.'

'A rare virtue among women!' The familiar mocking element was back, irritating Claudia.

'Sweeping generalisations are empty statements,' she said flatly. 'One might just as easily say all men are liars.'

'No doubt they are—ah, good! Here comes Maria and breakfast. Bea usually has a lie-in on Sundays.'

Claudia looked at him curiously. 'Don't you?'

'I wake at the same time each day. Habit——' he broke off as Becky ran towards them, her face accusing.

'You weren't in your bed, Claudia!'

'No, Becky, I woke early today.'

Becky turned to her father, demanding, 'It's Sunday. Are you staying home today?'

'Yes. You can come to the club with Aunt Bea and watch Claudia play tennis with me.' Saul smiled indulgently at the child and gave her a gentle push towards the table.

'Goody!' Becky prattled all through breakfast, then accompanied Claudia to the *porão* to open the trunk. Fortunately her racquets and tennis shoes lay on the tray on top, as Claudia had no intention of allowing Becky to see the contents underneath.

'I'll leave the rest until later,' she said, and relocked the trunk. 'Let's see if Aunt Bea's up and about.'

Maria and Lourdes departed after breakfast, not due to return until the following morning, and Bea took charge of Becky while Claudia went to change into her tennis gear. Her brief wrapover tennis skirt and tee-shirt top showed off her lithe, graceful figure and long legs to the best possible advantage, the white cotton knit of her shirt clinging to the curves of her high breasts and emphasising her neat waist. Claudia tied the laces of her tennis shoes firmly and secured her hair at the nape of her neck with a green ribbon, wondering if she needed a skirt for the short walk over to the club, and decided to play safe, adding the matching knee-length skirt and cotton blouson jacket that went with the outfit.

Bea examined Claudia approvingly in the kitchen where she was waiting for her.

'Saul's gone on ahead with Becky,' she said. 'You look very neat and businesslike, my dear.'

'I devoutly hope my game does the same!' Claudia's nerves were taut as Bea closed the door behind them and walked with her towards the gate.

'Don't be nervous, Claudia. It's not Wimbledon!'

The club bar was open, several people clustered round it, others sitting at the tables overlooking the courts, where a man's singles match was already in progress. All eyes seemed to turn in their direction as Bea and Claudia descended the steps and went towards the bar, where Saul, magnificent in white shirt and shorts, a light blue sweater knotted round his shoulders by the sleeves, was talking to two elderly men, Becky perched on a high stool beside him sucking orangeade through a straw. He looked up as he caught sight of Bea and Claudia.

'Ah, here they come!'

'Good morning,' said Bea. 'How are you John, Tom?'

Both men greeted her, short, dark, physically very similar, their kind faces creased in smiles.

'Claudia,' said Saul, 'meet John Trelaur, former Mine

Captain, Tom Enys, the best Drill Doctor west of the Tamar. This is Miss Claudia March.'

'She's my new gov'ness,' Becky informed them importantly.

Claudia received a warm welcome from both men, who began to tease Becky about having to watch her p's and q's from now on, then were obliged to explain to the curious child just what they meant.

'Ready?' asked Saul under cover of the conversation.

'As I'll ever be,' Claudia gave a little grimace. 'Where do I put my outer things?'

'Ladies' clockroom along there, just beyond the bar. I'll get on the court. Don't be long.'

'Yes, sir!' said Claudia smartly, and disappeared through the indicated door before he could respond. When she emerged Becky was loud in her praise of Claudia's outfit, embarrassingly so.

'You look smashing, Claudia, doesn't she, Uncle Tom?'

'A sight for sore eyes,' said Tom Enys, smiling in agreement.

'Saul's waiting for you on court, dear.' Bea smiled in encouragement. 'Good luck.'

Claudia's progress along the verandah and on to the court was made more nerve-raking by the knowledge that, added to the interested looks of the people sat at the tables, three pairs of male eyes were watching her cross the court with varying expressions; two with frank appreciation, the third blank as navy blue buttons as Claudia approached. Inwardly annoyed that Saul should subject her to this particular way of meeting two of his colleagues, Claudia's head came up proudly and she gave him a cool little smile as she reached the three men. One of them was a long-legged man with fair hair and gold-rimmed glasses, the same height as Saul but slighter and more rangy, with skin that showed a tendency to redden in the sun. His companion was younger, shorter by a head, swarthy and muscular with a thick black moustache and dark eyes that managed to convey respect and appreciation simultaneously as they rested on Claudia.

Saul took her by the arm.

'Claudia, I'd like you to meet Bob McClure, the geologist, and Manoel Araujo, one of the bright young engineers in my department. Gentlemen, allow me to present Miss Claudia March, who has been kind enough to leave the U.K. to teach my daughter and the Fonseca children.'

Feeling for the first time as though her exact function had now been clearly defined, Claudia smiled warmly at the two men, holding out her hand with a conventional 'How do you do.' Bob McClure shook it heartily, grinning in a friendly, disarming sort of way.

'Welcome to Campo d'Ouro, Miss March, I sincerely hope you'll like it here.'

'I already do,' Claudia assured him, and turned to give her hand to Manoel Araujo, who hesitated a second, then raised it to his lips for an instant.

'*Muito prazer, senhora*, allow me to add my good wishes to those of Bob.'

'Buy her a drink later,' Saul interrupted, 'but for the moment we'll all earn one with a little exercise.'

Claudia could see Becky on the edge of a chair at a table near the railing, with Bea and the two Cornishmen, all obviously prepared to watch with enjoyment.

With a fervent mental prayer to whatever patron saint had the job of looking after tennis players, Claudia began to knock up, sending balls back and forth over the net to Saul, whose sheer length of arm and leg augured only too plainly how difficult it would be to get a ball past him. Already familiar with his unexpected lightness of tread, it came as no surprise to Claudia to see the perfect co-ordination he displayed as he moved around the court with a speed not normally associated with someone of his proportions. At first her strokes were tentative, then eye and hand automatically began to function in unison, and Claudia grew bolder, hitting the ball at her opponent with a force Saul acknowledged with a raised eyebrow as he returned the compliment.

'Let's start,' he called, 'or the heat might get to you.'

Not if I can help it, vowed Claudia silently. She gave

him a nod and retrieved two balls in preparation for the
first serve. She threw the ball up high in a practised,
fluid motion, stretching every last inch of body and arm
as she came down on the ball with a strength many a
man might have envied, sending it over the net like a
bullet to land just inside the centre line of the service
court. Admittedly it was returned with interest, but
from then on Claudia's nerves steadied and she began
to enjoy herself, her brain cool as it automatically
calculated any weaknesses in Saul's game. There was no
weakness at all in his baseline play, and when she
slammed balls at his feet they came back with a force
that now and then defeated her, but doggedly she
stuck to her guns and the score went with service,
neither player conceding a break. Gradually she began
to introduce the occasional disguised little drop-shot
that fell just over the net, foiling Saul in his attempts to
reach them from the baseline despite his magnificent
bursts of speed. Nevertheless the score remained ding-
dong, with neither player gaining any advantage until
they reached a tie-break situation at the end of the set,
where Saul's powerhouse service prevailed, and Claudia
was defeated by means of three lightning-fast aces.

Saul vaulted across the net towards Claudia as a
spatter of applause sounded from the onlookers, to her
embarrassment, and Bob McClure and Manoel Araujo
came across from the other court, where they had
openly abandoned their game to watch. Saul gave her
an odd little bow, a smile of such genuine appreciation
on his normally impassive face that Claudia's heartbeat
might have quickened if it had not already been
pounding like a bongo drum with exertion, as she
suddenly realised she was very hot, very sweaty and
extremely tired.

'Claudia, I salute you,' he said simply.

She smiled shakily, her breath coming in laboured
gasps.

'Same to you, kind sir,' she panted.

Bob McClure loped up, the sun glinting on his
glasses, his face split from ear to ear in a grin of delight.

'Lady, you play a mean game! Before I beg the

honour of a game with you I guess I'd better get in some practice!'

'Parabéms, senhora!' The young Brazilian added his congratulations with sincere admiration.

Claudia felt embarrassed. Her aim had been to show Saul Treharne she was worth her salt in the sports department, not to make an exhibition of herself.

'I was stupid—I forgot to bring a towel,' she said apologetically, following Saul towards the exit gate, her legs like jelly.

'It's reassuring to find you have the odd little imperfection,' he said, with a barbed little grin. 'I had the forethought to bring two; Becky has them with her at the table.'

Claudia gave him an eloquent glance as she opened the gate to let her through to a rapturous reception from Becky, whose face was pink with excitement as she caught Claudia's arm in an excited grasp.

'I want to learn tennis, Claudia. Will you show me how?'

'Of course I will, then you can play with Daddy, too.'

The child's eyes sparkled as she ran to Bea to tell her. Bea's eyes twinkling merrily as she shook her head at Claudia.

'What in the world were you nervous about, dear girl?' She turned to look up at Saul. 'She almost beat you, my dear, your reputation is at stake!'

Saul grinned and handed a large blue towel to Claudia. She slung it round her shoulders, mopping at her forehead with one end.

'I'll have to resort to secret practice sessions with Bob to preserve my pride,' he said, straight-faced. 'Seriously, Claudia, you'd be wise to sponge yourself in the changing room and give yourself a good rub down before we claim the drinks Bob's about to stand us.'

Bea looked at Claudia's pale, perspiring face and said reasonably,

'It's only a step over to the house, Claudia. Why not run over and take a shower?'

Claudia agreed gratefully, and excusing herself to John Trelaur and Tom Enys, went to collect her skirt

and jacket from the cloakroom, Becky at her side
wanting to go with her to the house while she changed.
As they mounted the steps together Saul's voice halted
them.

'Claudia! What will you have when you come back—
your usual?'

Claudia nodded, smiling, and took Becky's hand to
walk jauntily back to the house, pleased at the
connotations of the word 'usual', which seemed to
indicate a permanency, a settled feeling, as though her
place in the Treharne household was an established,
welcome fact.

At lightning speed she showered and dressed,
hurrying into clean underwear and buttoning on a crisp
white cotton shirt which she tucked into the waistband of
the jade green trousers, which had been exquisitely
laundered and ironed by the invaluable Maria. Becky had
been delivering a running commentary about tennis up to
that point, but as Claudia tied the white rope belt and slid
her feet into white sandals she noticed Becky staring at
herself in the mirror with a black frown on her face.

'What's up, Becky?'

'This stupid dress is dirty,' grumbled the child,
pouting.

'Let's go and look for something else, then.'

Claudia rummaged through the hangers of exquisite
dresses in Becky's wardrobe until she found something
a little less elaborate, a sleeveless mint-green over
blouse with its own brief pleated skirt.

'How about this?'

Becky nodded unenthusiastically, but suffered
Claudia to strip off her dress and replace it with the
plainer outfit, in a fever of impatience to return to the
club. She danced on ahead as Claudia relocked the
house, but halted obediently at the gate in response to
Claudia's call, still very much on her mettle to show
how good she could be. Hand in hand they walked
more sedately back along the Club path, and descended
the steps to find Bea at a table, literally surrounded by
men, as Bob McClure and Manoel Araujo had now
joined John Trelaur, Tom Enys and Saul. They all rose

as one man as Claudia and Becky appeared, Bob instantly making for the bar, where a long gin and tonic materialised like magic from the cheerful, dark-skinned waiter in his immaculate white shirt and black bow tie.

Claudia sat down next to Bea amid a great deal of noise and cheerful teasing from the men as she took her first thirsty mouthful of her drink after acknowledging all the extravagant toasts aimed at her.

'Beginner's luck,' she said firmly, her face a little pink as she crossed one green-clad leg over the other and prepared to relax.

'You aren't trying to tell us that this was your first game of tennis?' said Saul severely. He hoisted Becky on to his knee, the startled look on the child's face evidence that this was not a common occurrence.

'It was my first game *here*,' said Claudia firmly, with a smile aimed at everyone in general.

'It surely won't be your last, Miss March,' said Bob with conviction. 'Where did you learn to play like that?'

'In college,' she answered, and turned to Tom Enys with a view to changing the subject, enquiring the meaning of the fascinating term 'Drill Doctor'. She was aware, out of the corner of her eye, that Saul was watching her as John Trelaur supplied the necessary information, as Tom Enys seemed a bit tongue-tied at explaining his special craft.

'The Drill Doctor's the chap who makes and sets the cutting-heads of the drills with diamonds——'

'Diamonds?' Claudia's eyes glittered in surprise.

'He means industrial diamonds, my dear,' put in Tom. 'I used to be responsible for forming new heads, or refurbishing existing ones, and not all had diamonds—some of them are made of special hard steel.'

'He was the best in the business,' said Saul, who obviously had great affection for the older man.

'Get on with you,' said Tom, embarrassed. 'Anyway, I trained young Sabino pretty well to follow me. I hear he don't do too badly.'

' "Young Sabino" must be all of fifty,' said Bob McClure with a grin, then looked at Saul expectantly. 'Feel like another game, old buddy?'

'Give me five minutes,' said Saul, and stood up, swinging Becky to the ground.

It was enlightening entertainment to watch the contrast in style between the two players. Bob countered Saul's fire and force with a game of craft and precision, placing his shots with as much care as his opponent allowed, endlessly retrieving and retrieving in a manner designed to wear down his opponent. At times it seemed he would succeed, but for Claudia the issue was never in doubt. She was certain Saul would win, and eventually the American conceded a service game and it was all over as Saul won the following game with four serves of devastating speed and accuracy Bob had no possibility of getting back over the net.

'Saul's on fine form today,' observed Bea, with a smiling glance at Claudia, who sat with Becky leaning against her shoulder, displaying signs of restiveness. The two men were hot and sweat-soaked as they came off court, the hot noonday sun having taken its toll. Bea rolled up her knitting and put it away, turning to her two fellow countrymen with a smile.

'Can I persuade you both to a pot luck sort of meal—you know I do it myself on Sundays, so you can't say you haven't been warned!'

They accepted with alacrity, as did Bob when Bea extended her invitation to include him.

'Yes, ma'am! With the greatest of pleasure. Be with you directly—just as long as it takes to shower.'

As the rest of the party made their way back to the house Saul gave a sly glance at Claudia and remarked,

'If you're stuck, Aunt Bea, perhaps Claudia might cook us something.'

There was a concerted laugh at the look of comic dismay on Claudia's face as she put up a hand in protest.

'I'm hopeless at quite a few things, but I must admit that cooking is my nadir!'

'What are the others, I wonder?' Saul's murmur was inaudible to the others as they followed more slowly.

'Don't worry, they'll become glaringly obvious the longer you know me.' Claudia shook back her hair, laughing, the shimmer of sunlight in her eyes prompting an answering smile in his, attractive as it was rare.

The impromptu lunch was a very pleasant affair, cold meats, including the delicious ham purchased in Boa Vista the day before, various salads, and an enormous pot of gnocchi, prepared by Maria the night before ready for heating up next day. The atmosphere was more like that of a picnic.

Bob McClure elected himself washer-up despite Bea's protests, and he and Claudia made surprisingly short work of the dishes while Bea put food away and generally tidied up. Saul, seeming at a loose end, lounged in the kitchen doorway and watched the workers at their labours.

'Being a bachelor I don't have a maid that lives in,' explained Bob to Claudia with a grin, methodically washing and rinsing plates with a practised hand. 'So I'm quite used to this sort of thing. Isilda always tells me to leave my dishes overnight for her in the morning, but my good New England upbringing considers that kind of tacky, so I do them myself. She thinks I'm weird, but no matter.'

'Well, aren't you?' said Saul lazily.

'I resent that, Treharne!' Obviously Bob didn't in the slightest, and suddenly he swung round. 'Hey, Saul, how about you and Claudia coming in to Boa Vista with me, Christmas Eve? The American Consul's giving a party. You'd be welcome.'

Claudia glanced at Saul, to find his eyes were fixed on her in speculation.

'That's kind of you, Bob,' he said slowly. 'But as it's Becky's first Christmas with me, I think I'd better be on hand. Claudia's free to do as she wishes, of course.'

It was crystal clear to Claudia that acceptance on her part was hardly likely to go down well with Saul, and although a rebellious section of her mind resented this, prompting her to say yes, the sensible side of her smiled at Bob with sincere gratitude and declined.

'That's very sweet of you, but in the circumstances I

think it best for me to stay here too. I've been here a very short time, really, and I'm still working on this altitude factor. I need my sleep, I'm afraid. Another time, perhaps?'

Any slight awkwardness arising from Bob's well-intentioned suggestion was promptly dispelled as a familiar Mercedes turned in through the gate and came to a halt in the drive.

'Hold everything!' said Bob with a grin. 'Here comes the *Patrão*.'

Saul was gone instantly, running lightly down the descending concrete path at the side of the house as Luc Fonseca got out of the big car and helped his wife out of the passenger seat with tender care. Saul closed the big garden gates swiftly as Luc shepherded his children out of the car, Emily standing on tiptoe as she held up her cheek for Saul's kiss. Even from the kitchen window Claudia could instantly see the difference in his manner as he greeted Emily, a curious protectiveness in his manner as he smiled down at her.

'She's a very special lady.'

Claudia started. She had forgotten Bob was standing behind her.

'Yes.' She smiled, blinking. 'Utterly natural and charming.'

'No more than you, honey.' Bob's eyes were earnest behind his glasses. 'Different maybe, but you've got a lot going for you, Claudia.'

'You're nice, Bob. Good for my ego.' Her smile became carefully carefree. 'I must go and call Bea. She went to her room to tidy up.'

Claudia was glad to retreat along the corridor, leaving the American to join the group outside, as she tapped on Bea's door.

'Emily and Luc are here with the children, Bea.'

Bea emerged at speed, immaculate to the last hair, in her tailored pink linen dress.

'Then I suppose that means it's time for tea now we've just managed to dispose of lunch,' she said cheerfully, her eyes keen on Claudia's face. 'Does all this activity make you homesick for your quiet

Sundays in England? My dear! What have I said?' Her forehead furrowed with concern as Claudia blinked to keep back the tears that suddenly glazed her eyes.

In an agony of embarrassment Claudia sniffed prosaically, dashing away the tears with a careless hand.

'*Are* you homesick, Claudia?' Bea persisted gently.

'No—really. Quite the reverse.' Claudia accepted the proffered handkerchief with gratitude. 'In fact I was just thinking how friendly you all are, and—and how pleasant a day it's been.' She shook her head impatiently. 'My God, you must think me a right idiot—I never cry, honestly!'

'It doesn't hurt now and again, you know! Now pop along to the bathroom and wash your face,' said Bea practically. 'Give yourself a minute, then come and join us.'

In the cool privacy of the bathroom Claudia dealt quickly with repairs, her tears too transient to do more than brighten her eyes a little, the lids unaffected. As she added a little more shadow to them her eyes stared back at her, full of a sudden, unwelcome knowledge. Her tears had been caused by sheer self-pity. *She* wanted to be the one Saul looked at with such tenderness, not Emily Fonseca. His protective manner was one Claudia craved for herself, and what was more, she wanted the copyright on it. A tearing spear of jealousy had impaled her as she watched Saul smiling at another woman in a way she wanted him to smile at *her*. Claudia sat down suddenly on the edge of the bath, limp with revelation. This feeling was presumably love. And for Saul Treharne, for heaven's sake! And what's more, if this was how love made one feel she could very well do without it.

Claudia took a deep breath and stood up, squaring her shoulders, then, carefully arranging her features into a gay smile of welcome, she went back to join the party.

CHAPTER TEN

FOR the next two days life was an odd mixture for Claudia, uneventful on the surface, apart from a few leisurely preparations for Christmas, the entire thought of which seemed unreal against a backdrop of blazing sunshine. The nights were different. In bed alone she slept little, tossing and turning as she tried to keep her mind away from Saul, and failed miserably. She, who had once thought nothing of exerting discipline over classrooms full of children, now found that discipline over her own wayward emotions was impossible. She kept remembering the heated, illicit encounter on the night of the storm, at times wondering if it had been a figment of her own imagination in the face of Saul's attitude towards her, at others hot with shame at the thought that should such a thing occur again she would have difficulty in calling a halt to his lovemaking.

Claudia was almost piqued to find that she was unlikely to be put to the test. Granted Saul had mellowed towards her, especially since their game of tennis, for some reason. There was less sparring and more genuine conversation, to Bea's evident relief, as Saul probed Claudia's mind, crossing swords with enjoyment over politics, literature and sport at the dinner table, a change for the better, admittedly, from the brief, barbed skirmishes of the first days after her arrival, but with never a hint of anything more personal. Presumably he had forgotten the incident that remained so vivid in Claudia's mind.

Bea functioned in something of the role of Greek chorus when all three were together, and when alone with Claudia she dropped quite naturally into the role of surrogate aunt. Becky had her moments of mutiny and tantrums still, but these were shortlived and getting fewer and farther between, as the merest reminder of Father Christmas's checking-up activities acted like

147

magic on her ill-humour, and effected a hasty transformation into a child well behaved enough to merit the hotly-craved bicycle. Claudia stifled any feelings of guilt on this score, and resolved privately to think of some other means of curbing Becky's volatile temper once the bicycle was safely in the child's possession.

By day it was easy for Claudia to lock her new-found feelings towards Saul behind a door in her mind, constantly aware of their existence, but refusing to let them out to threaten the new temperate climate prevailing between herself and her employer. At night in bed it was different. At times she comforted herself with the thought that at least Saul was less hostile towards her, apparently no longer tarring her with the same brush that his memories of Elaine wielded over women in general—excepting Bea, Emily and Thurza, of course. As Saul made no attempt to put their relationship on a footing any closer than one of impersonal friendliness, Claudia sometimes wondered what would have happened if her reaction to his unexpected assault had been unconditional surrender instead of eventual rebuff. Would he have taken it on to its natural conclusion, or would he have just decided she was a fully paid up member of the permissive society and withdrawn even more abruptly in cynical affirmation of his cold-blooded little experiment? Not that Claudia ever managed to convince herself that the blood of either participants had been noticeably cool on that occasion which had been memorable to her at least, if not to Saul.

On Christmas Eve Luc Fonseca annually held a party for the children of his employees in one of the company's big store-rooms, emptied and cleaned for the occasion, and provided with long white-covered tables laden with potato chips and sausages on sticks and all the other delicacies de rigueur at these occasions, to be washed down with gallons of fizzy drinks before games were played and the excitement mounted in expectation of Father Christmas's arrival, complete with toys, carefully chosen by Emily in advance and labelled with the names of the recipients.

'I think I'll be extremely weak-spirited and deny myself the pleasure of this particular occasion,' said Bea, with an air of guilt. 'Emily says it's very noisy and gets extremely hot, and being a vinegary old spinster I find the prospect of so much infantile exuberance positively daunting.'

'This is where I finally start to demonstrate my usefulness,' said Claudia promptly. 'Think of all the sports days I've helped organise—the party will be child's play for me, if you'll pardon the pun.'

Bea smiled gratefully.

'I must admit I don't fancy it much——'

'No problem,' said Saul decisively. 'Claudia and I are more than enough escort for one small five-year-old. Besides,' he added as an afterthought, 'Emily will be very glad of Claudia's experience, and I'll be on hand to watch over Becky.' He eyed his aunt sternly. 'I think you'd better rest up all day tomorrow, Aunt Bea, or you won't enjoy the evening at the Fonsecas on Christmas Day.'

'Maybe you're right,' said Bea meekly.

'You've been doing too much in the kitchen,' said Claudia gently, 'all those mince pies, brandy butter and a chocolate log, not to mention dozens of sausage rolls for the party.'

'Well, apparently people tend to drop in over the holiday,' said Bea conciliatingly. 'I thought it would be nice for Saul this year if we fostered the Christmas spirit as much as possible.'

'And I'm very grateful,' said Saul, an expression of tenderness in his normally hard voice that Claudia noted wistfully. 'This Christmas will be the best I've had in years, I know, but I not unaturally want you well enough to join in all the festivities.'

'Amen,' said Claudia fervently. 'How about staying in bed in the morning with a tempting breakfast tray and one of the paperbacks I unpacked from my trunk?'

'Excellent idea.' Saul gave Claudia a warm smile of approval. 'Becky's in good hands now we have Claudia, so you can take it easy.'

'Oh, very well,' said Bea, obviously ensnared by the

idea. 'Only stop fussing now and let's have coffee in the drawing room to let Lourdes clear away.'

Heavy rain overnight had damped down the dust, but otherwise had done little to lower the temperature, merely adding humidity to the heat next day. Saul arrived from work in good time to change into beautifully cut trousers of cream linen, worn with a thin shirt in cream and black stripes. Claudia, who had left changing until the last moment, sat down to lunch feeling distinctly dowdy in a rather elderly denim skirt and red tee-shirt, glad to see that Bea, who had not long risen, looked a great deal better after her rest. Saul's eyes rested on his daughter's face, querying the look of frowning preoccupation on her face as she disposed of her portion of meat loaf with a marked lack of enthusiasm.

'Problems, Becky?' he asked.

She heaved a great sigh and abandoned her lunch.

'Is Father Christmas Brazilian?'

Claudia and Bea avoided each other's eye as Saul blinked, searching for an answer.

'He doesn't really have a nationality, Becky,' he began with care.

'What's a nasher—what you said?' Her frown deepened.

'Well, I mean he's not British or Brazilian, he—he's just Father Christmas; a special person to all the children in the world.' Saul cast a comic look of anguish in Claudia's direction, but she merely smiled in bland encouragement, feeling there were times when fathers were best left to cope alone.

'How will he know my name?' persisted Becky.

'He knows everyone's name.' Saul spoke with the hearty emphasis that denotes inward doubt.

'Can he say the Brazilian names?'

Saul was on firmer ground now.

'He doesn't have to. He just hands the parcels to Uncle Luc and then Uncle Luc calls out the names.'

'Oh.' Becky gave this some thought and brightened. Uncle Luc would know *her* name well enough. Then her mouth drooped again. 'Will the other little girls wear dresses?'

'You bet! They're hot on frilly party dresses here—they all look like a lot of pretty little butterflies.'

This idea held no appeal for Becky, from the expression on her face, and hurriedly Claudia asked,

'Should I be fairly fancy too, then? I'd rather thought of wearing slacks if I'm to help with the games.'

Saul grinned maliciously.

'Not on your life! It's a frilly party dress for you too—only I suggest you choose one that's easy to launder. Things get fairly boisterous.'

Casting a mental eye over her wardrobe, Claudia doubted she possessed anything in the necessary category.

'Something cool,' added Bea, 'not necessarily elaborate.'

'I don't go in for frills much,' said Claudia wryly.

Becky's attention was caught.

'You do, Claudia,' she said reprovingly. 'You've got frills on some of your nighties.'

'Oh yes,' Claudia ignored the gleam in Saul's eye, 'so I have. But that's only for bed.'

Saul rose, murmuring in Claudia's ear as he passed her chair.

'Do you think Freud might have found that significant?'

Luckily Bea was occupied in discussing Becky's choice of party dress with the child, and Claudia's sudden rush of colour went unnoticed as she made for her bedroom in undisguised retreat from Saul's unexpected veer to personalities.

Her choice of dress finally fell on one of silk-lined Tana lawn in apple green, sleeveless and falling straight to her hips where numbers of tiny pleats swung from a sash in lawn of a darker green. Not precisely frilly, she thought, as she added small green beryl ear-studs to her lobes and brushed her hair into a heavy coil secured firmly on top of her head. Hardly her own idea of suitable costume for the rough and tumble of a children's party! She grinned as she remembered the track-suit worn on her last visit to the Orphanage Christmas Party, and hoped none of today's party-goers were likely to run amok with the ice-cream in her vicinity.

'Claudia!' Becky's voice held a definite cry for help, and Claudia quickly slid into her plaited kid mules and went to investigate.

Both Lourdes and Afra were holding out dresses for Becky's approval, while Bea looked on rather helplessly.

'Claudia!' Bea smiled in relief. 'Come and cast your vote. What do you think Becky should wear?'

After some argument Becky finally consented to wear a white organdie dress cut like a slip and ending in three pink-scalloped frills at the hip-line, chosen because it vaguely resembled Claudia's. Claudia took over the hairdressing and brushed out the rippling waves of silver-gilt hair, sweeping it up and away from the flawless, impatient face, and tying it at the crown of Becky's head with a length of pink silk ribbon, allowing the shining waterfall to hang free down the child's back. Pink-edged white socks and white patent leather shoes were the finishing touches, and Bea heaved a sigh of relief.

'Both of you look very beautiful,' she said, an opinion obviously shared by the two maids, for whom the child's hair was a constant source of wonder.

'Want to show Maria.' Becky shot off in the direction of the kitchen for more compliments en route to her father on the verandah. Bea looked at Claudia and smiled quiltily.

'I feel quite terrible about not making the effort to go.'

'Nonsense,' Claudia said instantly. 'Just make sure Maria has gallons of tea ready when we get back.'

Saul was waiting with weary patience as the two women emerged from the house, Becky's hand in his as she jigged up and down, eager to leave.

'This was about as frilly as I could get,' said Claudia, sketching an irreverent curtsy. 'Will I pass?'

The impatience left Saul's face as he deliberately subjected her to a head-to-toe scrutiny.

'Not bad at all,' he said casually.

'Come on, then,' Becky pulled his hand. 'We'll be late—bye-bye, Aunt Bea!' She waved and scampered down the steps.

'Bye-bye, darling, Have a lovely time.' Bea stood waving as Saul ran down the steps to drive the jeep out from its cool sanctuary under the house. She put a hand on Claudia's arm, unexpectedly, a little smile on her forthright features. 'Don't mind Saul, Claudia, he's not one to deal in superlatives, you know. I think you look absolutely lovely—and suitable.'

'Why, thank you.' Claudia was touched. 'I was only asking approval, not compliments, you know. See you later—and mind you put your feet up while we're out!' She went down the steps, carrying a napkin-covered basket filled to the brim with sausage rolls for the party and accepted Saul's proffered hand to spring up into the vehicle in a whirl of pleats that revealed rather more of her long legs than she would have preferred.

'Sorry,' she said shortly, and turned to see if Becky was sitting on the clean linen sheet Maria had provided to protect the white dress for at least the time it took to arrive at the party.

'Don't apologise.' Saul twisted round to look behind him as he reversed up the drive. 'Since I've seen you in tennis kit——' his eyes looked full into hers for a second as he swung the jeep out into the road, 'and otherwise, it seems irrelevant anyway.'

Claudia sat dumb as the jeep made the descent down the winding hill. What was up with Saul today? Was he reminding her that he, too, still remembered moments when things had been a great deal less than impersonal between them? She was silent and thoughtful until they reached the party location, which was a big barracks of a place, halfway between Casa d'Ouro and the mine. As Saul parked on the stretch of gravel outside the excited chatter from a mass of voluble children came swelling from the open doors of the building, and Becky was noticeably quiet, her face tense as she looked towards the source of the hubbub.

'What is it, Becky?' Claudia took the small hot hand as Saul relieved her of the basket.

'Will anyone speak English?' Becky turned blue eyes full of panic on her father.

'Jamie and Mark will be there.' Saul handed back the

basket to Claudia and scooped up the trembling child in his arms. 'I'll give you a lift so those rather smart shoes don't get dirty,' he said, his eyes meeting Claudia's over Becky's head with a fierce expression in them she interpreted as a sudden violent urge to protect his child from anything and everyone.

'Good idea,' said Claudia, and pointed out her own white sandals to Becky. 'Aren't you lucky—I wish someone were here to carry me!'

'But you're too big to be carried!' A smile broke out on Becky's face at the thought and her moment of panic was forgotten as she arrived at the party safe in the strong arms that set her down gently just inside the door at the precise moment that Jamie and Mark spotted the new arrival and came tearing towards them, excitedly pulling Becky away to meet other children, who absorbed her into their midst without question.

'I thought we might have a problem there for a moment.' Saul let out his breath in an audible sigh of relief as he watched his daughter run off without a backward glance.

'You did exactly the right thing,' said Claudia. 'Becky needs security, in every shape and form—*and* a bit of discipline,' she added with a smile. 'She's so enchanting to look at it's an effort to be firm with her on occasion.'

'I don't think you I can teach you much in that department!' Saul's face softened as he caught sight of Emily near the raised dais at the other end of the room and took Claudia's arm to lead her over to a line of chairs occupied by ladies of varying ages, their dresses elaborate and elegant, their jewellery impressive. As one woman their eyes turned to watch Claudia as she crossed the room with Saul, the basket still in one hand. Emily was bending to talk to an elderly woman, unaware of the newcomers until something in the rapt attention of the women nearby made her straighten to look round with curiosity, a wide smile of welcome on her face as she saw Claudia.

'Hello, you two, I didn't see you come in.'

Claudia regarded Emily with undisguised admiration.

Today the artless girl with the long flying hair was replaced by an elegant creature, every inch the wife of the *Patrao*, her hair in an intricate coil low on her neck, showing off magnificent aquamarine and diamond earrings and a matching pendant above the neckline of the intricately blue silk dress that swathed her slim figure.

'You look very expensive and haughty today,' said Saul smiling at her indulgently.

'I'm obliged to put on a show sometimes.' Emily made a little face. 'You look like Red Riding Hood with that basket, Claudia. Dump it somewhere and I'll introduce you to all these ladies.'

Claudia quailed inwardly, but meekly allowed herself to be led along the line of women while Emily pronounced complicated names and each woman politely welcomed Claudia to Campo d'Ouro. Saul went off to join Luc and Claudia soon forgot him in her efforts to keep track of Becky in the crowd of children, finding an unexpected ally in Jamie, who proved to be a very attentive escort. He took care that Becky found a place at table, and looked after her with touching diligence, seeing that she received her share of goodies with all the éclat of a much older boy.

Claudia worked with a will, helping Emily pass laden plates of food up and down the long table, pulling English crackers, arranging paper hats on heads.

Soon the tables were cleared and removed and the fun began in earnest. Emily took charge of the record-player while Claudia organised the children for Musical Chairs, Pass the Parcel and Grandmother's Footsteps, but when it came to 'Simon Says' she merely eliminated the transgressors while Luc roared out the instructions, her Portuguese scarcely up to the task. Despite its size the big room became very hot, and Claudia soon began to feel uncomfortably warm and sticky from her exertions, though none of this seemed to matter after looking up at one stage to find Saul's eyes fixed on her with undisguised warmth and approval.

There was a slight lull while drinks were consumed thirstly and Claudia had a breather, taken aback to find she was more breathless as a result of Saul's approval than from her participation in the games.

'I am much indebted to you, Claudia,' said Luc sincerely. He put an arm round his wife's shoulders. 'You have relieved Emily of much of the physical effort of the party.'

'I'm only too happy to help—I enjoy this sort of thing.' Claudia frankly mopped her forehead with a paper napkin, taking a surreptitious look across the room, but Saul had turned away to chat with some of the children's fathers. 'What happens now—more games?'

'The big climax,' announced Emily dramatically. 'The arrival of Papae Noel.'

'Ah!' Claudia leaned nearer. 'Who's in the starring role?'

'Tom Enys,' muttered Emily behind her hand, then broke off as her sons came running up with Becky in tow.

'Is Father Christmas coming yet,' Becky asked anxiously. 'They call him Papae Noel here, Claudia, did you know?'

Luc caught sight of Saul signalling near the far door and said triumphantly,

'He is arriving at this moment, *filinha*. Jamie, Mark, take Becky's hand.'

There was a great rush as all the children surged outside at the distant sound of bells. Saul caught up with Claudia as she followed.

'How are you doing? Everything all right?' he asked quietly.

Claudia nodded, smiling radiantly.

'Becky's having the time of her life.' Her eyes were alight with relief. 'I'm so pleased—I was very worried when we first arrived.'

'So was I!' He smiled down at her, taking her hand for a moment and squeezing it, to her surprise, but as they reached the door he stepped back to allow Claudia through with Emily and the moment was lost except for the pressure on her fingers, which still tingled from Saul's touch as she went outside and saw the reason for

all the excitement. Becky ran to her father, her face
white with anticipation.

'I can't see!' she said desperately.

Saul reached down and swung her up to perch on his
shoulder, and Claudia watched the child's eyes widen in
wonder, a lump in her own throat as she located the
source of the bells. A string of *burros*, little pack-mules,
were wending their way towards them along the red,
hard-packed earth road, a bell swinging from each
neck, a pannier on either side. At their head was a
larger animal, and astride it sat Father Christmas in all
his hot red and white glory, his face almost obscured by
his enormous white moustache and beard, sacks of toys
bulging from the panniers either side of his mount.

'Papae Noel, Papae Noel!' The cry went up in unison
as every child jumped up and down in a frenzy of
excitement before rushing towards the little cavalcade.
Instantly Becky struggled to get down in answer to
Jamie's imperious summons and ran off with him to
join the others as Father Christmas laboriously
dismounted, aided by dozens of willing hands as two
grinning young men bore the sacks of toys into the
building, followed by the burly figure in red, who led
the children into the big room like the Pied Piper.

Emily's maid had arrived by this time with a
wondering Lucy, who stared wide-eyed at all the
commotion from the haven of her mother's arms while
Luc distributed the presents as Father Christmas
handed them to him. Soon the room was a welter of
discarded wrapping paper as Becky stood hand in hand
with Jamie and Mark, the three faces tense and
expectant as they waited. Mark was soon the happy
owner of a sturdy truck, Lucy, a rag doll, and at long
last Luc handed Becky a large, flat box before passing
an identical parcel over to Jamie.

Becky tore back to Claudia, who helped her unwrap
a cowgirl outfit in white leather. Her eyes shone like
stars as she lifted out the brief, fringed skirt and bolero
and the miniature white Stetson, crowing with delight at
the finishing touch, a gun-belt with holsters and pistols.
Becky made a beeline for Saul, calling,

'Daddy, Daddy, look what I got!'

Saul spun round at her cry, his mask of restraint for once absent, revealing such a blaze of emotion in his eyes that Claudia turned away instinctively, unwilling for him to see she had witnessed the incident as he went down on his haunches to inspect his daughter's present. After such an emotional high it seemed only right that the party broke up soon after and Becky was driven home to recount the joys and triumphs of the afternoon to Bea until eventually even her inexhaustible energy ran out and she was persuaded to sleep after an extra long bedtime story from Claudia.

Claudia ate her dinner that evening in an atmosphere of euphoria, both from praise for her efforts at the party from Saul and from a definite rise in the temperature of his attitude towards her. Christmas spirit was high as all three enjoyed Filet Mignon and asparagus and a bottle of wine Saul had been saving for a special occasion.

'After all, what could be more special than Christmas Eve?' His eyes gleamed as he leaned across to fill Claudia's glass, a definite message in them she was at a loss to interpret, hoping it was something more significant than mere festive bonhomie. Whatever his intention, the result was a relaxed, happy atmosphere as Saul seemed intent on celebrating, pouring himself a mammoth brandy as they sat over coffee in the drawing-room afterwards. Claudia leaned back in her chair with a sigh of contentment as Bea confirmed the arrangements for the following day with Saul, wishing it were possible to crystallise and keep moments like this to store away and bring out in the future at less happy occasions.

'You look miles away, Claudia,' said Bea, smiling indulgently. 'Pleasant thoughts, I hope?'

Claudia blinked, flushing, and improvised rapidly.

'I—I was just remembering I have some odds and ends for Becky's stocking. Shall I fetch them to put with yours?'

There was a pregnant silence while Saul and Bea stared at her, their blankness ominous.

'My dear!' Bea put a hand to her mouth in consternation. 'I never gave a thought to a stocking!'

'One of those times when our inexperience becomes glaringly obvious.' Saul tossed off the remainder of his brandy and poured another, his eyes dismayingly shuttered once more as he turned back to Claudia. 'You might have mentioned it earlier.'

'I do apologise.' Claudia sat erect, her eyes glittering at him with offence. 'It never occurred to me that it would be necessary.'

'And why should it?' Bea regarded her nephew with surprised disapproval. 'The oversight is ours, not yours, Claudia.'

Saul shrugged impenitently.

'The fault is mine. Which doesn't alter the fact that Becky doesn't have a stocking. Knowing Elaine, I feel sure she bought one of those ready-filled affairs from Harrods and left it at that.'

'Which is hardly any help to us now,' said Bea with asperity.

Claudia intervened hastily.

'I have one or two little things, inexpensive odds and ends, really. I'm sure they'll be enough. At home one usually adds tangerines and so on, but out here where they grow in the garden they hardly seem appropriate.'

She watched with apprehension as Saul poured himself yet another brandy, drinking it in one draught before recollecting himself sufficiently to offer a liqueur to the two women. Neither accepted, more concerned with stocking-fillers, and Bea rose purposely to her feet.

'Fetch what you have, Claudia, and I'll just have a rummage through my room and see what I can turn up.'

Claudia went off to her bedroom and took the little bag of trifles from one of her suitcases, returning to Saul to find him alone at the verandah door, staring moodily out at the star-studded sky. He turned as Claudia put down her paper bag on the jacaranda table in front of the sofa, his face withdrawn and cold, his earlier mood vanished.

'I suppose you think I'm a bloody awful father,' he said morosely.

'No.' Claudia was cool and matter-of-fact. 'Just an inexperienced one.'

'You heard her say "Daddy" this afternoon?' Saul's tightly clenched jaw deepened the cleft in his chin as he scowled down into the contents of his glass.

Claudia nodded silently.

'The first time she'd ever said it.' He turned dark, bitter eyes on Claudia's watchful face. 'The only father she knew was Jack Connaught, Elaine's husband, though at least Elaine had some sense of fitness. Becky referred to him as "Uncle Jack".' He flung away and refilled his glass yet again before going on, his voice thickening perceptibly. 'What kind of father would forget that a little scrap like that would expect a Christmas stocking?'

Claudia was losing her patience. In a tone her former pupils would have recognised all too well she said, 'I think you're becoming maudlin. There'll be more than enough to fill a small stocking, and you've already bought her an extremely expensive bicycle, after all. Do keep *some* sense of proportion!'

Saul's look of blank surprise at her attack would have been funny at any other time, but it quickly dissolved into rage and Claudia quailed inwardly, deeply relieved as Bea appeared and he was forced to exert self-control with a visible effort. The mask was slipping a bit again, the result of an overdose of brandy, in Claudia's opinion. Bea sat beside her with her little haul, unaware of the tensions in the room as she produced her finds.

'I've done quite well,' she said with satisfaction. 'A little silver thimble I had as a child, two hair-slides I was keeping for her for tomorrow, a little pincushion in the shape of a mouse, and we could add one of those chocolates you brought from Boa Vista.'

Added to Claudia's contribution the result was pronounced extremely satisfactory, to Bea's relief.

'That's a load off my mind,' she said thankfully. 'I'll give them all to you then, dear, and you can pack them in a stocking. Will you creep in with it?'

'Why—yes, if you wish.' Claudia gave a quick glance

at Saul, but he was at the door again, his back to the room, the very set of his broad shoulders rancorous. Seething at the injustice of his attitude—after all, it was hardly her fault if the man had forogtten his daughter's stocking—she gathered up the little bundle.

'If you'll both excuse me I think I'll turn in; it could be an early start tomorrow.'

'Goodnight, dear. I shan't be too long myself.' Bea yawned. 'I'm quite tired.'

Claudia took her leave, winning only a wintry goodnight from Saul. And a Merry Christmas to you, too, she thought crossly. She dumped the bag on the bed and undressed with a regrettable lack of festive spirit, almost of a mind to keep back Saul's present next day, then decided to hand it over in the nature of coals of fire. Postponing the stocking filling for the time being, she decided to read for a while, lying against the pillows on top of the covers as the air cooled.

Claudia came to with a start, aware of having dozed. A look at her watch confirmed that it was only a little after twelve, and yawning, she got up to do something about Becky's stocking. She stood up still as she realised she had no suitable stocking to put the presents in. Becky's socks were tiny, Claudia's own tennis socks still nowhere near large enough. She sighed in exasperation. The little haul would look silly and forlorn in a pillowcase—one of Saul's socks would be the answer. Not relishing her quest very much, Claudia tied on her kimono and went on silent bare feet to the drawing-room, but it was in darkness, the doors to the verandah locked. Damn! Saul must have gone to bed already. She crept cautiously past his room, grinning as she heard faint snoring. Hardly surprising after all that brandy. Her heart stopped as Saul's door flew open, then she turned to run, but a long arm shot out, a hand closing on her shoulder with a grip like iron, pulling her back.

It was difficult to fight without making a noise, and Claudia had no desire to wake Bea, who must have been the one snoring. She writhed in desperate silence, struggling to free herself from Saul's vice-like hold, but it was no use. For someone who prided herself on her

fitness it was galling to be drawn inexorably towards
that broad chest, even while her mind registered relief
that Bea's gentle snoring could be still heard,
undisturbed.

The previous time Saul had held her off balance like
this she had been bemused, incapable of thought or
movement, but now, as her head tilted back, she gasped
in brandy fumes so strong she panicked, kicking her
feet against his bare shins in a fury of resistance as he
carried her into his room, the door clicking quietly shut
behind them as she was slung unceremoniously on the
bed like a sack of potatoes. As she tried to escape the
weight of his big body descended on hers without
mercy, winding her temporarily and making her
prisoner, with no possibility of movement, let alone
escape unless he allowed it. Gasping like a landed fish,
she stared acrimoniously into the face above her, the
expression on Saul's face visible in the light from the
single lamp. Her mouth dried as she realised it was as
mask-like as usual, but it was a different mask. For the
first time in her life she saw a man's face devoid of any
feeling other than lust, insulting in its impersonal
intensity, and she began to feel the first stirrings of fear,
coupled with a sensation of burning injustice. At this
rate she was likely to be out of a job before it had really
begun. Her struggles renewed.

'Let me up!' she whispered fiercely.

'After you'd gone to the trouble of visiting me in my
room?' Saul's brandy-laden whisper terminated on her
mouth as he began to kiss her with hard, slow kisses
that took away what remaining breath she had. His
breathing grew rapid, rasping, his kisses rougher,
wilder, his teeth grazing her lips. One of his hands
relinquished its hold to begin exploring the curves
beneath her kimono, pushing aside the thin cotton of
her nightdress until it tore. Claudia's brain woke up, the
intruding hand provoking anger instead of passion in
response as she twisted in rage beneath his touch.
Miraculously she managed to free one of her hands and
thrust the palm flat against his chin, pushing with all
her not inconsiderable strength until Saul's head went

back with a grunt, his vertebrae grinding together at the back of his neck. The involuntarily slackening of his hold gave her the opening she was looking for and she slithered like an eel from beneath him and landed on the floor beside the bed. The wrong side of the bed, it was true, but she was free. They both stood staring at each other, panting, the wide expanse of brown crumpled bedcover separating them.

Saul drew his robe together, tying the belt slowly, his eyes, black in the shadow above the pool of lamplight, holding Claudia's as she fumbled to make herself decent, her fingers clumsy now that the crisis was over. The silence grew heavy, unbearable as she looked away from him with distaste.

'Say something,' he said quietly.

'What would you like me to say?' Her eyes returned to his, glacial and scornful.

He shook his head and ran a hand through his hair, giving a shrug that, in another man, would have been one of embarrassment.

'I heard a slight noise.' His deep voice was barely audible. 'I had too much to drink. When I heard you outside my door I thought—you know very well what I thought. I apologise. Hell, what else can I say? Except that I'm now stone cold sober.' He stared across the width of the bed to where Claudia stood, poised, ready to run at his first move, hugging her dressing gown across her like a shield. 'Why *did* you come?'

'Would you believe I needed a sock to use for Becky's stocking? I hoped you might still be in the drawing-room. When I found everything in darkness I was just going back to my bedroom when you came at me through the door.' To Claudia's intense irritation his shoulders began to shake and he raised a fist to press it against his mouth. She walked with dignity around the bed and waved him out of her way with a disdainful gesture.

'Goodnight,' she said stonily.

'Wait.' He moved over to one of the doors in the jacaranda unit and opened a drawer, taking a pair of new white tennis socks from it. 'Will one of these do?'

'Thank you.' Claudia took the sock from him gingerly, as though she were taking a bone away from a dog, then turned on her heel.

'Claudia!' His voice halted her. She paused and looked at him, unsmiling. 'I really am sorry. I was drunk, and I apologise.'

She nodded with silent indifference.

'Will this—episode make any difference?'

'To what?' she asked coolly.

'To whether or not you stay.' The light was too dim for her to see his face clearly, but she could have sworn his eyes held a trace of entreaty.

'As you said the other day,' she reminded him, 'I'm here to educate your daughter, not to entertain you. Perhaps you could bear that in mind.'

Saul took a deep breath as though her shaft had struck home.

'Would it make any difference if I said it was the last thing I intended to happen?'

Claudia frowned angrily.

'You mean I'm the last person you'd consider making love to if you were sober!'

With the sudden lightness of foot that always surprised her Saul was at her side, holding her by the upper arms, twisting her round to look into her startled grey eyes, an unreadable expression in his own.

'I'm stone cold sober now, Claudia, just as I said,' he whispered.

This is where I start struggling again, she thought, as his face came nearer, but whatever impulses her brain was sending to her body they had little to do with resistance. Quite the reverse; as his mouth touched hers she began trembling deep inside her, but not with fright. It was the feeling remembered so vividly from the night of the storm. Saul's hands left her arms and slid round her body, which melted into his as though the desperate, bitter fight of a few minutes earlier had never happened. Her lips opened to his as she gave herself up without reservation to an embrace that gave rather than took as his lips left hers to wander over her eyelids and nose, moving down her chin to her throat, where they rested against the pulse throbbing there before moving back up to her mouth to settle with increasing pressure. Claudia's heavy eyelids opened gradually to show eyes whose normal crystalline clarity was clouded by the intensity of the feelings aroused in her by his lovemaking. She stared at him, reassured when she saw that, for the first time, Saul's eyes were alight with warmth, his whole expression transformed as he looked down at her.

'I must go,' she whispered.

He nodded, releasing her reluctantly.

'See you in the morning.'

'It *is* morning!' She smiled, a limpid joy in her look. 'Merry Christmas, Saul!'

'Merry Christmas, Claudia.' He stooped and kissed her gently, then bent to pick up something from the door. 'Here's your sock. Isn't that what you came for?'

'I got rather more than I bargained for, didn't I?'

With an impudent smile she went quietly into the hall, relieved to hear gentle snoring still issuing from the next room.

'I thought it was you,' she whispered.

'I never snore,' he said into her ear.

'How do you know?'

'There's one sure way of finding out!'

Defeated, she fled with silent laughter, aware that he watched her out of sight.

CHAPTER ELEVEN

CLAUDIA opened her eyes on Christmas morning to find Saul standing in the doorway with his daughter in his arms, clutching her bulging stocking to her chest, her eyes incandescent with excitement.

'Claudia,' Becky whispered, 'can we sit on your bed to look in my stocking?'

Saul gave her a rueful grin of apology as Claudia sat up groggily, smiling into her eyes over Becky's head, silently sending a message that Claudia instantly understood, relaxing against the pillows, careless of her tumbled hair. Saul himself looked as though he'd pulled on the nearest garments to hand. His hair was wildly untidy above a white cotton sweatshirt and a pair of much-washed denims clung to his long legs like a second skin. A dark growth of stubble added to a piratical effect that appealed to Claudia strongly.

'We've come to wish you Merry Christmas, Claudia,' he said, with a flash of white teeth in a smile that did strange things to her respiratory system and set the mood for a day of unalloyed happiness, from the exchange of presents after breakfast with Bea, to the hospitality of Emily and Luc at a lavish, convivial Christmas dinner at Casa d'Ouro. To Claudia's surprise and delight Saul had given her a necklace made of three strands of gold in different colours twisted together in a heavy chain, and she wore it with pride, secretly treasuring his obvious pleasure when he opened her own gift to him. Not a little of the day's harmony was due to Becky's joy in all her presents, mainly the bicycle, naturally, but the child was also enchanted with her doll and the clothes Claudia gave her, instantly demanding to change into pink tee-shirt, blue jeans and pink sneakers, refusing to change into anything more formal for the visit to Casa d'Ouro, which, as her bicycle had to go along too, was probably just as well.

After dinner, when all the children were finally out for the count, Luc put some slow dreamy music on the stereo, and Thurza, Bob and John sat chatting while Tom danced with Bea, Luc with Emily, and Claudia had her first experience of dancing with Saul. To her surprise he was not the best of dancers, but under the circumstances on the dimly lit verandah, it was enough to be held in his arms, moving only the requisite amount in time to the music, both of them glad of the excuse for physical contact.

'Have you enjoyed your first Christmas Day in Campo d'Ouro, Claudia?' asked Saul softly, his mouth close to her ear.

The word 'first' elated Claudia, with its promise of more Christmases to come, a hint of permanence that reassured her questioning heart. She tipped her head back to look up into his face as he moved her out of earshot of the others.

'For reasons many and varied, Mr Treharne, this has been far and away the best Christmas of my life!'

Boxing Day was bound to be an anti-climax, quiet by contrast, except for a morning spent at the tennis club, where Becky cycled endlessly from one end of the verandah to the other while Saul and Claudia played two sets of tennis in far more leisurely fashion than their previous game. Bea sat watching them while Afra kept an eye on Becky. Bea sat idly, without her knitting for once, content to watch the tennis in silence, the club deserted on this hot, overcast day, with everyone else apparently indoors, sleeping off the excesses of Christmas.

Afra was sent home before lunch, which was a simple, cold meal eaten on the verandah. Saul and Claudia ate heartily after their exercise, and so did Becky, despite eyes that drooped a little after her disturbed sleep of the night before with a ride from Casa d'Ouro in the middle of it. Bea looked pale to Claudia's worried eye, merely picking at her food, and after the meal was over announced that she was going to lie down for a while.

'Not too good today, Aunt Bea?' Saul looked searchingly at his aunt.

'Just tired, dear.' She smiled brightly. 'Serves me right, dancing at my age. I'll take advantage of your good nature, Claudia, and leave you with the lunch dishes, if you don't mind.'

'Of course not. Have a good rest.' Claudia and Saul watched the older woman out of sight, then sat down again to finish their coffee, their unspoken anxiety mutual. Saul glanced at his daughter, who sat with her chin on her hand, making patterns in the cream left at the bottom of her dessert dish, her eyes heavy with sleep.

'Just for once, Miss Treharne, don't you think even you might have a little rest on your bed?' he suggested, ruffling the top of her hair. 'Then you'll be full of beans later on to ride your bike again.'

Becky heaved a great sigh and agreed, to Claudia's surprise.

'My doll's tired too, I think she'd better lie down with me.'

'Good idea!' Claudia jumped up and held out her hand. 'Come on then, let's tuck you both up for a little while.'

When Claudia got back to the kitchen Saul was washing dishes. He turned with a smile as she closed the door quietly behind her.

'Everyone out for the count?'

Claudia nodded, avoiding his eye, suddenly ill at ease as she began drying plates at speed. Saul put a wet hand on her wrist and turned her towards him, lifting her face towards his with the other, smiling down into her eyes.

'Afraid to be alone with me?'

'No.'

'Why are you shying away like a nervous horse, then?'

Claudia made a face at him. 'You might be a little more flattering with your similes!'

'I *was* being flattering.' Saul held her away, giving her a straight-faced considering look from head to foot. 'Long slim legs, a mane of hair, nostrils that flare a little when you're nervous—like now!'

'All right, all right,' Claudia tugged free from his grasp and began putting away plates. 'I'm *not* nervous of being alone with you, anyway.'

He leaned against the kitchen table, his legs thrust out in front of him, and lit a cigarillo, watching her as usual through the smoke.

'You should be.'

She swung round to stare at him, her colour heightened.

'Why?'

'Because, dear Miss March,' he said, his voice slow and deliberate, the look in the blue darkness of his eyes emphasising the subtle sensuality of his tone, 'because I, too, would like to go to bed right now. Only sleeping isn't what I have in mind, at least not for some time. I want to take you with me and make love to you with infinite patience and at infinite length until sleeping in each other's arms was the natural, inevitable conclusion.'

Claudia stared at him, her colour high and her eyes bright and blank. She turned to look at the abacata trees outside the window, their leaves motionless in the sullen humidity of the still afternoon. His words hung in the air between them. Pushing her hair behind her ears, she pulled her cotton shirt away from her back where it clung to the dampness between her shoulder-blades, deliberately willing herself to be calm.

'It might be best to pretend you never said that.' She picked her words with care. 'I think I may have misled you. You have every right to think—to assume that I'm only too willing to fall in with your suggestion.' She swallowed hard, her eyes still gazing blindly in front of her. 'I should have made it clear from the outset that I could never play a dual role. Becky's governess by day and your—your companion by night is out of the question for me.'

The silence in the room was ominous. Claudia could feel Saul's eyes on her back as tangibly as though he were touching her.

'I regret having given you the wrong impression,' she went on, her mouth dry. 'When you specified a proficiency at sport I had no idea that the field of activity would be extended to the bedroom.' The words sounded so much worse than she intended that she could have cried the moment they were said.

'Are you suggesting that all that warm response I've been receiving was a figment of my overheated imagination? Or possibly I am to believe it was perhaps a mere transient manifestation of the Christmas spirit!'

The icy sneer in Saul's voice made Claudia writhe inwardly, all his former hostility returned in full force.

Claudia turned and looked at him, chilled to the core to see the familiar mask of indifference in place once more, his eyes shuttered and bored.

'We misunderstood each other,' she said huskily. 'I blame myself entirely. You had every right to think I—to think I was willing to let things progress further. I'm sorry, I'm just not in the market for——'

'That's enough,' he said savagely, and made for the open door, hurling the butt of his cigarillo out into the garden. 'You've made your point twice over. I'm not one of your pupils, Miss Schoolteacher, I managed to catch your drift first time round. Have no fear; you're free to pursue your life of blameless instruction totally unsullied by any male attentions.' Saul flung round in the doorway, his head thrown back, looking down his disfigured nose with a look of speculation calculated to insult. 'Unless, of course, it's only *my* particular attentions that displease. You may, of course, have some other target in mind.'

'Saul, please!' Claudia felt stricken. She put out her hands in appeal. 'Surely you can understand——'

'Of course I can.' Saul relaxed, his wrath abruptly gone. 'Women are pathetically easy to understand—I learned that early in life.' He gave her a mocking salute. 'I leave you to meditate on the joys of abstinence alone and unmolested. Tell my aunt I shall be out for dinner.'

Claudia watched, dry-eyed, from the window as Saul strode past the side of the house. He backed the jeep out of the *pordo* and reversed up the drive and out into the road, sweeping the vehicle round in a noisy, brake-squealing arc before gunning the vehicle down the hill and out of sight. Claudia remained where she was for some time, wondering just where he was going, unheralded and unexpected at that time of day. She knew nothing of his life before Bea came to live with him. Perhaps there were several places down in the town where he was sure of a welcome, and probably a great deal more. Claudia gritted her teeth at the thought that possibly there was just one place. Some beautiful local lady who was accustomed to joining Saul in all the activities outlined so temptingly in his proposed way to spend the afternoon, and no doubt a great deal more adept at it than his daughter's governess was ever likely to be at this rate.

Claudia cursed herself for a fool as she sat at the scrubbed table in the big kitchen, chin on hand, wishing herself back to the day before with all its attendant joy and warmth. She should just have laughed at Saul, of course, and turned his sensuous words aside with subtle dexterity, leaving his self-esteem intact. Instead of which her attitude had been one of antediluvian rectitude, like some Victorian prunes-and-prisms spinster drawing her skirts aside from contact with man's baser instincts. He could hardly have been serious about taking her to bed with his aunt in the next room and his child likely to wake at any time.

The more Claudia thought about it the more she wished she'd kept her silly mouth shut. She was relieved when she heard Becky's call and her miserable reverie had to be abandoned for the joys of running round the garden paths after the intrepid cyclist, whose batteries had been recharged to an exhausting extent by her unaccustomed afternoon nap. When she joined them Bea was surprised to learn that Saul would be out for dinner, her curiosity as to his whereabouts increased when Claudia was unable to supply any details, only her obvious embarrassment leading Bea to change the subject out of sheer kindness.

Claudia felt little embarrassment in Saul's presence in the days that followed, for the simple reason that his household was graced by it very little. He was seldom home to lunch and often dined out, on the perfunctory pretext of pressure of work needing extra sessions with Bob McClure or Luc, or Manoel Araujo. When Bea suggested Saul bring his colleages home for some of these necessary working dinners he refused, on the plea of boredom for the ladies, and thereafter she held her peace. Luckily Becky was absorbed with her new toys and apparently found Saul's absence a familiar recurrence. Claudia, however, missed Saul's dominating presence with an intensity that it was difficult to hide.

She was relieved when, a couple of days after Christmas, the much-anticipated lessons actually began, though the schoolroom eventually chosen was in Casa d'Ouro, where so many rooms were at their disposal it was considered impractical to use the only spare room in Saul's house, so the books and equipment were installed in a large, airy room looking out on the front garden of Casa d'Ouro, away from the macaws, and Claudia began to perform the function for which she had been hired.

In the beginning the children found the regular hours of schoolwork restrictive, short though they were, but Claudia made their first lessons so much like play their attention was quickly caught, and, as suspected, Becky was a bright, intelligent child who absorbed knowledge with an ease that put Jamie on his mettle to keep up with her despite his slight seniority. Mark pottered happily with less complicated lessons, and Claudia found no difficulty in controlling three small children after the numbers she had been used to teaching, though the very youth of her pupils was a challenge to her, and she never lost sight of her responsibility towards shaping their entire future attitude towards the discipline of education.

The new routine was welcome, passing the day very effectively. Luc sent a car for Becky and Claudia every morning, and again to drive them home in the afternoon, and on days when Saul was out for lunch Bea often went with them to Casa d'Ouro, and passed the time chatting to Thurza and Emily. The first week went by fairly uneventfully. Becky grew less and less temperamental as her energies were concentrated on the lessons that proved to be far more pleasurable than the child had expected, and Bea became more relaxed as the responsibility of taking care of a young, difficult child was taken out of her hands completely. She was obviously concerned by Saul's renewed absences from the house, but never discussed the subject with Claudia, who was left to think about it endlessly in private, on times heartsore, at others angry at the lengths to which Saul was carrying his displeasure.

Claudia and Emily lingered over coffee after lunch on the day before New Year's Eve. Thurza had gone for her rest, Bea had stayed at home, and the children were playing in the garden, glad of the freedom after a morning of lessons.

Emily gave Claudia a thoughtful look.

'Bea says there's an atmosphere at home, Claudia; at least when Saul's there, which I gather is practically never.'

'I must have said something which offended him.'

'Must have been quite something!'

'Saul's behaving irrationally.' Claudia got to her feet restlessly and leaned her hands on the verandah rail. 'All right, so he's angry with me. Why should he let that deprive Becky of his company?'

Emily joined her, waving a hand towards the children, where Becky was playing quite happily with the others.

'Becky's doing very well, Claudia. She probably takes his absence for granted.'

Claudia lifted the hair away from her neck, her face troubled.

'Maybe you're right. I just hope it's not worrying Bea too much. I feel so guilty.'

'Well, stop it, you goose. I'm sure *you* aren't worrying her.'

'She doesn't seem well, Emily. I wish she'd visit the doctor.'

Emily nodded. 'Thurza has already broached the subject in her usual forthright way and I gather Bea agreed.'

Reassured, Claudia went off to chase up her reluctant pupils for their short afternoon session, secretly as little inclined for lessons as they were and comforting them with the thought that the next two days were holidays.

The following day was overcast and humid, with an oppressive atmosphere that intensified the uneasiness Claudia felt when Saul came home for lunch for once. She was relieved when the tall figure of Bob McClure loped up the steps behind Saul's forbidding figure, praying the American's relaxed company would lighten the atmosphere over the lunch-table.

'I've just been telling Saul here that you two ought to come into town with me tonight,' Bob said persuasively.

Saul shook his head, turning from something Becky was telling him.

'No, thanks—not for me.' He turned expressionless eyes on Claudia. 'There's nothing to prevent Claudia from taking you up on your offer, of course.'

'Good idea,' said Bea with approval. 'Why don't you, Claudia?'

'Oh, I don't think so.' Claudia smiled at Bob and went on doggedly with her chicken casserole. 'It's such a long way.'

'You went there with Daddy,' remarked Becky. 'Remember, Claudia?'

Claudia felt the colour rise in her cheeks.

'But that was for some necessary shopping,' she said hastily, and drank some ice-water, conscious of Saul's saturnine glance on her face.

Bob smiled goodnaturedly, giving a slightly baffled look at Saul.

'I promise to drive real slow, Claudia—come on, why don't you? If old stick-in-the-mud here won't budge, it doesn't mean you have to stay home too. What do you say, Miss Bea?'

'Oh, I'm in entire agreement,' said Bea heartily, then turned sharply as Claudia gave a sudden gasp and clapped her napkin to her mouth, rising precipitately to her feet with a muttered apology as she fled from the verandah, leaving the men staring after with varying expressions on their faces.

Bea followed Claudia to the bathroom in concern.

'What is it my dear? You're very pale—are you feeling ill?'.

Claudia shook her head with a lopsided grin.

'I've broken a tooth.' Beads of perspiration stood out on her forehead. 'I think there was a fragment of bone in my chicken and I bit hard on it.'

'Oh, my dear!' Bea put her arm round Claudia's waist. 'Is it very painful?'

Claudia nodded dumbly, momentarily speechless with the agony of an exposed nerve-end, making an effort as Becky appeared in the doorway, large-eyed.

'It's all right, poppet. A spot of toothache, that's all.'

'Dentist for you, my dear,' said Bea with decision. 'I'll get Saul to organise it.'

'Oh, please——' Claudia gasped, but Bea had gone. A small hand slid into Claudia's and Becky looked up at her anxiously.

'Are you hurting, Claudia?'

'Don't worry, I'll live—let's go back to the others.'

Claudia could hear Saul on the phone in the study as she and Becky went back to the verandah.

'Bad luck, honey. Is it grim?' Bob's pleasant face shone with sympathy.

'One of my teeth just snapped in half.' Claudia smiled with caution. 'The reward for filling my mouth too full!' She looked up as Saul came back and stood over her, his frown anxious instead of hostile.

'How do you feel?'

The slight warmth in his voice more than compensated for sharp twinges in her jaw, and Claudia smiled up at him gamely.

'Fine. Minus half a molar, that's all.'

'The earliest appointment I could get for you is at five with my dentist in Boa Vista. I'll get back early and take you in——'

'No need, old buddy,' cut in Bob. 'I was going in anyway. I'll be glad to take Claudia.'

The fleeting warmth was gone from Saul's face instantly and he moved back.

'By all means,' he said stiffly.

Claudia looked on helplessly as Saul provided Bob with the dentist's address, her toothache almost forgotten in her resentment. It was burningly obvious that he was only too glad to shift the responsibility for her on to Bob. Nevertheless, there was an odd expression on his face when he looked down at her before leaving after lunch. Staring mutely into his face, Claudia could have sworn a flicker of emotion showed in his hard eyes for an instant as he said goodbye.

'I leave you in Bob's hands, then,' he said.

'So I see,' she said flatly.

'I was under the impression you'd prefer that.'

'Were you really?' The throbbing in her jaw cancelled out any effort at manners.

To Claudia's surprise Saul stretched out a hand, the clasp of his fingers tight on her own for a moment.

'Claudia——' he said huskily.

'Come on, Saul,' interrupted Bob cheerfully. 'I'll be back for you about three, honey.'

Saul dropped her hand and turned away with a jerk, making for the steps without a backward glance, and Claudia watched him go in frustration, barely capable of a polite thank you to Bob as he hurried off in Saul's wake. She could have wept. A toothache would have been a negligible price to pay for a trip into Boa Vista with Saul. Aware that she was losing her battle against tears, she made excuses to Bea and Becky and fled to her bedroom to cry hot, silent tears into her pillow, until the pain in her tooth drove her in search of aspirin to blunt the anguish, wishing there were some wonder pill she could swallow for the ache in her heart.

CHAPTER TWELVE

CLAUDIA emerged from her encounter with the dentist a new woman. The street lights glittered like baubles among the thick dark greenery of the trees lining the main Avenida as she strolled through the dusk with Bob, a temporary cap on her tooth, almost lightheaded with the relief from pain. Boa Vista was electric with the atmosphere of *festa* as they made their way along the crowded pavements, the passers-by in party mood and ready to celebrate New Year's Eve.

'I feel terrific. All the knots in my nervous system are delightfully unravelled.' Claudia smiled gaily at Bob as they crossed the wide thoroughfare. 'I hate dentists—they bring out the coward in me.'

'You look a whole lot better, honey.' He grinned down at her and led her in the direction of a small bar.

'How about a drink here, then a couple of hours in a nice air-conditioned cinema watching the new Dustin Hoffman film. Afterwards I'll buy you dinner.'

Claudia tried to hide her dismay, by no means overjoyed by Bob's programme.

'Oh, but I thought we were going straight back. I'll be expected——'

He shook his fair head, patently pleased with himself as he seated her at one of the small marble-topped tables in the cool, dimly-lit bar.

'Sort of depending on how you felt, I told Saul what I had in mind, and he was all for it.'

'He was?' Claudia's eyes gleamed like the ice-cubes in the drink the waiter set in front of her. She smoothed her heavy hair back from her face and smiled brightly. 'In that case how can I refuse? O.K., you're on.'

Claudia enjoyed the film, firmly controlling the wrath bubbling deep down at the thought of being granted permission by Saul to remain in Boa Vista to do so. She took less pleasure in the meal that followed. The dentist's injection had begun to wear off and chewing aggravated the slight throbbing that started up again in her jaw, and she demurred when Bob suggested going on to a party at the house of some American friends afterwards.

'That would make us very late, Bob. Besides, I'm not exactly dressed for it.' She flicked the skirt of her maize linen dress disparagingly.

'You look great, Claudia. Come on, honey,' Bob urged. 'Saul won't expect us back early. Anyway, we can leave straight after midnight, and Hank and Nancy are nice people. You'll like them.'

Her heart sinking, Claudia gave in, guilty at the thought that Bob's New Year's Eve would be affected if he was obliged to take her home early. From that point on her throbbing jaw made it difficult to focus on the rest of the evening, and she remembered very little afterwards of the noisy, highly animated party at a large white house in a lush tropical garden with a swimming pool. Strident music played while waiters circulated endlessly with drinks and mine host presided over a barbecue with great good humour while his guests lined up for the fruits of his labours.

Claudia was welcomed with open arms by Hank and Nancy Riessen and introduced to many more people whose names were difficult to catch above the noise. With a determined effort to forget her sore mouth she smiled and drank, smiled and chatted, smiled until her lips felt stiff and Bob was delighted she was having such a great time. What had been a moderately pleasant evening turned into a marathon of endurance until midnight when everyone screamed good wishes and kissed everyone else, and still Claudia went on smiling until she had grave fears her face would be set in the same meaningless rictus for all time. It finally relaxed when Bob was eventually persuaded to leave, almost an hour later, by which time she was bone-weary, not merely from aftermath of her dental ordeal but from nagging worry about Saul's reception when she got home. Taking herself to task for being so wet as to care about the wretched man's opinions, Claudia settled herself in Bob's Lincoln Continental with a sigh of relief. It was more than likely that Saul was in bed and asleep, utterly indifferent as to how her evening had been spent or how late she was in getting back.

Bob was blessedly silent on the return journey, to Claudia's gratitude. The temporary anodyne of champagne had quietened down her throbbing mouth, but depression crept over her insidiously as the softly-sprung car undulated its way around bends and over ruts. To her surprise its motion was far worse for any incipient nausea than the rattling of Saul's jeep. As she thought of Saul she longed with a sudden passion for his massive, dominant presence beside her instead of Bob's kind, amiable company. It was no use. She stared at what was visible of the road in the beam of the headlights, as abruptly struck by the truth as though this were the road to Damascus. Claudia sat upright, her eyes narrowed. This was all so silly. When she got home she would go to Saul with her pride in her pocket and deliver herself up to him on whatever terms he wanted. For her the battle was over. She settled back in her seat with a sigh, her mind blissfully occupied with the possibility that defeat might just turn out to be victory after all.

'Are you all right, honey?' Bob sounded anxious.

'I'm fine, really. A bit tired, that's all.'

'I should have gotten away earlier,' he said remorsefully. 'Just a few more miles now.'

They were precisely three miles short of Campo d'Ouro when things began to go wrong. The car slowed and began to make some very disquieting noises, finally jerking to a halt plumb in the middle of a bend.

'Holy cow!' Bob leapt out of the car, torch in hand, looking under the bonnet in frantic efforts to find the fault. After a time he stuck his head back through the window and looked at Claudia in agonised apology.

'I'm sorry, honey, but could you possibly help me push the car off the road? We're obstructing any other traffic like this.'

Other traffic! Claudia would have cheerfully sold her soul for the sight of another car, truck, mule-cart, anything, but aware that at this time of night it was hardly likely. Balancing on the rough road surface on the high heels of her fragile sandals, she pushed with a will in response to Bob's shouted instructions until the car was as much off the road as it was possible for it to be. She held the torch and shone it under the bonnet in the places Bob indicated until he was forced to give up in frustration, to the accompaniment of a few highly-coloured oaths.

'Forgive the language, Claudia, and me too for stranding us miles from anywhere like this. I guess we'd better sit in the car until——'

'No,' said Claudia forcibly. 'We walk.'

'Walk? You can't be serious!' Bob's glasses glinted in the light of the torch, and Claudia smiled in spite of herself, well able to picture the horror in the eyes behind them. Her own mind was made up. Late they might be, but no way was she sitting meekly in that car until help arrived—if it ever did. If they set out on foot at least she would have *tried* to get home. No doubt it was a very faint hope, but Saul just might feel more kindly disposed towards her if she had made some kind of effort.

After only a few hundred yards of stumbling along she deeply regretted her decision. Bob's torch helped a little, but the road surface was rough and uneven, with dangerous loose stones in abundance. Her sandals soon began to rub blisters on her bare feet, but Claudia trudged on doggedly, her hand in Bob's for support, neither of them sparing the energy to talk apart from the odd stifled curse from the American, whom she could hardly blame for thinking it was madness even to attempt to reach Campo d'Ouro on foot. Soon Claudia's whole world became centred in her feet, which grew rapidly more swollen and painful every step they took. Several times she stumbled, wrenching an ankle a little, but rigidly stopped herself from complaining. Her concentration on just putting one foot after another was so intense as they toiled up a particularly steep incline she was past registering the noise of a vehicle in the distance until it was almost on them. Bob squeezed her hand with painful enthusiasm as he saw the headlights of something large gaining on them.

'Thank the Lord, honey—I think it's a truck!'

It was. A very ancient, battered lorry drew up alongside them with a squeal of brakes, its cab overflowing with a family from Campo d'Ouro returning from festivities with relatives in Boa Vista. Somehow Claudia was squashed in among several children and their mother, everyone loud with exclamations of sympathy as Bob explained their plight. The driver was apologetic as he surveyed Bob's dimensions and regretfully indicated the open back of the truck as the only space available for one with so long a leg. In no position to quibble, Bob scrambled up into the lorry and they were off, the head of the family goodnaturedly insisting on driving them right to the gates of the Treharne house before setting them down.

Claudia flatly refused to let Bob see her inside the house, wincing with pain as he set her on her feet after lifting her out of the truck. After reiterated thanks to their saviours she took off her sandals as the truck sputtered noisily away down the hill, turning down Bob's support as she prepared to hobble down the drive.

'No, really, Bob, thanks just the same. It's been a long night—God knows what time it is—so you go on home and I'll see myself inside. Goodnight, and thank you for taking me to the dentist.'

'I guess the last bit ruined the entire evening—I'm truly sorry, Claudia.'

Bob sounded utterly miserable in the darkness, but Claudia was too exhausted to essay much comfort.

'Don't worry, it couldn't be helped—I really must get off these feet. Goodnight, Bob.'

She crept gingerly down the drive on her abused feet, almost collpasing with fright as she cannoned into the figure that waited in the dark at the foot of the steps.

'Where in God's name have you *been*?' Saul shook her savagely, like a dog with a rat. 'Are you awarc of the time?'

It was the last straw. Abandoning her earlier resolve to throw herself into his arms and pour out her love and devotion, Claudia slapped him hard across the jaw instead, connecting more by luck than by science but making Saul's head jerk back, if only in surprise.

'And a Happy New Year to you, too, Mr Rochester!' There was pure venom in her voice as she hobbled up to the verandah, every step a victory of mind over matter. It had been her intention to keep on going until she reached her room, but once inside the drawing-room the lure of the nearest chair was too much and she sank down on it, her face screwed up in a ferocious scowl as a defence against the urge to howl like a baby.

'Why are you limping?' Saul stood over her in a towering rage, his mouth compressed as his eyes fixed on her feet. 'What the hell happened to you?'

'Where would you like me to begin?' Her eyes gleamed back at him in defiance.

'Did you manage to fit in a visit to the dentist, for starters!' He remained where he was, looming suffocatingly close, rubbing his jaw where her fist had landed.

He was still fully dressed, a half-full glass of whisky on one of the tables evidence of his occupation while he waited for her.

'Of course I did,' she snapped. 'It's the reason why I went in the first place. I've had a temporary cap and I have to go back next week.'

'McClure said he intended persuading you to stay in town for dinner,' he said bitingly. 'It must have been quite a meal!'

'Bob was set on going to a party afterwards—the last thing I myself wanted, but it *is* New Year's Eve, in case you've forgotten, and I knew I'd ruin Bob's evening if I insisted on coming back early.' Claudia's eyes opened wide suddenly, their clarity intense as they fastened on his. 'After all,' she said deliberately, 'I was fairly sure my absence would hardly be mourned very much.'

Neither moved, staring at each other angrily, their eyes locked as if trying to read each other's minds. Claudia lay in the chair, numb, her dress limp and crumpled, her eyes huge in her colourless face, her anger and defiance draining away to leave her defenceless before Saul's searching look. She winced as he went down on one knee and picked up one of her feet.

'How did you get these blisters?' He shook his head. 'Did McClure make you *walk* home, for God's sake?'

'No. I made *him* walk!' Claudia began to laugh softly, helplessly, her mirth submerging her until it was impossible to stop and tears ran down her cheeks. Saul bent and took her by the shoulders, shaking her again sharply, her laughter quenched in an instant at the touch of his hands. He released her and went across to the tray of drinks on the table, pouring a generous amount of brandy into a glass.

'Drink this.' He thrust it into her hand.

Claudia looked at it doubtfully. 'I don't know that I should—I had wine at dinner and champagne at the party.'

'What time did you leave?'

'Oneish.' Her eyes widened as she glanced at her watch. 'Good heavens, it's past three!' She gulped down the brandy, careless of any ill effects.

Saul stood, arms folded, his patience plainly at an end.

'Explain, Claudia. If you left the party at one, what happened between then and now?'

Her tongue loosened by the brandy, Claudia began on the account of the wretched journey, at first annoyed when Saul's lips began to twitch, then even to herself the sorry tale of the hike in the darkness with her reluctant escort began to sound ludicrous, and when she came to the part where she was squeezed into the cab of a rather vintage truck with a family of kind festive Brazilians while Bob finished the trip in more Spartan fasion in the back, she was grinning as widely as Saul.

'He was wearing such an elegant beige linen suit,' mourned Claudia. 'Heaven knows what condition it was in afterwards!'

'Hard luck.' Saul was unmoved. 'He should have checked the car before he went. In too much of a hurry to get you to himself, no doubt.'

'It wasn't Bob's fault the car broke down, Saul. Besides, he thought we should wait in the car until something came along.'

'I'll bet he did!' He raised an eyebrow at her, his eyes gleaming. 'Why didn't you?'

Claudia's eyes fell, her cheeks tingeing with colour.

'I wanted to get home.'

Saul looked pointedly at the sandals lying discarded by her chair. She glared at him.

'Next time I'll take my hiking boots!' Her shoulders slumped. 'Besides, I was afraid nothing *would* come along to pick us up, and three miles or so didn't sound too terrible in theory, only when we started to walk.'

'Was that the only reason?'

'No. But it's the only one you're going to get.' Claudia got up awkwardly, wincing as she put her weight on her feet.

'Oh, for God's sake!' Saul swooped and picked her up bodily, carrying her in silence through the hall and setting her down just inside the bathroom door. 'There should be some antiseptic in the medicine chest—pour a good dollop into your bathwater, then get yourself to bed. I'll come and put something on those blisters when you're ready.'

'There's no need,' whispered Claudia furiously. 'I can manage!'

'You can't risk infection in this climate—be sensible, woman!'

Claudia pulled a face as he closed the door softly behind him, then did as he said, lowering her aching body into the hot water gradually, gritting her teeth as the antiseptic stung her feet and regretting it instantly as her jaw gave a warning throb. She lay for only a minute or two, much as she would have loved to linger, then wrapped herself in one of the crimson bathsheets and tiptoed to her room, shrugging her nightdress over her head as a tap sounded on the door. Wrapping her kimono round her she let Saul in.

'Lie on the bed,' he ordered. 'I'll put some antiseptic salve on your feet—it might be as well to keep your dressing gown on and lie on top of the covers tonight.'

Claudia obeyed, too tired for any protest as Saul pushed pillows behind her head and slid the folded towel beneath her feet. His hands were surprisingly gentle as he smoothed on the cooling ointment, its effect blissfully analgesic on the sore skin. Claudia relaxed and closed her eyes with a sigh as he finished.

'Did I hurt you?' His deep voice was soft, without its dictatorial note for once, and her eyes flew open to peer warily at him as he leaned above her.

'No.' She managed a saucy little smile. 'Sorry to be a nuisance. I don't need much medical attention as a rule.'

Saul smiled at her spontaneously, his teeth white in the darkness of his face, a glint in his eyes clearly visible in the subdued light of the bedside lamp.

'How would you describe today's ailments? Foot and mouth?'

Claudia clapped a hand to her mouth to stifle the laughter bubbling up inside her, her body shaking slightly.

'Hey,' he murmured, leaning closer, 'not hysterical again, are you? Must I shake you again?'

She shook her head in disapproval, taking her hand away from her mouth.

'No way! Three times in succession is a bit over the top—in danger of getting hooked, in fact.'

The laughter faded from Saul's face and he leaned nearer.

'Too late, Claudia. I *am* hooked already.'

Her breathing felt constricted as she lay there, her eyes wary as she considered his undramatic statement.

'Did you hear me?' he persisted softly, and leaned lower.

She nodded, mesmerised, unable to look away from the disturbing warmth in his eyes.

'Well?' he prompted, his hands now on either side of her.

Her eyelids fluttered and she moved her head restlessly.

'I don't know what you want me to say,' she muttered.

'Liar!'

Claudia was torn. This would seem the right moment to tell him she was—was what? Available? The term seemed strangely vulgar in this particular context. She stared uncertainly into the strong face above her as Saul's broad shoulders blocked out the room, the scent of his skin enveloping her in a haze of excitement, his big body almost in contact with hers, yet not quite. She could push him away. The choice was hers. Before she could make it Saul suddenly levered himself up with one agile movement and left her without a word. Claudia lay deflated, her dilemma settled for her, wondering if her silence had been the reason for his departure. She would never understand this enigmatic, maddening man. So he was hooked, was he! It would have made her considerably happier if he had seen fit to explain just precisely what he was hooked *on*. Never end a sentence with a preposition, Claudia, she scolded herself, with an attempt at humour, but she seemed to have run the gamut of all the emotions she possessed, except for surprise, as the door opened again. Saul shut it

noiselessly behind him and came over to the bed,
looming large in the dim light.

Annoyed at his cool assumption that he was welcome
to come and go in her bedroom as she wished, she
demanded,

'Why are you here?'

She stared blankly as Saul merely smiled faintly and
sat on the edge of the bed with his back to her and bent
to take off his rope-soled shoes. He turned and lifted
her farther over on the bed, then swung his legs up and
settled himself comfortably beside her, sharing her
banked pillows.

'You can't stay here!' She slid away from him in
agitation, but he put out a hand and yanked her back,
holding her against him in the crook of his arm. 'Saul—
please! Becky——'

'Becky's at Casa d'Ouro. She was at a loose end after
you left so I took her over to Emily when I drove Bea
to see Dr Machado this afternoon.'

'What!' Claudia twisted frantically in his grasp.
'What was the matter? Was she ill—why didn't you say
at once——'

'Calm down, sweetheart!' Saul pulled her wholly into
his arms, smoothing her hair as he held her close.
Claudia was silenced by the endearment, her body tense
as he explained. 'She made the appointment days ago,
but didn't want to worry any of us. She only told me
yesterday when she asked me to run her up to the
hospital.'

'But you offered to take me to the dentist at
lunchtime.' Claudia raised her head from his shoulder
to look up into Saul's face, something she found there
making her pulse behave erratically.

'When you were in pain I forgot everything else,' he
said simply. 'Even poor Aunt Bea's appointment went
out of my head—which, I might add, amused her no
end.'

Claudia forced her mind from this dangerously
fascinating topic.

'But what exactly is wrong with Bea?'

'A touch of high blood pressure, but nothing some

medication and a lot of rest won't put right, I'm profoundly thankful to say.'

Claudia melted against him in relief, burrowing her face into his neck.

'Oh, Saul, I'm so glad! I had thoughts of heart trouble—all sorts of things. I've known her for only a short time, I know, but I've come to care for her very much.'

His arms tightened round her.

'You've known me the same length of time, Claudia.'
She nodded blindly. 'Yes.'

'What do you mean—"Yes"?'

She raised an arm and mopped her damp eyes with the sleeve of her kimono. 'Just yes.' She refused to look up at him, suddenly shy now that the moment of truth had arrived. 'If you mean do I care for you too, yes. Am I hooked on you, yes. Do I want you to stay here all night, yes!' She got no further as her face was turned up to his, their mouths coming together in a sweet violence that cancelled out the need to say any more for some time. They slid to lie full length, holding each other close with an aching need that grew more intense with each passing moment, his mouth caressing hers at first gently, then with heat and persuasion as their breathing quickened and their bodies began to move instinctively against each other in a rhythm as natural as breathing. As his mouth left hers to travel lower, a thought occurred to Claudia.

'Saul,' she said huskily, and shivered as his mouth moved lower.

Saul paused reluctantly and looked down into her eyes, his breath quickening as he saw the smoky tinge in their clarity.

'What is it, my lovely one?'

A tremor ran through her at his words, and she closed her eyes in wonder, unable to credit the light of tenderness in his.

'You can't really stay,' she said, her hands restless on his shoulders. 'Aunt Bea——'

Saul chuckled and held her closer.

'For the time being Aunt Bea is to take two sleeping

pills at night. Dr Machado says she needs undisturbed rest, and when I checked on her just now she was fathoms deep in sleep.'

'Oh.'

Even in the subdued light it was possible to see the great wave of colour that swept up Claudia's face. Very slowly Saul slid the kimono from her shoulders and followed suit with the ribbons holding up her thin white cotton nightdress. With infinite care he peeled it the whole length of her body, taking such an unconscionable time about it that Claudia lay in an agony of shyness, deeply aware of his eyes on her even though her own were tightly shut. She knew that this was what her words had invited, but now that it was all actually happening she felt diffident, ridiculously timorous for a woman of her age.

'Open your eyes, Claudia.' The caress in Saul's voice was as potent as the touch of his hands. Her lids lifted slowly, weighted by a new, consuming languor, then flew wide as she realised he was as naked as herself. Her eyes grew wild as they glittered at him in near panic, then the time for hesitation and doubt was over as he secured her against him in the seduction of skin on skin, the shock of it sending great ripples of feeling through her as his mouth and hands took possession of her body with a mastery that cancelled out fear, leaving only a pure refinement of longing that ignored the first painful instant as their bodies came together, and gloried in the wave upon wave of sensation that followed. For long, breathless moments he held her inexorably at the very brink of the unknown, then plunged with her into the fulfilment that lay beyond.

For long silent minutes they lay motionless in the aftermath of their loving, until, one by one, other senses began to reawaken in Claudia, reminding her that she needed to breathe, which was something of an impossibility under the circumstances. She stirred, and Saul rolled over on his back, holding her close against him.

'How are your feet?' he asked lazily.

'What feet?'

He chuckled, smoothing strands of hair away from her moist, hot forehead.

'Saul?' Claudia pushed herself up on her elbows to look down into his face. 'Is it always like that?'

The look of indulgence in his dark blue eyes was almost identical to the one usually reserved for Becky.

'It's a considerable source of wonder to me that somewhere among all that education you received this part was neglected.'

Claudia' s head lifted proudly.

'It was never compulsory on any of my courses.'

Saul held her away, shaking her slightly, his eyes suddenly serious.

'Do you think I'm complaining?' He brought her against him convulsively. 'To revert to your question, no. It is *not* always like that. This time it was our voyage of discovery and it will never be quite the same again. On the other hand, it was the merest foretaste—the best is yet to come.'

Claudia wriggled a little.

'I suppose it was painfully obvious that it was my maiden voyage!'

Saul pulled her head down to his, kissing her hard.

'Of course it was, you goose. Apart from that one unmistakable moment, you were so surprised by everything!'

'Stupefied, you mean!'

They lay together in contentment for a while before Claudia stirred unwillingly.

'It's almost morning. Shouldn't you go back to your room?'

Saul's head turned towards her on the pillow, his eyes filled with gratifyingly frank pleasure as they rested on her body, her skin luminous in the first pale glimmer of light filtering through the curtains.

'One or two things to clear up,' he said in a matter-of-fact way that caused a little curl of disquiet deep inside Claudia. She stiffened.

'Oh?'

'On the subject of value for money.'

Her mouth dried. 'Go on.'

Saul heaved himself up to lean against the carved headboard.

'I've hit on the very best solution possible.'

'So tell me.' Claudia turned wary eyes on his smug face.

'Certainly. Instead of employing you as governess I marry you instead. I get free tuition for Becky, Becky gets a mother as well as a teacher, Bea gains a niece and you get all the security you'll ever want.' He grinned in triumph at the expressions competing for mastery on her face.

Claudia slid off the bed and retrieved her kimono from the floor, aware of a need for protection as she tried to assimulate the statement made in such a casual manner. She pushed her hair behind her ears and sat on the dressing-table stool, looking appraisingly at the brown, relaxed body of the man on the bed. Saul drew the sheet over his lower half with blatant mock-modesty as he waited for her reply, wondering if she knew how different and how desirable she looked with her hair all anyhow, and her eyes diamond-bright in her flushed face as they examined his face in doubt.

'Is that a proposal, or a mere business proposition?'

'A proposal, of course. Surely it was obvious as such?' It was hard to recognise her grim, dour Mr Rochester in this elated male creature who was occupying her bed in such flagrant nudity.

'Not all that easily. Perhaps you could elucidate a little?'

'With pleasure.' Saul slid off the bed and stepped into his cotton slacks, zipping them up as he turned to her, the casual intimacy making her blink. He held out his arms. 'Come here.'

Claudia went. He shook her slightly.

'Saul!' Her tone was threatening.

'Sorry—I must break the habit. As I was saying, Miss March, will you marry me if I ask you very nicely, because in the short time I've been privileged to know you——' Saul paused, all his raillery abruptly gone, 'I've discovered that I can't for the life of me think how I ever survived without you before. I was joking about the teaching bit. You don't have to.'

'Of course I want to. I love teaching children.' A radiance was beginning to glow in Claudia's eyes, as she buried her face against him.

Saul shrugged, his arms almost cracking her ribs.

'The salient point I'm trying to make is that I love you,' he said huskily, 'and I hope to God you feel the same.'

'Of course I do. Why didn't you say all that in the first place?' She shook him crossly, or attempted to. She tipped her head back to look up at him with mock impatience. 'Why wrap it up in all that superfluity?'

'I wasn't sure how you'd answer.' To her astonishment she felt the arms round her tremble slightly.

'After last night? I'm afriad I must insist you make an honest woman of me!'

Saul drew back, his lips pursed judicially, his head on one side as he considered her demand, then he nodded graciously.

'Very well—on condition you make it worth my while.'

Claudia slid from his grasp and stood away from him, one eyebrow raised, hands on hips, the black silk of her kimono parting to give a glimpse of long slim leg. She ran her tongue round her lips and tilted her head back, her eyes narrowed to a sultry glimmer beneath half-closed lids as she stared into the dark face above her, unholy joy consuming her as she saw the colour rise in his face and his breathing begin to quicken.

'How do you propose I should do that?' Her voice was husky with provocation. 'Are you one of those chauvinists who consider woman's place is in the home?'

Saul pulled her back into his arms roughly.

'I'm not interested in other women, Orphan Annie. If you mean you're the woman I want in my home you're dead right. In my home and in my bed, for ever and ever, amen.'

Deeply satisfied, Claudia closed her eyes in rapture and slid her arms round his neck.

'Well?' he demanded, his hands hard on her waist. 'Nothing to say for once?'

She shook her head and eyed him questioningly.

'You mean that if I marry you I don't get a salary?'

Saul shrugged, his eyes dancing.

'The Fonsecas will pay you, the same as usual.'

'And how will you pay me?'

'In kind, my darling, in kind!'